RHYTHM

A NOVEL

Robin Meloy Goldsby

ISBN: 1-4196-9939-3
ISBN-13: 9781419699399

Library of Congress Control Number: 2008903102

This is a Bass Lion book, published in the United States by BookSurge.

Visit www.booksurge.com to order additional copies.

Front cover image by Simon Podgorsek. All rights reserved. Used by permission.

Author photograph by Andreas Biesenbach, Cologne, Germany

Book design by BookSurge

Manufactured in the United States of America

For my parents, Bob and Ann Rawsthorne.
For my children, Curtis and Julia Goldsby.
Love, like good music, travels well from
one generation to the next.

Prologue

I rock my spoon back and forth in time to the music and watch the ice cream slide around. It's funny how the last little scoop always tastes the best – a half-melted, half-frozen, creamy-dreamy bite. I listen to the pulse of my mother's congas. She sounds like a groovy Latino locomotive, chugging her way through a perfect Manhattan night.

Music and strawberry ice cream – it doesn't get much better than this.

But something's not right. A horrible whining noise fills the club, growing louder and louder with each split second. The band stops playing. A waiter leaps over the bar, almost knocking me off the stool. I spin around and see orange flames framing the stage like a strange piece of performance art. A thick column of pewter-colored smoke streams from the little window above the dressing room door.

The players – unaware of the danger behind them – stare at the audience with puzzled looks. My mother swats at the burning embers tumbling onto her congas, as smoldering scraps of fabric land in her hair. She scans the audience, looking for me. Her eyes travel to the press table, but I'm not there. Panic consumes the room. The crowd pushes towards the exit and blocks my view of the stage.

"Mommy!" I cry. "I'm here! Over here, Mommy!" There's a sickening gush of sound, then a deafening thud – like wind slamming a door shut.

"Mommy! Over here!"

My words are smothered by shouts and a blast of fire and smoke.

PART I: 1986

Songs Without Words

"You have to be a helluva good drummer to be better than no drummer at all." I was six years old when my mother, dressed in black stretch pants and a faded Pittsburgh Steelers sweatshirt, put a pair of drumsticks in my hands and said those words to me for the first time.

Her drum kit – a classic 1962 champagne-sparkle Gretsch set – still sits in the corner of the living room. On calm winter days, the weak afternoon sun slants through the prism of our bay window, and tiny dust particles – brought to life by the sunbeams – flicker past the grand piano and skip around Mom's old snare drum. In this delicate light, the buffed surface of the drum shimmers and glows, and – if I stare at it long enough – begins to look like melted gold.

In one of my earliest memories, Mom and I are chasing glimmering bits of sunshine through the living room, pretending our drumsticks are magic wands. We play with the light until it disappears, then, laughing, she leads me back to the drums, and teaches me – with her calloused hand on my skinny arm – how to play a rhythm as simple and steady as the beating of my heart.

Here's the way it goes, I imagine her saying. *Listen and you'll hear.*

These days, memories of Mom sneak up on me. Sometimes – like when I'm struggling to braid my dark blond hair – her light brown face stares back at me from the bathroom mirror. *Look*, I think, *it's her!* Or when I laugh at one of Dad's silly jokes, and it strikes me – from the way he avoids my eyes – that I probably sound a lot like her. Or when I turn on the television late at night and there she is – fired up and playing her ass off – on a re-run of the Curly Dobson show. The only female, she stands behind the other nine musicians, on a riser next to the drummer and the bass player, striking her conga drums with enough force to blow the music right out of the television set and into my bedroom, where I dance, sing, and cry, not always in that order.

People say I look like her, and I do, just a little, but there's no way I'll ever shine the way she did. She was really beautiful.

My mother was a percussionist. I'm a drummer. Most people don't understand the difference. A drummer plays the drums. A percussionist plays everything else, or at least that's what Mom used to say. She started out on the drums, but switched to congas and bongos, marimba, vibraphone, xylophone, and all of the cool things a person can whack that have nothing to do with a drum set. She was also a wicked tambourine player, which sounds like a joke if you never got a chance to hear her play the tambourine, but she could make that thing speak, I swear.

She always carried a big black bag of percussion instruments with her – some of them looked like goat bladders or dried-up vegetables or shrunken heads.

"Una buena congera es como una hechicera," she used to say when I begged her to tell me how she would get a really cool sound out of an object that looked like an old turkey leg bone. "A good percussionist is like a magician. And a magician never reveals her secrets. Learn to play the drums first. Then I'll show you how this other stuff works."

I never did get a chance to learn – she died holding onto her magic. But when I was little the promise of learning to play the turkey leg was enough to inspire me to practice. On my sixth birthday I started taking drum lessons from Mr. Hammill. He came to our house every Thursday afternoon for one hour that usually stretched into two. I begged Mom to teach me herself, but she refused, claiming that parents and music teachers should remain separate parts of a kid's life. That used to bug me, but now – when I think back on it – I realize she started teaching me about rhythm from the day I was born. I mean, we couldn't even walk across the street without her counting off the tempo. She was my teacher; she just pretended not to be.

Mr. Hammill's pushy attitude worked for me. With a slippery voice that played against the precision of the exercises he assigned, he convinced me to practice more, to work harder. But really, he didn't teach me anything I hadn't already learned from my mother. I went along with the whole scheme – practicing my paradiddles and ratamacues, organizing my lessons, and soaking up Mom's praise like a thirsty sponge.

"Tu eres mi cielo," she used to say.

You're my little heaven.

Although I studied standard rudimental snare drum techniques and began my studies on the drum set by playing swing, rock, and Latin beats, I fell in love with R&B and funk music pretty early on. Mom played the Aretha Franklin "Respect" recording for me while I was still in kindergarten, and I've been hooked ever since. There's something about a solid funky groove that makes me feel like I'm inside a fizzy drink, bubbling up to the top of an overflowing glass. I don't get that feeling from any other kind of music. For as long as I can remember, I've been listening to – and playing along with – Aretha Franklin and James Brown. They're like Gods to me. Since Mom died, the fizz is sort of gone, but still, it's my kind of music.

My favorite snapshot of Mom rests on the night table in my room. In the photo, she's wearing tight red leather pants and a sparkly pink top. She's carrying me on one hip and a conga drum on the other. My dad is the coolest guy I know, but you'd never guess it from this photo – he's wearing a tuxedo, a flowered lei and a purple velvet sombrero. His head is thrown back, and he's laughing. The scribbled date on the photo says June 17, 1971, one day before my first birthday. I'd leap headfirst into that picture if I could.

I've scattered photos of Mom all over our home in Sewickley Heights, Pennsylvania. They're placed on tabletops and windowsills; tiny silvery shrines to the memory of Helen Bowman, framed in perfect sterling circles or squares purchased at Tiffany or Cartier or one of those places that sells pretty things to fancy people. Right after my thirteenth birthday – on the first anniversary of Mom's death – Dad gave me a collection of fifty photos, each one framed and wrapped in sky-blue paper. Since most of the photos were ones I had never seen, every picture took me on another little journey into Mom's past. Dad would tell the story behind a snapshot, and then we'd sit there and try not to cry. "Look," he would say. "Here's your Mom with Dizzy Gillespie in Sweden, here she is riding a bike through the forest in Bavaria, here she is at Café des Artistes on the night I proposed to her, here she is eating French fries at a Pittsburgh Pirates game – "

Here she is, here she is, here she is. But not really.

Sometimes it seems like Mom's spirit is wedged between the silver bars of those frames, trapped in the past, stuck forever in the rooms of a high-rent memory jail. Or maybe it's me who's stuck. I wish I could help us escape. But I'm not very good at helping. When it counted, I couldn't help her at all.

It took me three days to open all of the packages. Dad told me to arrange the photos any way I wanted to, that they were mine to keep and carry with me for the rest of my life.

"They're small," he said. "They don't weigh much."

At first, hell-bent on giving Mom the tribute she deserved, I propped all fifty of them on small tables around the drum set. But the sparkle of the drums and the silver of the frames made the corner of the living room look like a cheesy catering hall, which I knew Mom would have hated. She played in too many of those places when she was starting her career. I'm not completely sure, but I think the last thing she would have wanted was to have her house looking like the back ballroom of Niko Keriotis's Crystal Palace.

So I began to experiment. Me, a thirteen year old masquerading as an interior decorator, arranging photos of my dead mother in places where I could see her and remember her in some nice way. It took me a couple of months to get it just right. Years later, I still get into silly fights with Mary One – our live-in housekeeper – who moves my photos around when she thinks I'm not looking.

Mary One is part of the family. She isn't retarded, not at all, but we think there's something loose in her brain, in a good way. Or maybe she's one of those idiot-savant people I keep hearing about on *Sixty Minutes,* except without the idiot part. She's really kind of brilliant, at least musically. A long time ago, when I was in kindergarten, Mom met Mary in the restroom of the

Tikki-Tikki Supper Club. The Tikki-Tikki – a huge Indonesian restaurant that was eventually torn down and replaced by a Kmart – featured chubby Pittsburgh girls performing big-butt versions of the hula. The girls were accompanied by authentic Samoan drummers who squirted lighter fluid on the heads of their congas and played through the flames. It was our idea of excellent entertainment and we used to love to go there.

One time, when I was home with a cold, Mom went by herself to check out a couple of Balinese percussion instruments she had heard were for sale. At intermission she made the transaction, hung out with two musicians named Dali and Sid – then retreated to the restroom so she didn't have to watch the second half of the show, which starred a midget running across a bed of red-hot spikes.

In the ladies' room, Mom couldn't help but notice Mary, a new restroom attendant who was cleaning the Tikki-Tikki toilets while singing "My Sweet Hunk O' Trash," an old Billie Holiday tune not often heard in the restrooms of Western Pennsylvania. Mary, who stood four and a half feet tall, had bright orange hair, freckles, and a smile that covered most of her face. She wore a rainbow-colored grass skirt and black sneakers with lightning bolts on them. I'm not sure if it was the outfit or the song, but Mary charmed the common sense out of my mother. After three trips to the Tikki-Tikki ladies' room, a lot of smooth talking, and several financial negotiations, Mom hired Mary to be our combination live-in housekeeper and nanny. I was five years old at the time and Mom convinced me that having a nanny who could sing just like Billie Holiday was pretty much the best thing that could happen to a kid.

Mary, whose full name is Mary Henderson, brought a lot of extra joy to our home, but after awhile Mom and Dad noticed that she wasn't really getting any work done. Mary spent most of her time on the toilet in our guest bathroom. She didn't have to actually use the potty – I mean, she didn't have intestinal problems or anything – she just enjoyed sitting there, lid down, with her little legs sticking straight out in front of her. Every morning, after making my breakfast and washing a dish or two, she'd head right into the bathroom where she'd spend most of the day, singing verse after verse of Billie Holiday classics. She liked to leave the door open, so we heard everything, over and over and over again. I'm pretty sure I was the only five-year old in Sewickley Heights who knew all the lyrics to "Strange Fruit."

Mom didn't have the heart to fire Mary One, so she hired another Mary, Mary Hogg – pronounced *Hogue* – to look after me and clean up after the first Mary. We could have used their proper names, but I was five years old and calling them Mary One and Mary Two made perfect sense. The names stuck.

Mary Two comes from England and dresses in a grey woolen suit with thick white stockings – all British and proper – but she cusses like a truck driver. Years ago, she had been fired by Binky Pendleton, a neighbor with tons of cash and not an ounce of sense – because she claimed Mary Two used too many bad words. Mom, who couldn't stand Binky, insisted that anyone fired by her would turn out to be a perfectly fine employee. In those days our house was overrun by visiting musicians, writers, and assorted artistic gypsies – so Mary Two's generous use of the f-word hardly mattered to us one bit. She fit right in. The Marys took care of each other, and sometimes they even took care of the house and me. Both of them still live in the west wing.

Lucky for us, Mary Two persuaded Mary One to keep the guest bathroom door closed. We had gotten used to the sight of Mary One sitting there, but sometimes she scared our visitors. Once, a bass player named Carlos, who had wrinkled skin the color of roasted walnuts, blood-shot eyes, and a soft spot for tall bottles of Rolling Rock beer and – I suspect – some mysterious chemical substances, wandered past the guest bathroom, heard Mary One singing selections from *Porgy and Bess*, and turned as white as snow. He was convinced that a miniature redheaded version of Billie had been dropped from heaven straight onto our toilet seat. He ran out of the house yelling something about rehab. It took Mom a couple of months to get him to return for another jam session.

Sewickley Heights – Pittsburgh's version of old money swank – sits high in the hills outside the city. Lots of extravagant people live here, but we're the only family I know with a maid for our maid. Dad and I have shared a home with both Marys for so long that we can't imagine living any other way. I think Dad had hoped the Marys would pitch in and take over for Mom after she died, but they didn't even try – it's almost like they knew they could never replace her. In some ways, I think the Marys miss Mom just as much as I do. This makes me love them more, even though they drive me a little crazy sometimes. For instance, Mary One is always flipping out about mom's photos. She doesn't like the way I've arranged them. Not one bit.

"Mary One, did you move the photo of Mom in Miami again?"

"Jane, I keep on tellin' you. Your mama is half-naked in that photo. You want your suitors to be eyeballing her in that itty-bitty skirt she's wearing? And if it weren't for those shaker things she's holding you'd be able to see her bosom."

"Those shaker things are called maracas. You know that. And I have no suitors."

"Still it ain't right. I put that picture down in the basement, next to the furnace. Your suitors ain't going down there. And that picture of her carrying you home from the hospital? In case you're looking for it, I told Mary Two to hang it up over the front door."

"Mary Two hung a photo in a sterling silver frame outside?"

"Yes, Jane, and I can report that Mary Two was not real happy about doing it. You know how she hates ladders. She cussed me out something fierce. But you know, that's one picture we're proud of – the day your mama left the drums long enough to bring you into this world. Getting you born was the smartest thing she ever did."

I haul the ladder outside, remove the photo from the front door, and return it to its place next to the drum set, where it belongs.

Once a month or so, when Mom was still here, we would organize a concert for Dad and the Marys. I'd play drum set, Mom would set up her marimba or congas and we'd go nuts together. We'd rock, we'd groove, we'd make so much noise that the big crystal chandelier in the living room seemed to rattle and swing. Dad would do his Three Rivers Stadium cheer, Mary One would cover her ears and make repeated requests for "God Bless the Child," and Mary Two – with her puffy face and upside-down smile – would clap with two fingers, muttering that we ought to learn some of the nice ballads from *Jesus Christ Superstar*. But in those days, we hated playing anything slow.

Three years ago, when my mother was killed in a New York City nightclub fire, our living room was eaten alive by silence, broken only by the chirp of Mary One singing a few bars of "Good Morning Heartache," or the swish of Mary Two's pale yellow rag as she dusted the piano and marimba. Dad wanted to talk to me about the details of the fire, but I refused. I can be pretty stubborn – it's one of the traits I've inherited from Mom. He asked questions, I stared at the wall. He paced. I fumed, mad that he wanted to talk, even madder when he stopped trying.

Chirp, swish, pace, fume – on and on we went, for months. I thought my head would explode from the nothingness of my life.

Dad stopped pacing and returned to work. I continued to fume, sitting in my room and waiting for a reason to stop feeling sad and guilty. That never happened. So I resumed my weekly lessons with Mr. Hammill. Thankful for an activity, I practiced the drums, hours and hours every day, pounding out exercises, forcing new rhythm patterns under my skin and into my hands and feet. I worked like a maniac, I did all of the things that Mom would have wanted me to do. Hoping she would hear me, I hit the drums as hard as I could.

I might have continued to play concerts for Dad and the Marys, but I couldn't stand the idea. Alone, I would have sounded silly – like Garfunkel without Simon, half a Smothers, Ike minus Tina. So I stopped. I refused to play for anyone but Mom's spirit. I figured she must have been drifting around out there somewhere.

Yeah, right.

I actually thought if I played loudly enough, she'd drop in for a visit, that she'd tell me she loved me, and that she forgave me. Then she would wrap her arms around me, one last time, and I'd have a chance to say I'm sorry.

Two weeks after the fire – a few days after I had been released from the hospital – Dad held a big memorial service for Mom at St. Peter's on the East Side of Manhattan, the jazz musicians' church. Tucked away on my bookshelf is a copy of her obituary, along with an article about the service: *Major and Minor Musical Celebrities Pay Tribute to Percussionist Helen Bowman.*

I'm told there were speeches, songs with meaningful lyrics, and instrumental pieces performed by Mom's friends. But I only remember the scent of too many white roses, the scratch of Dad's jacket against my cheek, the rustle of Grandma Isabella's linen dress, the stinging rawness of my nose, the sticky air in the sanctuary, my grandfather's initialed handkerchief, the sobs that shamed me, the clumsy hugs of Mom's colleagues, and, most of all, the glare of the snappy blue sky as we exited the church on Lexington Avenue. I looked up, and heaven seemed like an empty mirror.

I'm so sorry Jane.

Your mother was so proud of you.

Be strong Jane, that's what your mother would want.

Helen was a beautiful woman, a great musician.

I'm so sorry, so sorry, so sorry.

No one, not even Dad, knew that Helen Bowman's death was my fault.

We cried and cried and cried at the beginning, all of us. We're still trying to get past it, really. To move on, to turn the stupid page, to "buck up" as Mary Two says. We have our separate grief-busting techniques – Dad wanders from the kitchen to his office, where he writes mystery novels that keep his imagination occupied with stories more dramatic than his own. Mary One sings – occasionally leaving the guest bathroom to stare out the window. Mary Two curses as she scrubs and scrapes invisible grime from the floors and countertops, walls and staircases. And I practice the drums. We're all doing what we've always done – but the fun has been sucked out of our lives and replaced by a chilly emptiness. We've all got a bad case of brain freeze. Or maybe it's soul freeze.

Three years have passed since she died. Sometimes our home in Sewickley Heights seems like a stuffy museum that no one visits – a luxury warehouse for fifty silver-framed photographs, percussion instruments that have become polished pieces of furniture, and weepy statue-people with limbs carved from slabs of soft stone. Hard as I play, as much as I try to hold onto the memory of my mother, it grows fainter, like the fading chimes of an ice cream truck driving away.

Come back! I want to shout. *Please. Come back.*

If there's a sound more hollow than the thump of a broken heart, I don't know what it is.

Under Latin Skies

Mom's name – Helen Jane Ames Bowman – doesn't conjure up the image of a hard playing, heavy-hitting Latin-jazz *congera*, but that's exactly what she was. She inherited her love of Afro-Cuban music from her own mother, Isabella Vargas Ames, who was from a rich Cuban family that immigrated to Miami in 1945.

Isabella, a sizzling singer in a Cuban mambo band, met Jack Ames – owner of the Flamingo Hotel and Nightclub – on the strip in Miami Beach. She was eighteen at the time. I've got pictures of Grandma from back then. Mocha colored, she was a flashier, more glamorous version of my mother. She liked to squeeze her curvy body into skin-tight sequined evening gowns. The dresses were always red. No dusty rose or deep burgundy for Isabella – her reds were explosive, like a fire, a volcano, or a hot-blooded sun in a violet sky, burning its way into the ocean.

As the guys in my school would say, Isabella was stacked like a brick house. Back in 1945, I think they said hubba-hubba.

Isabella's husband, Jack Ames, was a tall green-eyed chunk of man with movie-star hair the color of marigolds. As the story goes, he strolled into the Flamingo one afternoon to check out some fabric samples for new bar stools, just as Isabella was catapulting onstage to start her first rehearsal with the hotel band. Turned on by her throaty voice and the sway of her hips, he fell in love. When the song was over, he rushed to the stage to introduce himself, tripped over one of the bar stools, and broke his ankle. Isabella leapt from the stage to help him, and has stayed by his side ever since.

In the late 1940's, doing the hootchie-cootchie every night in front of hundreds of drunken men wasn't considered a reputable occupation for a married Cuban Catholic woman. In spite of this, or maybe because of it, Isabella's fame grew. She earned the respect of her Cuban musical colleagues, including Desi Arnaz, who featured her with his band whenever he played in Miami. When Isabella snagged the attention of Machito, the popular Latin-jazz bandleader whose sharp-edged rhythms and restless arrangements had started the craze for Afro-Cuban music, her climb to celebrity accelerated at a pace matched only by the steamy tempo of the music itself.

Every Saturday night, at the end of her third set, Isabella Vargas Ames would lead a conga line of drunken party-goers through the nightclub and outside onto the Starlight Terrace overlooking Miami Beach. As the column of dancers curled around the wooden bridge leading to the pavilion on the sand, the throb of Machito's music would clash with the rhythm of the crashing waves. Isabella guided the procession, a voluptuous silhouette backlit by the moon, leading her parade to a place that made her happy.

* * *

Isabella – known on the marquee as the "Mistress of Mambo" – discovered she was pregnant just as her popularity began to peak. She was six months into her pregnancy when the zipper of her red dress refused to close. She decided to stop performing, much to Jack's relief. Poor Jack had grown weary of fending off the conga line of men waiting outside Isabella's dressing room door every night. He sold the Flamingo to Meyer Lansky and took his earnings to New York City, where he and Isabella invested in Manhattan real estate. One of the buildings they purchased was a large brownstone on East 48th Street. That's where my mom – Helen – was born, in the back bedroom that faced the garden. Isabella filled the courtyard with pale pink roses and wisteria vines that climbed to such mind-blowing heights that they became legendary in New York garden circles. The wisteria is still there, stretching and cracking the earth with roots as thick as the legs I walk on.

Everyone assumed that after Helen was born the "Mistress of Mambo" would return to the stage. The red dress fit again, but she refused to wear it. Instead, Isabella devoted her time to her daughter and her home. She became one of New York City's best-loved society wives – the flashy Cuban trophy hanging on the arm of her rich handsome husband. She claimed she had no regrets about giving up her career, but Mom never quite believed her.

Mom once tried to get Isabella to admit that Jack had forced her to quit, but she denied it. To me, Grandpa Jack never seemed like the kind of guy who would force anyone to do anything, but who knows, 1948 was a very different time. My theory is that Isabella quit because she wanted a change. She never lost her passion for music; she only lost her need to perform in front of hooting crowds of inebriated night-clubbers.

"Mi amor," she once said to me, her only grandchild, as she turned up the recording of the Machito Orchestra playing Dizzy Gillespie's "Exuberante," and shimmied across her front parlor with a tray of sugary rum cocktails. "Hay musical doquiera y me sóbran ganas para distrutar."

Music is everywhere. Who needs a stage?

No one could coax her back into the business. Everyone tried; Dizzy, Desi, Machito, and Tito called and visited often, but no offer was enough to tempt her. Mom liked to say that Grandma was the Greta Garbo of Cuban music, bowing out early and leaving a trail of freaked-out Mambo fans praying for her return.

Not that it matters now. Grandma Isabella has Alzheimer's disease. She started spiraling into oblivion right after my mother died. They say a baby's reaction to terror is to sleep. Maybe Isabella's illness is the old-person version of that.

Grandma Isabella and Grandpa Jack still live in their big Manhattan home, assisted by round-the-clock nursing care, cooks and maids. Ever since Mom died, I've been checking the faces of my leftover family, searching for some trace of my-self in them. Whenever I see Isabella, childlike and ancient, being consumed – one piece at a time – by the black hole in her memory, she looks more and more like the pictures of me as a young girl, as a baby, even. It's like I'm watching myself being born and dying, all at once.

I've inherited Grandma's love of music, her sense of humor, and her weakness for fried plantains. I visit her in New York City every two months and hope that she recognizes something of herself in me. But most of the time, she just stares, straight ahead, hunting for memories she'll never find. She doesn't know who I am anymore, which makes me really sad. Then again, she doesn't remember how my mother died, and Grandpa Jack says that's a blessing.

But here's the thing: she still knows the melody to "Mambo Diablo." And when I visit her and model one of her over-the-top red dresses, she smiles. Not at me – at the dress. If I play a recording of Desi Arnaz's "Babalu" for her, she dances – too broken and spaced-out to talk, but still alive enough to lead an imaginary conga line through her empty sitting room.

She has forgotten us, but the music – that she remembers.

* * *

Yesterday, I got a letter from Grandpa Jack. Like all of his letters, it's hand-written on ivory monogrammed stationery – selected by Isabella years ago. I hold the heavy sheet of water-marked paper in one hand, and run my fingers across the words with the other. His letters always comfort me, but I have to force myself to read them. Sometimes I can't stand his kindness.

Dearest Jane,

How are things at school? I enjoyed your visit last weekend so much. Your grandma really perks up when you're here. Maybe you don't see it, but she gets so much out of your trips to New York. Did you notice the way she tapped her foot when you played that old Dizzy record for her on Saturday night? After you left, I put on the same re-cording, and she actually tried to have a conversation with me. It sounded more like rhythmic babbling than talking, but I'm sure, in her own way, she was saying something significant. Thank you for finding that record and having the savvy to play it for her.

I look at your school picture almost every day, and I can't believe how much you resemble your mother. You have her eyes, you know. One time, when Helen was about your age, she told me she hoped that someday she'd have a daughter. At the time, she was so immersed in her music; I couldn't imagine that she'd ever have a family. But she looked at me with those resolute eyes of hers and said she was determined to have everything she wanted.

I know you're having a hard time, my dear Jane. I see how you've changed since your mother passed away. I remain confident that you'll come to terms with what happened and find a way to make your life, and your mother's life, meaningful. When I look into your eyes, I remember her. And I'm reminded that Helen did indeed get everything she wanted.

You're my little heaven.
Love,
Grandpa Jack

I brush away the tears and shove the letter into my top dresser drawer. Then I open the drawer, take the letter out, and read it over and over.

Natural Woman, Natural Man

I go to Penn Academy, a private school located in Sewickley Heights, Pennsylvania. Most of my classmates have fathers who dress in dark gray three-piece suits during the week, but – when the weekend rolls around – trade them for jewel-colored outfits with embroidered alligators and ponies. The mothers, decked out in creamy cashmere sweaters, braided gold jewelry, and pastel tweed skirts from Talbot's, stay busy managing their staffs and children, hosting gin and tonic lawn parties, and decorating their homes in suitable shades of beige.

With my odd combination of dark skin and light hair, renegade-writer Dad, and dead mother, I'm the Penn Academy black sheep. My friend Leo says I could qualify to be the school mascot.

Early on I discovered I was unlikely to spot a drum set, bongos or even a pathetic kid's shaker toy in the corners of my classmates' living rooms. When I was four, I was shocked to learn that other mothers didn't go out at night with a conga drum, a beat-up leather tote bag, and a bunch of cool musicians dressed in black turtlenecks. The other mothers didn't wear tube-tops or commute from Pittsburgh to New York on the weekends. The other mothers combed their hair and served pecan-cheese balls at cocktail parties. They didn't consume tubs of Isaly's black raspberry ice cream, lift weights, or let their daughters experiment with bronze glitter eye shadow. "Pity," Mom would say.

"They haven't a clue what they're missing. *Quizá pore so es que son tan borrachos.* Maybe that's why they drink so much gin."

My dad – the author Sam Bowman – stays home all day writing novels about people who live in a place that sounds just like Sewickley Heights. The characters of his books sip martinis, talk about the stock market, and kill each other when they think no one is looking. Loyal fans come from all over to get Dad's autograph when he does a book signing, but his books cause a little paranoia around here. Our neighbors worry that he might be writing about them – although as far as I know, no one in the Heights has ever clobbered his wife with a seven iron and buried her in the dahlia bed to be dug up by a Vietnamese pot-bellied pig. That's the plot of his latest book. When I tell Dad that the neighbors might chill out if he changed his style, or at least the setting of his stories, he just laughs at me.

"Maybe you could write a novel about life in New Zealand or Montreal or something?" I say. "Binky Pendleton is gonna have a heart attack if you don't stop writing about Sewickley Heights."

"I don't write about Sewickley Heights."

"I know, but it sounds like Sewickley Heights."

"You can only write what you know," Dad says. Then he smiles and shrugs and that's the end of the conversation.

Dad is lanky in a cowboy kind of way – not that there are many cowboys in this neighborhood. He has long brown hair that he wears in a ponytail because he's too lazy to go and get a haircut. Once I overheard my math teacher telling an assistant that *Sam Bowman is a long cool drink of water,* whatever the heck that means. Half of the girls in my school have big fat crushes on Dad; his rough face and rangy body seem to make them act even sillier than they already are. The girls at P.A. sort of snub me, but whenever Dad shows up, they flock around me like baby ducks.

Dad grew up in Fox Chapel, another fancy part of Pittsburgh, where his parents still live. Grandma Millicent and Grandpa Vernon encouraged him to continue writing after he had a story published – at the age of twelve – in the magazine section of the Pittsburgh Post-Gazette. Never mind that the story – written in rhymed couplets – was about a teenage girl who kills her demented aunt with a bowl of poison quince marmalade. The story showed promise, and his parents advised him to keep at it.

Sam attended Columbia, graduated, and began working on his first novel while living in New York City. That's where he first saw – and heard – Helen, who was sitting in at Roseland with an all-star percussion line-up featuring the "Big Three" percussionists of Latin jazz: Tito Puente, Tito Rodriguez, and Machito. Sam, who had taken a date to the club, sat at a table right next to the stage, where the music was so loud it made the seat of his chair vibrate. In between tunes, as Helen was wiping sweat from her face with a towel and trying to catch her breath before the next count-off, she caught Sam smiling at her. She smiled back.

"I never believed in love at first sight," Mom once told me. "Until I locked eyes with your dad. When it happened, I felt as if a fast-running river was rushing through me, headed straight towards an open sea of forever-ness. I knew he was the one. When you fall in love Janey, I hope it happens just this way for you."

An open sea of forever-ness.

Mom said stuff like that. No wonder Dad fell in love with her.

With the bass player's help, Helen slipped her phone number to Sam, who called her as soon as he returned home, very late. Helen took a cab to his apartment on Riverside Drive, and pretty much moved in that night.

I was born a year later, after Sam had convinced Helen to move back to Pittsburgh with him. His parents had purchased the Sewickley Heights estate for Sam and Helen as a wedding gift, his trust fund had kicked in, and there was no reason why Helen couldn't fly back and forth to New York whenever she liked. Not to be outdone, Isabella and Jack gave my parents a renovated three-bedroom apartment in their 48th Street brownstone, to be used whenever Helen came to the city for a gig or a visit. This apartment became our weekend home when Helen began taping the Curly Dobson show in 1975. We still stay there when we visit Grandma Isabella and Grandpa Jack. My room has a view of the courtyard and Isabella's wisteria.

Mom was talented, confident, and in love with my father. She had me, a huge house, a great sense of humor, a couple of kooky maids, a career she adored, parents who loved her, a passion for her music, and enough money to last several lifetimes. Like Grandpa Jack said, she got everything she wanted.

"It's easy to be an artist when you've got money," Mom used to say. "In fact, it's almost an obligation."

Helen, unlike Isabella, didn't allow motherhood to interrupt her career. If anything, she played more. Mom gave me a lot of gifts during the twelve years I had with her, but that was probably the best of them all.

"Sigue adelante hija," she used to say. "Pase lo que pase."
Keep going, my daughter. No matter what.

Helen worked in a field that had never welcomed women, but if that bothered her, we never knew it. Girl singers, like Grandma Isabella, were one thing. Standing in front of a band in a pretty dress, singing a pretty song with a pretty voice was, almost, an accepted profession for a woman. But female percussionists were an oddity. When Helen attended college in the mid-sixties, she wasn't permitted to join the school jazz band. No girls allowed, no questions asked. Still, she was driven – big time. She quit school and doubled up on her private lessons. She played sessions, she studied, she worked a thousand horrible gigs in low-life clubs and tacky catering halls, and then, when she was ready, she asked Isabella to call her old friend Dizzy Gillespie. After listening to Helen play, Dizzy hired her for a six-week European tour, and introduced her to musicians like Mario Bauzá and Patato Valdés.

Helen joined the biggest boys' club in the world. Slapping the pants off a conga drum – plowing through hard-charging renditions of salsas and Merengues, traveling on a band bus full of chain-smoking heavy-drinking jazz cats, Helen was hardly the poster child for a Sewickley Heights society wife. But Sam – who was considered by many women to be the catch of the decade – chose her. Or maybe it was the other way around. Maybe Helen chose him.

I worry about Dad these days. I don't know why I can't talk to him about Mom. Three years after her death, we still tiptoe around the subject, avoiding conversations that might remind us that she's really gone. I have this chronic ache in the back of my throat that comes from wanting to cry. Maybe dad feels like that, too.

One of the silver-framed photos holds a picture of Sam and Helen on their wedding day at the William Penn Hotel in downtown Pittsburgh. Mom, dressed in a sleek bridal gown made of bright pink silk, appears to be tugging on Dad's arm, trying to get him to follow her up a narrow staircase. The movement in the picture smudges his features, and he seems confused. That's the way he always looks these days in real life – stuck on a staircase, pulled by a ghost.

Think

I ask Leonard Wainwright, my only real friend at Penn Academy, for advice about Dad. Leo is fifteen, like me, but I figure he might have the male perspective nailed down, so I invite him over on a Saturday morning. Leo and I have always hung out together, mainly because we share the same warped sense of humor. It all started in the first grade at Penn Academy, where we had a teacher named Mrs. Dick. When she introduced herself on the first day of school, I almost fell out of my chair laughing. The only other kid in the class who cracked a smile was Leo, who informed me that Mrs. Dick's husband was named Richard and was called Dick for short. Dick Dick. We laughed and laughed over that. We've been together ever since – nothing like first grade toilet humor to cement a friendship.

Today, Leo and I sit at my family's enormous kitchen table, one of my favorite places in the house. Embedded in the table-top is a mosaic of well-chosen scraps of Mexican tile, the colors swirling and forming a starburst pattern in shades of amber, terra cotta, and sunflower yellow. The table might be a work of art, but – because of the bumpy surface – it's a tricky place to eat. We're always spilling something. Just last night I cut a piece of pork chop, the knife skidded, and the bone slid off the plate with enough force to knock over my Fresca. Mary Two doesn't respond well to these emergencies. She's always bugging Dad to buy a "proper fuckin' breakfast nook." But that's not likely to happen. We're not a breakfast nook type of family.

"Jesus had a breakfast nook," says Mary Two. Before she moved from London to Sewickley Heights, Pennsylvania, Mary Two had worked as a housekeeper for the actor playing Jesus in the West End production of *Jesus Christ Superstar.*

"Jesus also had a smoked glass coffee table, a lava lamp, and several boyfriends," says Leo.

"Bite your tongue, laddy," says Mary Two.

"Hey, you're the one who told us that," says Leo.

"Yes, but it's not for public knowledge," says Mary Two. "Jesus was very good to me, at least until he got fired. The bloody producers of that show sacked him just because he started to get famous and asked for more money. Those theater people are fuckin' vultures, they are. Imagine, firing my Jesus."

"Whatever happened to your Jesus?" asks Leo. "Have you stayed in touch with him?"

"Last I heard he was tending bar at a pub in Piccadilly Circus," says Mary Two. "Once you've played Jesus, there's no-where to go but down."

I've positioned one of the silver-framed pictures of Mom on a counter right across from my seat at the kitchen table. In this picture, my mother sits cross-legged on top of the mosaic table, with me, age three, on her lap. We're eating cookies and laughing. I like to think that she made the cookies, but I'm sure she didn't.

Mary Two puts out a plate of maple rolls for Leo and me, then she sets down two cups of tea. Leo and I hate tea, but Mary Two is determined to teach us to love it.

"English Breakfast Tea, Earl Grey. The best," she mumbles. "Be careful at the table, Leo, you're sitting in a particularly un-steady spot. Keep your hands on the cup at all times. Don't want a fuckin' mess now, do we?" Mary Two bustles out of the room. She's a champion bustler.

After we're sure she has disappeared, we dump the tea in the sink and make chocolate milk. From the hallway we hear the sound of Mary One in the bathroom, singing a song about razors and guns.

"You know," says Leo. "Mary One has genuine talent, but she really ought to rethink that "Pigfoot" number. It's weird."

I get up and close the kitchen door, which will start both Marys gossiping about what Leo and I are doing in here. He's a boy, I'm a girl, and we're both fifteen. Of course they'll gossip. Who cares?

"So what do you think about Dad?" I hate this. Even with Leo, I can't stand talking about anything that might lead to a discussion of Mom's death. But I've got to start somewhere. "Dad seems so, I don't know, depressed or something."

"Your dad can't get over your mom," Leo says. "He doesn't want to."

"I can't get over her either," I say. "And believe me, I want to. Maybe he has the same problem."

"Maybe you don't want to either," Leo says.

"Oh right," I say. "Like I'm interested in spending the rest of my life watching Curly Dobson re-runs and crying."

"So don't watch them."

"Sure. I never thought of that."

"And as far as your dad goes, he needs to get out of this house every once in awhile. He spends all day writing about people dying when the very thing he's trying to do is forget about someone dying. I mean, doesn't that seem a little perverse to you?"

"Good word, Leo. Perverse. Anyway, Dad gets out. He goes to the store with Mary Two, all the time. And the two of them have long talks."

"Mary Two? How much fun can that be for him? I can just hear her cussing out the dairy department manager at the Giant Eagle. 'What do you bloody mean you don't have any fuckin' buttermilk?'"

"Okay, okay, I get it. But last month, see, he did a huge tour of bookstores in Utah. He told me he met hundreds of loyal fans and signed books until his hand cramped."

"That's not getting out Jane, that's working."

"What are you trying to say here Leo? That he needs to start dating?"

"Well, yeah, that's exactly what I'm saying."

"So. Who?"

"Good question." Leo's eyes drift to the kitchen window.

"You can't possibly be thinking of Daphne Shuttleworth across the street?"

There's a long silent pause.

"Leo?"

"Yeah, well, she's divorced."

"She also has a stable full of horses and a face to match."

Leo and I like to categorize people into one of three face-types: cookie, bird, or horse. This game – invented by a local Pittsburgh celebrity named Josie Carey – can be very entertaining when played in a public space – a mall, a sports stadium, or an airline terminal. Here's a fact: More cookie-faces live in Pittsburgh than in New York. New York is full of bird-faces. Cookie-face and bird-face are not so bad, but horse-face is generally awful. You see a lot of horse-face in this community. Too much money and inbreeding, I guess. I'm bird. Leo is cookie. Mary One is bird, and Mary Two is an extremely rare cross-breed of bird and horse.

"Right," says Leo. "Mrs. Shuttleworth is definitely horse – in a certain light she's a dead ringer for Secretariat."

"And even without the horse-face, do you honestly think Dad is the type to go on fox hunts? He has never been on a horse in his life, as far as I know. Not even a pony."

"Hi-ho Silver, away!"

"Stop it Leo. Right now."

"What about Pamela Dunbar?"

"You mean Mrs. Smythe's gardener?"

"Right. She's bird."

"She's also nineteen, Leo."

"Right. Young bird. Spring chicken. Some men like that."

"You're impossible. Forget the spring chicken."

"You asked for my help."

"I didn't think you'd respond with the Episcopal version of *The Dating Game*."

"I'm telling you, a little female companionship would work wonders."

"He's surrounded by females, Leo."

"Right, a drum-pounding teenage daughter, a maid who sits on the toilet singing 'Gimme a Pigfoot and a Bottle of Beer' and a second maid who looks like Margaret Thatcher on a bad-hair day."

"Mary One and Mary Two are not just maids, Leo, they're family. Do not insult them, it pisses me off."

"Right. Sorry. You know I'm a huge fan of both of them. But your dad needs more than the Marys."

"I guess you've got a point."

"Give me a little time," says Leo, "and I'll think of someone perfect."

"Yeah, right," I say.

"And you know what else?" says Leo. "Your face is all red. How come any time we touch on any subject connected to your mom you look like a tomato ready to explode?"

"Leo."

"What?"

"Never mind."

"You need to talk to someone about your feelings."

"You've been watching too many TV talk shows."

"True. And talking about your feelings is a big theme. According to numerous experts, if you don't talk, you really could blow up."

"Dad keeps taking me to these stupid shrinks, but I can't make myself talk to them."

"Why?"

"I don't want to talk about – " I swallow.

"That night?"

"Yeah, I don't want to talk about that night."

"Why?"

"Don't know. Afraid, I guess."

"Jane, look. There's nothing left to be afraid of. There was a terrible fire. Your mom died. You almost died yourself. These are the facts, and I know, in some ways, you accept them. But it seems like there's something else you need to talk about. You've been hiding something from everyone, including me. What happened that night, before the fire? Did you have a fight with your mom?"

"No! Leo, stop. Now. Man, you sound like my shrink of the month. He keeps hammering at me to *talk talk talk*. There's nothing to talk about. I just need time, to, I don't know, process what happened."

"You've had three years."

"Yeah, well I might need thirty, Dr. Wainwright."

"You could talk to me, Jane. It might help."

"I could. But not yet. I'm not ready." I trace a tiny mosaic flower on the tabletop with my finger. "Please, Leo."

"Don't wait too long, tomato-head." Leo stands up, jostles the table, and spills chocolate milk all over my favorite James Brown t-shirt.

My Mother's Eyes

These days I don't play the drums for anyone other than Mr. Hammill and myself. I'm sure Dad and the Marys can hear me when I practice, and Leo told me once that when he rides past our house on his bike he can feel the ground shaking, but I think he's making that up.

Before Mom died, I'd go onstage with her every so often and bang out a number at the end of her concerts. The audience loved it, and it was super-cool for me. Mom even bought me a black turtleneck. Trying to avoid a *Partridge Family* vibe, she limited my appearances to school vacations or concerts that took place in the afternoon or early evening. Once, when I was nine, I almost played with her on the Curly Dobson Show. The program's producer had heard me play with Mom at a New York City Jazzmobile concert and invited me to appear with the Curly Dobson Band during one of their brief on-camera appearances.

The night Mom took me to the rehearsal and taping, Curly sat alone at a big desk, next to the over-stuffed sapphire blue sofa where he interviewed his celebrity guests. Curly – half cookie-face, half horse-face – was bald, which struck me as very funny. He had the biggest hands I'd ever seen – fingers like bananas. He sat, lump-like, looking over his script and mumbling to himself about last minute changes. I thought he looked like a complete crazy person.

"Water!" he screamed, and an assistant quickly approached the stage with a bottle of Evian and a towel to mop his glistening head. "I'm so bloated," he announced to no one in particular. "All I had for lunch was a bagel and a glass of scotch, and now look at me. I'm schvitzin' like a fat girl and I can barely close my pants." My mother gave me *the look* – the one that meant I wasn't supposed to laugh, but I couldn't help myself. I bent down and pretended like I was tying my shoes.

The band waited for a cue to begin playing the interlude music that would lead them into the next commercial break. I sat at a red Slingerland drum set that had been adjusted for my height. For the next tune, a funky rendition of "Mercy Mercy Mercy," I was slated to play alongside my mother and guitar hotshot Bardo Hopper. As Mom reached down to tuck in my shirt, I caught a glimpse of the three of us on the television monitor. We looked like we were trapped in a little box, and all of the sudden I felt silly.

"Mom, I don't want to be on television."

"You don't? I thought you were excited about this."

"Not anymore. I quit."

"Why? It'll be fun."

"This isn't fun. It's boring. All we do is stand here and wait, and when we do play they make us stop right away."

"That's because we're doing a sound check, sweetie. And camera blocking always takes a long time."

"These lights are too hot. And that guitar guy stinks."

"Jane, Bardo Hopper is one of the best guitar players in the world."

"Yeah, I know, but he stinks, like he smells bad."

"Oh. Well you're right about that. Good thing you're not sitting next to Conrad in the trumpet section, he's even worse.

He's on a weird fish diet and he smells like old cod. But they're good musicians, so I've learned to live with the smell."

"So what do I have to do to get fired?"

"Nothing at all, honey. I'll fire you. If you're going to be a musician, you better get used to it." Mom took the Production Assistant aside, explained that I'd resigned from my position, and asked her to escort me to the green room, where I waited out the rehearsal by practicing press rolls on my practice pad. Later that night, when the studio audience showed up and they began taping the show for real, Mom sneaked me onto the bandstand, where I sat, hidden from view, at my mother's feet. Looking up at her from the floor, she seemed like a golden giant to me, dancing around the conga drum, her bright brown eyes throwing sparks of love in my direction every time she glanced down to check if I was still there.

Seven years later, when the re-run of that particular show airs, I sit frozen on my bed, watching my mother's face as she gazes away from the camera and smiles down at the floor, where I kneel, hidden and safe. I know she's looking at me, but no one else would ever guess.

* * *

I think my friend Leo is gay, but he doesn't know it. Not yet. No one knows, except me, and I'm not about to tell him because I'm not exactly an expert on these things. The kids at school think we're an item, which is fine with both of us. I'm not interested in any of the boys at Penn Academy. There are some nice guys there, like Raymond Browning, who is a math whiz and helps me with biology experiments – but I can tell he is interested in doing more with me than dissecting frogs and

memorizing geometry formulas. So I avoid him. The last thing I
want right now is a boyfriend. I can't imagine that I'll ever want
one, but Mary Two keeps telling me that these feelings sneak
up on a young woman, so who knows. I listen to the girls in the
locker room – some of them younger than me – babbling on and
on about who is doing what, and it makes my stomach flip. I
wonder why they're rushing into grown-up land like speeding
trains, when they could be kids just a little while longer. Being
a kid is a good thing.

Penn Academy isn't known for its music department. We
have a marching band, but I can't picture myself in a sailor's
hat with a synthetic purple ostrich plume on it, playing march-
tempo versions of "Smoke on the Water" or "Wild Thing,"
which seem to be the only two selections in their repertoire.

Leo, in a good-hearted attempt to get me to play in public, dragged me to a band rehearsal one afternoon last August.
Penn Academy is a teeny-tiny school, and there are only fifteen kids in the marching band. You can't really choreograph
sophisticated marching band formations with fifteen kids, but
that has never stopped Mr. Dilernia, the band director, from trying. Astonished, we hung out in the bleacher seats and watched
him force the band into a serpentine pattern that was supposed
to wrap around the fifty-yard line and spell out **P.A.** for Penn
Academy.

No matter how Mr. Dilernia arranged the kids, they always
bumped into each other before unwinding into a formation that
looked exactly like a crooked line. I felt really sorry for the boys
who had to stand in the spots where the periods should have
been. They were both trombone players, which is humiliating
enough, but then they had to crouch down on the ground so

that the "period" effect would be more evident. After hours of practicing this routine in the blistering sun, Mr. Dilernia threw his arms up in the air and shouted that maybe the band should try for a simple figure eight formation.

"Maybe they should form the number one," said Leo. "That would be easier."

About a month after the marching band experiment, Leo decided I should investigate playing drum set with the Penn Academy Orchestra. This scheme seemed slightly better than the marching band idea, mainly because the orchestra practiced indoors, had hipper outfits to wear at performances, and never ever played "Smoke on the Water." But they did play horrible orchestral arrangements of pop tunes like "Song Sung Blue" and "Born Free." Last year, at the big Spring Fling Concert, they played a frightening version of "2001, A Space Odyssey," which had a really dorky timpani part that sounded especially bad since no one had a clue about tuning the timpani. And the *Space Odyssey* trumpet player kept playing higher and higher, with each screeching note less steady than the last – well really, I thought my brain might explode. But to be a good sport I told Leo I'd at least check out an orchestra rehearsal. On the day I showed up, all of the musicians were in the art studio, painting pictures of their instruments. Suddenly I understood why they always sounded so horrible. Instead of practicing, they were wasting time in an arts and crafts corner, making acrylic paintings of oboes and French horns. It's nice to be able to draw a viola, but it's even nicer to be able to play one. I made an excuse about having a stomach ache and got out of the art room just as Mr. Dilernia was headed in my direction with a watercolor kit and an apron.

So, having given up on musical opportunities at school, I keep playing at home, alone and with records. I listen to a lot of Mom's favorite recordings, the Latin-jazz stuff that made her so happy, records like Woody Herman's *Early Autumn* with Candido and José Mangual, *Gillespiana* with Dizzy, Ray Barretto and Candido, or the 1972 Art Blakey recording *Child's Dance*, featuring Ray Mantilla on conga. Beautiful. Beats the hell out of "Born Free."

I have my own R&B, funk, and fusion favorites – classics driven by amazing drummers like Clyde Stubblefield, Steve Gadd, or Peter Erskine. Peter is such a killer drummer. Sometimes, when I'm snoozing through Senorita Mulkowski's Spanish lecture – the last class of the day for me at Penn Academy – I dream about racing home so I can listen to Peter playing on this track called "Birdland" from *8:30*, my favorite Weather Report record. Then I'll put on Steve Gadd and listen to the way he grooves on my Steely Dan records. So much to hear, not enough time. There's this new guy on the drum scene, Dennis Chambers – playing with George Clinton and Funkadelic – who makes me crazy, he's so good.

When I feel like my energy is low, I'll put on a James Brown recording and hear the pop of the rhythm guitar lashing out like a leather whip, and the way the bass pushes the bottom of the music up to a place where I can grab on and go for a ride – and I know I'm onto something I can understand. I feel, I don't know, rescued. I try to explain to Leo that this is the kind of music I want to play. He squints at me, and nods.

"But you can't just keep playing with records."

"Why not?" I ask.

"Because you're too good for that. Other people need to hear you. Maybe not school kids or Mr. Dilernia, but there are other people out there who will love hearing you, that's for sure."

I have, until this point, never considered that my music should be for anyone other than my Mom and myself. Except for the silver-framed photos, my music is all I have left of her. And I don't want to share.

"You have a gift, Jane," Leo says, as if he's reading my mind. "Like your mom, like your grandmother. You have to do something with your talent. Isabella quit and Helen died. It's up to you to carry on for them."

"Man, Leo, do you have to be so dramatic?"

"Well, it's true. You're wasting your talent. Helen and Isabella would want you to get out there and play. For the whole world. It's time to stop being so selfish. We've got to find a way."

"What difference does it make where I play, as long as I'm playing?"

"You're practicing. I don't think that's the same thing as rehearsing and performing with other musicians. I don't know why it isn't the same. But it isn't."

I'm pissed off at Leo, but I can see from the look on his face that he loves me in his Leo way. He's the only person my age who gets it, sort of. He understands that playing the drums – the way I play them – is the one thing that keeps me going. Practicing distracts me from remembering: Remembering her, remembering us, remembering the way a pointless fire, brilliant and cruel, lit up the sky with my childhood.

Do Right Woman

Leo's mother, the social wonder woman Sara "Spanky" Wainwright, heads the committees of four separate charities in Pittsburgh, and serves on the boards of the Pittsburgh Symphony, the Pittsburgh Ballet, and the Pittsburgh Foundation. When Spanky isn't raising funds, she's raising hell. She's a rebel in a Chanel suit and Gucci shoes, an activist with manicured hands and two-hundred dollar blond highlights.

"Leo, darling," Spanky says to Leo when I'm hanging out at his house over Christmas. "Emerald green – especially when enhanced with just a tad of teal – is a smashing color for you. That cardigan looks ever so fabulous with your eyes. But must you clutter the effect with that hideous red t-shirt?"

"Chill out, Spanky!" says Leo. "I thought the red and green color-combo was pretty snazzy. And besides, Jane gave me this shirt for Christmas."

"Yeah," I say. "That's a picture of the Commodores on the front."

"What's a Commodore?" asks Spanky.

"They're a funk band that – "

"Never mind that Jane," says Leo. "Tell her where you bought it."

"Yeah, right," I say. "I ordered it from an organization that donates their profits to a children's rescue fund in Ethiopia. Dad told me about them. A lot of musicians are participating in the fund drive, and –"

"Good heavens darling, what a perfectly wooooooonderful idea," Spanky says. "You must give me their contact information. We could work that into next month's fundraiser at Penn Academy. Buy a Commodore, feed a child. Something like that."

Most of the neighbors in Sewickley Heights worship Spanky Wainwright, but they're also a little scared of her. My mother said that Spanky always strutted into the Penn Academy PTA meetings like she owned the school. Maybe she does. In this neighborhood, you never know.

When Spanky snaps her fingers, the rich folks of Pittsburgh flock around her like sheep with wallets. But it's more than money she's after. Every year Spanky wins re-election as president of the PTA, causing parents all over Sewickley Heights to shake in fear of the complicated craft projects she's bound to organize. Spanky wants *commitment*, and she gets it. For instance, two years ago she decided we needed hand-embroidered holiday tablecloths for the cafeteria. I'm not sure how she managed it, but before the end of the winter term the school linen closet was stocked with over a hundred hand-made tablecloths cross-stitched with Halloween pumpkins, Thanksgiving turkeys, Valentine's hearts, and Easter eggs. Mary One embroidered a cloth with a spring motif, featuring dancing black swans. Mary Two opted for a President's Day theme. How she cross-stitched an exact likeness of Abraham Lincoln on a piece of mint-green linen is beyond me, but then again, Mary Two is the only person I know with custom-fitted thimbles for all ten of her fingers. She once told me her sewing skills came from months of repairing *Jesus Christ Superstar* costumes.

"Oh, they had a costume department alright, but Jesus preferred my stitching. In many of Jesus' scenes, he wore a simple

Calvin Klein loincloth with a comfort-fit waistband. Those were easy to mend. But that 'Garden of Gethsemane' scene was fuckin' brutal, it was," says Mary Two. "Every time Jesus fell on his knees he ripped a hole in his flowing robe. And guess who had to repair it? It really pissed me off that they didn't treat him better, let me tell you."

"How do you say that, anyway?" asks Leo. "Geth – what?"

"Geth-se-ma-ne" says Mary Two. "A bugger of a word, that one. The Jesus who had the job before my Jesus was named Seth – I swear to God. And Seth – he was a good Jesus, too – got fired cause he had so much trouble pronouncing Gethsemane – really, swear to God. You'd think with a name like Seth – but he always got tongue-tied, poor bloke. I swear to God."

Every winter Spanky organizes a "Spruce Up the School Week," and all of us, parents and kids alike, paint cheerful murals on the corridor walls and maps of third world countries in the cafeteria. She's clever, that Spanky. We can't complain about the cafeteria food while we're staring at maps of places where there's no food at all.

It's hard for me to get into this school activity stuff. Most of the time, when I'm not practicing or hanging out with Leo, I feel sort of sad. Or maybe lonely is a better word. But if I don't at least pretend to participate, everyone at home freaks out, the teachers start looking at me with that *poor Jane her mother is dead* look, and before I know it, the principal is calling Dad and telling him to take me back to one of those loopy shrinks. Who needs that? Better to suck it up and fake a little school spirit.

This year we're baking cookies and cupcakes to raise money for poor people in Costa Rica. I often wonder why we can't just collect the money instead of going through the baking ritual, but Spanky insists that this kind of teamwork builds our sense of community and, at the same time, encourages us to help the needy. I guess she's right, but it's hard for me to see the connection between the poster of the starving girl and the platters of Rice Krispie treats and triple fudge brownies on the decorated table in the Penn Academy cafeteria. This year the big hit seems to be a concoction called "trash," which looks like five kinds of crappy breakfast cereal mixed with sugar and covered with melted margarine.

There's an unspoken rule about not involving maids or nannies in school activities, but since my mom is dead, Spanky and her various committees have let me slide. Dad is a really good father, but I've never been able to drag him to parent-student events, especially the ones involving craft projects. So I rely on the Marys. Last fall Mary One painted an eight-foot tall Billie Holiday on the wall outside of the school gymnasium. The idea had been to paint sports figures, but Mary One didn't grasp the concept. Or maybe she did and she chose to ignore it. Anyway, that stupid horse-faced Mr. Mann, the sports teacher with the huge biceps and a brain the size of a bean, assumed that because Mary was painting a person with dark skin on the wall next to the gym that the subject must have been some kind of athlete, probably a female javelin thrower. You'd think the feather boa might have tipped him off.

From the size of the painting, some of the kids thought Billie might have been a basketball player, but I cleared that up right away. Mr. Mann wanted to cover Mary One's work of art with a life-sized poster of Mark Spitz in his stars and stripes bikini, but Leo – who questioned the merit of attending a school where no one could identify Billie Holiday – decided to take a stand. He told Spanky that if Mr. Mann covered Billie with Mark Spitz we would both quit school and move to West

Virginia. We won. Billie stayed on the corridor wall, surrounded by Roberto Clemente, Franco Harris, and some triple-jump guy whose name I can never remember. Leo, who sings in the school choir, suggested to Mr. Dilernia that the choir perform one of Billie's songs for the dedication of the newly decorated hallway, and they brayed their way through a rich-suburban-kid version of "Ain't Nobody's Business If I Do." Mary One cried a little at the ceremony, but I'm not sure why. I thought the whole thing was kind of cute until the choir charged into the third chorus of the song and began clapping – encouraged by an uptight Mr. Dilernia – on "one" and "three," which made the song sound a lot like Pittsburgh Steelers football chant.

Mary Two takes care of the bake sales for me, and I'm grateful because I've inherited my mother's inability to make anything more than a peanut butter sandwich. Mary Two likes to cook, but she makes weird English food that's either gray or gooey, and sometimes both. For bake sales, Mary Two insists on making her famous Butterscotch Marshmallow Trifle, a dessert that tastes okay, but looks pretty much like dog vomit. It's not a big seller at P.A. bake sales. Every year, to spare Mary Two's feelings, Leo and I pool our allowance money and buy out Mary Two's Butterscotch Marshmallow Trifle before she shows up. We choke down as much as we can, then – feeling queasy and guilty – stuff the leftover goop in the cafeteria garbage cans.

* * *

Leo is a gentle version of his mother. He lacks her social ambition, but outdoes her when it comes to focus. When an idea snatches his attention, he clings to it until he finds a way to make it work. Sometimes he fools me. I'll think he has forgotten some whacky scheme he has dreamed up, and then, months later, he'll reach his goal, surprising everybody but himself. Like the time he told me he wanted to win the Western Pennsylvania Young Inventor's Competition, when he had never in his life invented anything. Leo had never built model airplanes; he had never owned a chemistry set, a rock tumbler machine, a short wave radio kit, or any of those educational toys that encourage scientific thinking. About as close as Leo had gotten to inventing was the time he cleaned out Mary Two's spice rack, dumped everything into a bucket, added milk, two packets of strawberry Jell-O, just a tad of Vodka and a spoonful of Tang, and claimed to have invented the Elixir of Life. Mary Two got steaming mad when she attempted to make her famous "Last Supper Chicken Curry" recipe and discovered that the curry powder was missing, but we kept quiet, convinced that Leo was about to strike it rich with a potion that would help us stay six years old forever. Sadly, the Elixir of Life, which was stashed on a shelf downstairs, grew moldy, leaked, and made the basement smell for days. When Mary Two went to investigate the cause of the big stink, she found a Tupperware box – holding the Elixir of Life – dripping a foul-smelling Technicolor paste all over my mother's stored collection of Brazilian rain sticks. After that, Leo stopped inventing. Until he entered the Young Inventor's Competition.

"I know I can do it," he said. "I just need to invent an invention."

"Fine," I said, just don't do it at our house. "Mary Two is still scraping moldy Tang off the floor in the storage room. Use Spanky's kitchen."

I thought he had given up, but two months later the contest people announced that Leo had won in the ten-and-under category with Leo's Lego Eliminator, a vacuum cleaner for Lego's. He had used huge quantities of duct tape, an old bag-pipe he discovered in Spanky's attic, and an ancient electric fan – the kind that threatens to chop off your fingers and rip your hair out by the roots. Leo's Lego Eliminator sucked up the annoying blocks in world-record time, storing them safely inside the dusty guts of the bagpipe until the next play date. Cool. The machine made a weird droning noise that reminded me of an Old Spice commercial – but it was effective. He took the twenty-five dollar prize and bought himself the Lego Superset. Typical Leo.

* * *

Leo and I plod through the school year, and I forget that he has promised to find a girlfriend for dad and a place for me to play with other musicians. But he hasn't forgotten.

I don't much like Sewickley Heights during the winter months. The February wind hums a gloomy-doomy dirge, and the clouds are the color of a cement driveway. So I stay inside even more than usual, practicing, staring out the bay window and wondering why the sun has disappeared. One dingy Sunday afternoon, the doorbell chimes. We have a cool doorbell; it plays the first few bars of "Chain of Fools," one of my favorite tunes. It was a gift from Mom and Dad for my ninth birthday. I'm sweating like a pig cause I've been practicing for three hours and I'm right in the middle of a marathon "Funky Drummer" session, attempting to copy Clyde Stubblefield's groove. Clyde makes it sound so easy, but it's not. I'm mad that I have to stop playing to answer the door, but the Marys are wearing earplugs, and Dad is busy writing. I go to the foyer and peer through the leaded glass window, expecting a couple of Jehovah's Witnesses or a Girl Scout selling boxed shortbread cookies. Instead I see Leo standing next to a striking woman with glossy skin, almost the same shade as the Steinway in my living room. Leo sees me peeking through the glass. He smiles and nods.

Just then, the sun breaks through the murky Pittsburgh sky and the woman becomes backlit, a cashmere-clad silhouette of long muscles and strong bones. As I grasp the brass knob of the heavy oak door, I catch a glimpse of one of the silver-framed snapshots sitting on the granite table under the foyer mirror. In the photo, Mom is buttoning her coat, preparing to go outdoors. There's something mysterious about the look on her face. She stares out at me from inside the fancy frame, like a fortuneteller bundled in a bright red parka.

My hands and feet tingle and I feel like I've been dipped in warm water. I do the only sensible thing – I open the door, and let in the light.

Convince Me

The icy air burns my cheeks.

"Hi!" says Leo.

"Hello," says the mystery woman.

"Hello." My mouth is dry and I'm gawking.

"Are you going to invite us in?" says Leo. "Are you okay? You look like ET or something."

"Yeah, I'm fine," I say, switching to my formal voice. "Just having a temporary lapse of courtesy. Please, yes, come in. It's awfully cold out there, even for February." Leo and the woman to walk into the foyer. She's tall, almost six feet, and her hair is braided and piled high on her head. The contours of her face are razor sharp, her uncovered neck long and graceful. She's pure bird, an eagle soaring straight into my home. As she passes me, I notice tiny pearl earrings. I think of Christmas – she smells like cinnamon and cloves. Again, I feel warm.

"Miss Blue," says Leo in his best formal introduction voice. "Allow me to introduce Jane Bowman, the drummer I was telling you about. Jane, may I present Miss Olivia Blue." Then, as if Miss Blue isn't there, he whispers to me, "She's a music teacher – a really good one!"

My heart sinks. I don't want another music teacher. But I want this woman in my house – more than anything – so I proceed with the meeting and greeting drill and offer my hand to her.

"How do you do?" I say with precise Penn Academy diction. Leo and I are awfully good at this social crap. Pretty scary for a couple of fifteen year-olds, but that's what happens to kids growing up in Sewickley Heights – we learn to be polite while muttering obscenities to ourselves. I feel funny about what I'm wearing – gym shorts and a cut-off t-shirt. It's my favorite practice outfit.

"Very well, thank you. And you?"

"Very well, thank you," I say. Olivia Blue peels off her soft leather gloves and places them in her quilted suede handbag. I take her coat, fold it over my arms, and hold it in front of me like wooly armor. I look at Leo. He's bubbling with glee, but he contains himself and waits for Miss Blue to speak.

"I heard you playing from the driveway. We stood outside for quite awhile listening." She lowers her voice to a whisper and raises one eyebrow. "That was some very funky shit – sounded like you were playing along with a Clyde Stubblefield track."

"Uh, yes, that's exactly right." Did I hear her right? Did she really say *funky shit*? And how does she know about Clyde Stubblefield? Holy cow.

"Clyde Stubblefield is a master," she says.

"You've got that right," I say. "Yeah."

"I *knew* this was gonna be cool," says Leo.

"You might try hitting that bass drum a little harder." says Miss Blue. "Give it some juice. No need to sound like a wimp. After all, the song is called '*Funky* Drummer,' isn't it?" Miss Blue smiles at me, then she glances in the heavy mahogany-framed mirror hanging over the hallway table. She pats her hair, looks down, and sees the framed picture of my mom. She picks it up.

"Ah, Helen Bowman. Leo told me your mother was a percussionist, but I didn't realize you were Helen's daughter. Didn't make the connection, although I should have. I'd forgotten that she lived in this area for a few years. She was a fine musician, Jane. The best. I'm sorry you lost her. What a terrible tragedy."

"Thank you." My eyes clog with tears. I never cry in front of strangers. Ever. Miss Blue stares at me for a second, and a soft breeze brushes against the back of my neck. She hands the photo to me, and I return it to its place on the table. Back where it belongs.

"So!" Olivia Blue lifts her eyes and peers through the arched entranceway into the living room. "Looks like you've got yourself a nice little Gretsch drum set there. That's a collector's item, you know." She pauses, waiting to be invited into the living room.

"Yes, it belonged to my mother." I don't want Olivia Blue to go into the living room, but I don't want her to leave either. I wish Leo would help me with this, but he's standing in the corner, arms crossed and grinning, like he's waiting for a circus matinee to begin.

"Let's go back to the kitchen," I say. "It's more comfortable there. Would you like something to drink?"

Suddenly, Mary Two explodes out of the kitchen with huge cooking mitts on each arm. She stops in her tracks when she spots Olivia Blue. "Bollocks! Company! Jesus, Mary, and fuckin' Joseph! We've got company!" she shrieks, and then bustles back into the kitchen.

"Uh, that's Mary Two, she lives with us, and she's wearing earplugs," I explain to Miss Blue. "That's why she's shouting.

And except for Leo, we don't have many visitors these days, so I suspect she's excited. And please excuse the bad language, she really can't help herself."

"Nothing I haven't heard before," says Miss Blue, laughing.

"Guess what? She used to clean house for Jesus," says Leo. "When she was in London, she – "

Passion's a distraction
Worth a fraction of the cost
Just because there's an attraction
Doesn't mean the stars are crossed,
Look into my eyes before my common sense is lost,
Convince me I should fall in love with you.

"Who is that?" says Miss Blue.

Leo, noticing that I'm a little overwhelmed, says, "That's Mary One," he says. "She lives here, too."

"She sounds just like Billie Holiday," says Miss Blue. "Remarkable. Really remarkable. And that's one of Billie's most obscure songs. Hardly anyone knows it. "

"'Convince Me' is one of Mary One's better numbers," says Leo. "But you don't wanna be around when she starts in on 'Pigfoot.'"

Too chaotic, too hypnotic,
An exotic silent race,
I'm resisting, you're insisting,
I'll survive your next embrace . . .

"Do you folks have a music studio in there?" she asks, looking puzzled and pointing to the door.

"No, Miss Blue, that's just the guest bathroom," I say.

"You know," says Leo, winking. "The powder room."

"The powder room?" says Miss Blue, just as Mary Two hustles back into the hallway and begins to pound on the bathroom door.

"Mary One, we've got company," yells Mary Two. "Listen to me right now, Canary! Take out the earplugs, stop the brayin' and come out here and greet our guest."

"NO!"

"Please."

"Don't be botherin' me in here," shouts Mary One from behind the door. I ain't comin' out 'til I'm ready. You know what to do. Serve up a couple of them scone things and boil up some of that tea you're so crazy about."

"Well, doesn't that sound great?" says Miss Blue. "Do you have another restroom I might use before we get settled?"

"Yes, sure," I say. "Miss Mary Two, will you please show Miss Blue to the bathroom upstairs?"

"The yellow one, the floral one, or the red one?"

"Uh, it doesn't matter."

"The red one's cleaner."

"Fine, then, the red one."

"On the other hand the yellow one was painted just last week," says Mary Two, "and we did just buy that lovely new toilet seat."

I'm ready to die of embarrassment.

"You know," says Olivia Blue. "I love the color red. Let's go for that." She smiles at me.

"I'll put the water on for tea," I say as Mary Two and Miss Blue head to the staircase. Leo and I go into the kitchen.

"Okay Leo, what's this about?" I whisper.

"Isn't she cool?" says Leo. "I heard she sang back-ups on a session with Aretha, and that she knows George Benson personally."

"Really?" I say.

"Really. Cool, right?" says Leo.

"I don't know if cool is the word, but yes, she's – uh – unique. But why is she here?"

"Spanky threw a fund-raiser brunch this morning for the school where Miss Blue teaches. The party was at our house. Miss Blue was the guest of honor. You should hear her talk about music."

"I hope she didn't use the *funky shit* terminology in front of Binky Pendleton and Daphney Shuttleworth."

"No! She *charmed* them, Jane. I'll bet she cleans up on donations."

"Where does she teach?"

"Allegheny Gatehouse."

"That rehab place?"

"Miss Blue says it's a school for teenagers with problems."

"Yeah, well that usually means gangs and dope."

"Probably. But the way she describes it, the school is focusing on arts programs to get these kids turned around. You know, paint a picture, play an instrument, kick the habit, break the cycle."

"I'm sure it's not so simple Leo," I say. "Okay, so where do I fit into this?"

"She needs a drummer."

"What?"

"She needs a drummer in her school band."

"Man, Leo. I can't go play drums for a bunch of juvenile delinquents."

"Come on, where's your spirit of adventure? It's an R&B band, Jane. You wouldn't be playing the "Theme From Rocky" or "The William Tell Overture" like you would with Mr. Dilernia. You'd be playing some *funky shit*. More your style." Leo's smile is wider than the Monongahela River. "Just talk to her."

The teakettle whistles and Miss Blue sweeps into the kitchen with Mary Two scurrying behind her, still wearing the cooking mitts and holding a toilet scrub brush in one hand.

"Oh my sweet baby Jesus!" Mary Two yells. "Where are my fuckin' manners?" She opens a kitchen cabinet, and without even looking, tosses the toilet brush inside.

"Have a seat, Miss Blue," says Leo.

"This is a lovely home, Jane," she says. "So many beautiful things. This table for instance. It's a work of art. Where did you find it?"

"I'm not sure where it's from exactly," I say. "My mother bought it from an artist while she was on tour in Mexico. Cozumel, I think."

Mary Two places a plate of scones on the table and sets out the china teacups. The cups are Wedgwood, from Grandma Millicent, and the china is so thin it's almost translucent. I can't remember the last time we used them.

"Hold onto your cups, I'm about to pour," says Mary Two.

"The mosaic makes the table surface a little unsteady and you have to protect yourself from spills and burns," explains a very serious Leo to Miss Blue. We brace ourselves and Mary Two pours the scalding liquid. Mary One begins to sing again from the bathroom.

Love is too quixotic,
An erotic treasure chest,
Perhaps I should leave town,
And give my heart a needed rest,
Or I could simply kiss you, put my judgment to the test,
Convince me I should fall in love with you.

"Exquisite," says Miss Blue.

I don't know if Miss Blue is talking about Mary's voice, the table, or the tea. I get up and close the door. My house seems like a complete lunatic asylum.

"So Leo tells me you're one helluva drummer," says Miss Blue. "You know, you have to be a helluva good drummer to be better than no drummer at all."

I choke on my tea.

"What did you say?" I sputter.

"'You have to be a helluva good drummer to be better than no drummer at all – Chet Baker said that."

"Oh. Oh. Oh yeah. My mom used to say that, too. I thought, um, I thought she made it up."

"Didn't your mom play with Chet in the early seventies?"

"Yeah, she did."

"He must have said that to her then."

"Guess so." I shrug and look away.

"Anyway, from what I heard while we were standing outside, I'd say Leo is right. You're one helluva good drummer. Looks like this young man knows what he's talking about."

"I have a future as a talent scout," Leo says. "Or maybe an agent. You think William Morris is looking for anyone? I could start in the mailroom and work my way to the top ..."

"I'll get right to the point," says Miss Blue. "I'm a music teacher and music therapist at Allegheny Gatehouse. It's a school for troubled teenage boys, most of whom come from unfortunate circumstances."

"You know," says Leo, clutching my arm. His face is flushed with excitement, "Broken families! Jailed fathers! Abusive mothers! Living rooms that are drug dens!" He sounds like a commercial for the *Geraldo* show.

"Actually Leo, many of our children are simply poor. Those other things you mentioned are the odious fringe benefits of poverty. We do have a number of boys who have had serious drug problems. They go through a six-month rehabilitation program before they arrive in my classroom. They're clean, but they might be empty and sad, and it's my job to put some joy back into their lives. Music can help. Melody and rhythm – combined with the discipline of learning to play an instrument – work their magic more often than you might think."

"Is Allegheny Gatehouse sort of a second chance place?" asks Leo.

"No Leo, I'd say for most of these kids it's a first chance place. Learning to play a tune might not seem to have anything to do with the real world, but for these kids it's the first step to creating a little bit of order in their lives. A few of my boys have become professional musicians, many of them are factory workers and mechanics, several of them are teachers, one of them is training to be a surgeon. Music, you know, can give a kid confidence. And options."

And with that, Miss Blue lowers her sparkling eyes, picks up her teacup, and takes a delicate sip.

Holy cow. I know I should say something, but *what?* This is probably my cue to stand up and shout *I want to help!!!* But

I know if I do I'll be signing up for something I can't handle. It would be easy to ask my dad to write a check and wish her well, but that's not why she's here.

"Leo tells me you want to play with other musicians," she says.

I twirl the spoon in my tea, hoping to find a response in the bottom of my cup.

"And I need a really good drummer," she continues. "The boys in the Gatehouse Band are advanced students of music. Either they had some training before they got to the school, or they practiced and studied very hard once they began private lessons at the Gatehouse. Our boys live at the school, and have round-the-clock access to practice facilities. And some of them practice for many hours each day. We've had a policy of not bringing in musicians from the outside, but I'm ready to change that rule so that we can start to sound like a genuine band. I've got some talented boys this year, and they deserve a real drummer. Can't have an R&B band without a drummer! I've got several intermediate-level drummers who will be good enough in a couple of years, but right now, I need someone who can groove. Hard."

I squirm, trying to think of one simple reason to say no. Leo kicks me under the table.

"I don't want to," I say.

"Yes you do," says Leo.

"No, I really don't," I say. The tears that have been building up burst from my eyes and spill down my face.

She pauses for a minute, and waits for me to stop crying. I hold my breath, and pinch the inside corners of my eyes.

"You've experienced a lot of sadness for a such a young woman. You lost your mother when you were, what, eleven years old?"

"Twelve," says Leo, because he knows I can't talk. "She was twelve years old when the fire killed her mother. It happened three years ago."

"You have much healing to do yourself, Jane. Just like my boys. Not all of my kids make it, you know. Music gives them hope, but sometimes that's not enough."

I blink, catch my breath, and look away.

"Sometimes we're trapped by emotions we can't understand," she says. Miss Blue takes my hand and holds it for a moment.

"You call me when you're ready. I think I can help you look back. Then maybe you'll be able to move forward." She reaches into the pocket of her suit jacket, pulls out a card, and slides it across the bumpy table.

Olivia Blue, Music Teacher

I stare at the card and try to focus on the letters. On the back is her phone number.

"I'll be going now," says Miss Blue. "Leo, perhaps you can see me to the door. "Goodbye, Jane." She turns to leave, but spins around to face me again. "Your mother is gone, Jane. But you're still here. And so is your music."

Leo, looking pale, holds the kitchen door open for Miss Blue and mouths the word *sorry* in my direction. Mary One sings from the guest bathroom, another song about moonlight, drunken men, and stolen kisses. Miss Blue leaves. I lay my throbbing head against the cool tiles of my mother's unstable kitchen table and close my swollen eyes.

Take It to the Bridge

I spend the rest of the day in my room, listening over and over again to one of Mom's favorite old recordings – James Moody and the Modernists playing "Tin Tin Deo" with Chano Pozo. It was recorded in 1948, the year she was born, but sounds as hip as anything I've ever heard. I put on a cassette of Mom playing the same piece, an unreleased track from a session she did with Woody Herman's band, and I'm stung by the music's spirit. It takes the edge off my bad mood and makes me feel – in spite of everything – like I should get off my butt and dance.

Dad knocks on the door. He's holding a plate of leftover scones and two glasses of chocolate milk. It's late, and he's wearing something that looks like pajamas, even though I know it's his daytime outfit. When he catches me looking at him, he stands a little straighter and combs his messy hair with one hand.

He misses her. I want to be enough for him, but I'm not, just like he's not enough for me. He turns down the stereo, just a little, so we can talk, and perches on the edge of my cow-print sofa, the one Mom bought for me when I was a little girl. It looks ridiculous now, like doll furniture.

"Jane." He brushes crumbs from his plaid flannel shirt. "Mary Two told me you had a visitor today. She said you were pretty upset. I hope you're feeling better. You want to talk about it?"

"I don't know," I'm pissed off at Mary Two for tattling on me.

"What are you listening to?"

"I don't know." But I do know. It's Mom.

"That's your mother playing on the *Con Alma* session with Woody and Barretta, isn't it? I forgot about that tape. I'll have to borrow it from you some day."

I pretend to ignore him. We sit and listen for three or four minutes.

"Jane."

"What? Can't you see I'm trying to listen to music?"

"You need to talk to me. It's been three years and – "

"And I'm fine. I survived, okay? I'm completely fine. Fine, fine, fine. How many times do we have to go through this?"

"If you won't talk to Dr. Moore or Dr. Bragdon – "

"Or Dr. Landers or Dr. Ly?" I say. "Or how about Dr. Constance, Dad? She was real nice. She forced me to draw pictures, and kept pushing a box of tissues at me like I was supposed to break down at any moment. I'm not a baby and I don't need to talk."

"Yes you do."

"No I don't."

"That's not what the experts say."

"I don't care."

"Please, Jane."

"Stop, okay? Just stop. I'm so sick of this."

"Okay," he says. "I'm sorry."

"And stop being sorry, this isn't your fault."

"Sorry."

"Dad."

"Okay. I'll shut up."

"Thank you." We sit next to each other, listening to Mom's recording, saying nothing. It's something we're both good at – spacing out. I look at the measuring tape on the wall, the one that kept track of my size when I was little. Mom made the last pencil mark three years ago.

I break the silence. "Dad, look, this woman – her name is Olivia Blue – she wants me to play in her band. She teaches at Allegheny Gatehouse and they need a drummer."

"Oh, I see. Interesting. The Gatehouse is the reform school for boys in Edgewood isn't it?"

"Reform school, rehab place, there are a bunch of names for it. Miss Blue says it's a place for troubled boys to work out their feelings through music."

"Sounds like a worthwhile endeavor," says Sam. "I can't say I'd want my teenage daughter playing at a halfway house for boys, though. Don't some of those kids have criminal records? Sounds dangerous. What did you say?"

"I said no."

"Can't blame you for that. I'm sure you have good reasons."

"See, that's the problem. I don't know why I said no. It's not because it's Allegheny Gatehouse, I would have said no if she had a band at Episcopal Trinity or Carnegie Hall. That's what's bothering me. I want to play, but I don't want to play. Or maybe I just don't want anyone to hear me play. It doesn't add up. I love music. Why am I afraid to play with other kids or let anyone hear me? It was easy to say no to the dorky Penn Academy band and orchestra, it's not the kind of music I want to play anyway. But I have a feeling I would love Miss Blue's band. There's something about her that seems very right to me. Like we'd be a good fit, you know what I mean?"

"Yes, I do. You can sense that in a person, that good fit thing."

We dunk our scones in chocolate milk. And all of the sudden – out of desperation, defeat, or maybe even desire – I say: "I'm thinking about calling her and seeing if I can check out a rehearsal. Would that be okay?"

My father laughs. "Yes Jane, I think it's a good idea," he says. "You remember what your mother used to say? 'Can't cancel till you book it.' Give it a try and you can always back out later. I read an article about Olivia Blue in last month's *Pittsburgh Magazine*. Sounds like she's a very dedicated teacher. I'd like to come with you to the first rehearsal, if that's okay – I'm not sure if I like the idea of you and Mary Two driving through that part of Pittsburgh by yourselves."

"Yeah Dad, that's okay. You can come with me." I look around my bedroom at the vintage posters of James Brown and Aretha, the silver framed photos of my mother, the canopy bed built for an eight year old princess, the record collection gathered on the hand-painted bookcase in the corner. It's a room stuck in a time warp. Dad smiles at me with his big cookie-face and I notice the web of wrinkles collecting at the corners of his eyes.

"*Keep going,*" Mom used to say.

An entire planet of music is spinning past me, and I'm trapped here in a shrine to my stupid sadness. Time to join the party. Maybe I was just waiting to be asked. I turn off the stereo, race to the telephone, clutching Miss Blue's satiny business card in my sweaty hand, and call to accept her invitation.

Zoom

The following Wednesday afternoon, Dad and I drive to Allegheny Gatehouse, a big red brick building squatting in the middle of a run-down community. From outside, the building looks angry and intimidating. Inside, it's different. The small lobby holds a colorful art gallery – the walls lined with pictures made by residents of the school. Some of the paintings look like the ones hanging in the hallways at Penn Academy – there are pictures of sunflowers and bridges, dark corridors and empty hands.

We fill out a couple of visitor information forms and the guard buzzes us through the heavy steel door. The hallways are deserted and the sound of my feet on the stone staircase plays against the nervous thumping of my heart. I'm sure my cheeks are scarlet. Leo would call me tomato-head.

Leo begged to come with us, but I said no. In a way, I don't even want Dad here, but getting to the Gatehouse on my own would have been a major problem. Together, we climb the granite stairs leading to Miss Blue's classroom on the second floor.

All at once, Dad starts talking. "I'll be right outside, Jane. I brought some work with me. I need to outline the next few chapters of my book. I'm almost finished with the first draft, but I've got a technical problem in the last section. I've got to figure out what to do with Mrs. Lather's corpse once the pig digs her up. Any ideas?"

"You could have the murderer bury her in the sand trap by the eighteenth hole. I mean, he's a golfer, right?"

"Hey, that's good! You might be on to something there. I'll work on it." He pauses. "Jane, I love you. You know that."

"Yeah, Dad, I know that. I love you, too."

"Your mother would be proud of you for trying this today."

"I know that, too." We look away from each other.

"Give a shout if you need anything. I'll be right here." He plops down onto the gray speckled floor, his long legs sprawled in front of him. "Go on, now. Everything will be fine." He opens his notebook, and starts leafing through the pages.

I take a deep breath of the crackling air, knock on door 201, and step into the room. I see at least a dozen teenage boys, wearing blue pants and sweaters, white shirts, and striped ties. They are chattering and unpacking their instruments. When they spot me, they stop what they're doing and stare.

"Hi," I say. Funny, they don't look like juvenile delinquents. They look like kids.

Miss Blue, who is at the far end of the room organizing music, whirls around and says: "Jane! So happy to see you. Boys, please say hello and introduce yourselves to Jane Bowman. She is here today to audition for the drum chair."

Audition?

Some of the boys roll their eyes and some of them sort of grunt and snort. I think I hear a muffled snicker. I don't know whether to cover my face, run away, punch a couple of them, or stand there and take it. Before I can decide, Miss Blue cuts in.

"Enough!" she says in a voice that's both quiet and stern. "I asked you to introduce yourselves. I'll be with you in a moment Jane, as soon as I organize these charts."

RHYTHM

The boys form a single file line, and one by one they shake my hand.

"Carlos, bass guitar."

"Robert, keyboards."

"James, guitar."

"Emmanuel, first and only trumpet."

"David, alto sax."

"Joseph, alto sax."

"Rodney, alto sax."

Sort of heavy on the altos, I think.

"Marvin, tenor sax."

"Allan, lead vocals."

"Octavious, background vocals, rap, and announcements."

Announcements?

"Oscar, percussion."

"André, piano."

"How do you do?" I say over and over again. Their faces are different shades of copper and bronze, and their expressions range from disgust to boredom to delight. I do a quick calculation: Twelve musicians, total – a rhythm section without a drummer, four saxophones, one trumpet, a singer and a rapper. Could be worse.

The strap of the cymbal bag cuts into my shoulder. I change it to the other side.

"Olivia says you're funky – that's cool, cuz I ain't never seen no rich girl who can hit. Can you really play, rich girl?" says André, half under his breath. He's jive. He's trying to vibe me and mess with my head, but it doesn't work. I've watched my mother handle situations like this.

"Yeah, I can play," I say. "Can you?" He laughs, struts back to an upright Yamaha piano, and shoves it into place, turning to make sure I'm watching him flex his muscles. I am.

The boys resume setting up for their rehearsal. I spot the drum set in the back of the room, covered with a tan blanket. Miss Blue catches me eyeing it. "Go ahead," she says. "It's not a Gretsch, but I think it will do."

I pull the cloth away from the drums. Oh man, this is so cool! It's a Yamaha Recording Custom kit, made of birch, with gleaming chrome tuning lugs that stretch from the top to the bottom of each drum. Steve Gadd, one of the drum Gods, plays a set like this, finished in black lacquer. The drums in Miss Blue's rehearsal studio have a cherry wood finish, which makes the kit look like a giant jewel box waiting to be opened. It's much larger than what I play at home. This set has a twenty-two inch kick drum, a sixteen-inch floor tom, two mounted toms and two more rack toms off to the right. It's beautiful, just beautiful! The cymbals look nice – spanking new Zildjians – but since I lugged Mom's cymbals from home, I figure I might as well use them.

The cacophony of twelve musicians warming up is like no other sound in the world. Hot licks resonate through the room and throw shards of energy into the far corners. It's a prism of sound, tone playing against tone, buzzing with promise. I reach into my bag and grab my favorite pair of Vic Firth 5A sticks, heavy enough to make some noise, light enough to handle. As I begin to warm up, the boys check me out. I pretend to ignore them, and they pretend to ignore me, but I feel their eyes on me. Their heads and ears tilt in my direction. I keep testing and checking the drums. I'd tune the floor tom differently if I had time, but this will do, for now.

Miss Blue distributes the music. "Jane, I forgot to ask you if you read."

"It's not my favorite thing in the world, but yeah, I do. Mr. Hammill insists on it."

"Bravo for Mr. Hammill," says Miss Blue. "I had a little chat with him yesterday. He told me you've worked hard on the piece we're going to play first, and that you're damn good at it." She hands me a basic lead sheet for 'Give it Up or Turnit-a Loose.' When I see the title, I want to jump up and down and shout, but I don't because I notice the boys staring at me again. "Give it Up" is one of my favorite tracks. It's also one of the most difficult grooves I've ever tried to learn. I've been studying Nate Jones's technique on this piece with Mr. Hammill, and after months of hard work, I've learned to keep a constant sixteenth note pattern running just underneath the surface of my skin. Sometimes, when I practice at home, I swear I can feel my pulse hooking up with the syncopation of the kick drum.

"We're playing lots of new tunes," says Miss Blue, "but I like the boys to understand the roots of funk. Gives them a sense of where their favorite contemporary music comes from."

"Yeah," I say. "That's important. I know when I . . ."

"We'll talk later, Jane," says Miss Blue. "Let's get this rehearsal started. Good luck." I adjust my drum stool a little and look over the chart. Nice of her to pick something I'm familiar with. The chart is bare bones, but I know exactly how to play this groove: there's an eighth-note open and closed high-hat pattern, and a load of ghosted snare drum hits. Those things combined with the lack of a solid downbeat make it kind of slippery to play. I remember when I started working on this piece, I felt like a spastic mess. If I hadn't been listening and practicing this groove for so long, I'd be in big trouble right now. Miss Blue strides to the podium in front of the band. Instantly, the noise level of the room drops.

"It's going to be both strange and wonderful for all of you today," she says. "Some of you have never played with a real drummer. Some of you remember playing with Franklin and think that no drummer in the world would be good enough to replace him."

Who is Franklin?

"And you'd be correct to think that," says Miss Blue. "Franklin was an amazing drummer. Like magic, the way he played."

Who is Franklin?

"And no one can ever replace him. But we don't want to replace him. We will treasure Franklin's memory and the magic of his music, forever."

Who the hell is Franklin?

"This is the first time these drums have been played since we lost Franklin. Let's have a moment of silence, right now, and honor him."

I raise my eyebrows and lower my head in respect but I can't help thinking that I'm about to fight a battle that I can't win. I want to ask what happened to Franklin, but I'm afraid. Did he graduate? Is he dead? Did he join the army? What?

"To Franklin!" says Miss Blue.

"To Franklin!" we respond.

"Sit up straight, kids, and remember who you are! You're fighters, you're workers, you're *musicians*. Now let's kick some ass," says Miss Blue. "Jane, you said you know this song, right?"

"Oh yeah, I've played it a couple of times." I say.

"So we'll take your tempo, then," she says, smiling at me. "Count it off."

And I do.

Passage

At dinnertime, Leo, Dad, Mary One, Mary Two, and I sit together at the big kitchen table and I tell them about my first rehearsal.

"Did they look like criminals?" asks Leo.

"No, they looked like you and me," I say. "But better dressed."

"So, tell us again. What did André the piano player say when he heard you play?" asks Leo. "He must have been blown away!"

"He smiled at me a few times, but that was his only reaction. He has this little sideways smile. He's sort of cute, that André. And he plays great. All these fat chords with really cool voicings."

"I'm confused about the Franklin part of the story,' says Dad. "Did anyone ever say what happened to him?"

"No," I say. "And I was too wimpy to ask."

"Did they serve refreshments?" says Mary Two.

"It's a funk band, not a bridge club," I say. "But refreshments wouldn't have been a bad idea."

"Next time I'll make some sugar cookies!" she says.

"I sat right outside the rehearsal room the entire time," says Dad. "Those guys sound really good. I can't believe most of them are Jane's age. How does Miss Blue do it?"

"André told me she has local music teachers and jazz musicians teaching private lessons to the kids there," I say. "A few of the teachers are volunteers, most of them are being paid through funding by people like Spanky. I found out that the drums were donated by Volkwein's Music Store on the North Side."

"And Jane sounded like a million bucks playing them," says Dad. "It's one thing to hear her practicing by herself, it's another to hear her play with a band. You were groovin,' honey."

A smiling Mary One cuts her stuffed chicken breast into precise half-inch cubes.

"So tell us again," says Leo. "What did you play first?"

"It was like a James Brown festival. First we played 'Give it Up or Turnit-a Loose,' then we played 'Get Up' and 'Papa's Got a Brand New Bag,' and then Miss Blue got out a new chart, some arrangement of a song written by André – the cute piano player. It's called 'Better Place' and has this super cool 12/8 feel to it, which is really tricky for a drummer cause if you play every eighth note it ends up sounding like some kind of weird waltz-march. Miss Blue says I have to be discreet and figure out exactly which eighth notes to play, which ones to ghost, and which ones to accent. That's how to get the music to breathe. You know who was really good at this? This drummer named Clayton Fillyau – he spent three years with James Brown and he was a master of the 12/8 feel. Miss Blue told us all about him."

Leo's eyes glaze over. Actually the only one who under-stands what I'm saying is Mary One. She nods and taps her fork on the table in 12/8 time. I know I've lost the rest of them, but I can't help myself, and I keep babbling.

"So Miss Blue said what I played wasn't exactly right and that I'll need to practice and listen to some recordings with Clayton Fillyau on them. Then, get this; she actually gave me a couple of cassettes to work with. When the rehearsal was over the trumpet player – his name is Emmanuel – he came over and said that I was pretty decent, which doesn't sound like a very nice thing to say but I remember from Mom that these trumpet players don't like to give out compliments, so I figure saying that I was pretty decent means that he thinks I'm good."

"What?" says Leo. "It's like a secret code or something?"

"You *are* good, Jane," says Dad. "You know that." Sometimes my dad sounds so much like a Dad.

"More chicken?" says Mary Two. "It's stuffed with Pepperidge Farm croutons."

"What about the other guys?" asks Leo. "Did they have anything to say?"

"No. They sort of ignored me. But that happened to Mom sometimes."

"More rice pilaf?" says Mary Two. "Uncle Ben's!"

I've been talking so much I haven't eaten much of my dinner. I shovel a fork full of vegetable mush into my mouth just as Leo asks: "When's the next rehearsal?"

"I think Friday," I say. "Miss Blue said she would call me tonight. Evidently the guys were going to vote on whether or not they want me in the band. They stuck around to vote after I left. I hope I make it."

"Of course you will!" shouts Mary One. We are stunned to hear her speak at the table. She usually eats her meals in silence and then retreats to the guest bathroom. "Those boys don't vote you in," she continues, "I go and wup 'em with that old snow shovel in the cellar."

"Thank you, Mary One," I'm touched that she would defend me. I have a fleeting image of Mary One, all four and a half feet of her, chasing hunky André around the music room with a snow shovel. I'd put my money on Mary One.

"Jell-O, anyone?" says Mary Two, just as Leo sends his salad plate skidding across the table.

"Jesus m'beads," shouts Mary Two, catching the plate just before it crashes to the floor.

"Sorry!" says Leo.

I laugh.

"No Jell-O for me, Mary Two," says Dad.

I laugh again, for no reason.

And it strikes me – that for the first time in three years – we sound almost like a normal family.

* * *

Miss Blue phones to tell me the boys have elected to keep me, but on probation.

Probation? My heart sinks, but I recover, fast. Now I'm pissed.

"But – Miss Blue, I thought I played great. I mean – I did play great. And, I – I didn't even want to do this in the first place, but I convinced myself it would be good for me. I showed up, I played – really Miss Blue, I played my damn ass off, and now you're telling me those boys *don't know* if I'm any good?"

"They like the way you play, don't get me wrong, Jane," says Miss Blue.

"I played my ass off!" My voice is rising, but I can feel my confidence draining away.

"They just aren't completely sure. It will take awhile before they stop comparing you to Franklin."

"Well excuse me for being nosy, Miss Blue, but what's the story with this Franklin? Did he get shot or something?"

"No, Jane. He goes to medical school. Harvard. Franklin Boswell is one of Allegheny Gatehouse's biggest success stories. He received his high school diploma from us, and then he was awarded a full scholarship to Carnegie Mellon University, where he studied biology. While he was in college, he showed up at the Gatehouse three times a week to rehearse with us. But now he's too far away. Franklin has become a hero to these boys. They miss him."

"Well that's just great. How am I supposed to compete with Dr. Boswell?" I say.

"You shouldn't compete with anyone, Jane," says Miss Blue. "Keep your eyes on your own paper. You just keep playing the way you play, and the boys will adjust. You're a fine drummer, a different kind of drummer from Franklin, but just as talented. Remember, Franklin was twenty-two years old when he left us. That's seven years older than you are now. That's seven years of practicing hard, playing with a band three times a week, seven years of living and doing and absorbing what's going on around him. Seven years of listening.

"There are some things you'll need to work on. Mainly, you need to turn off that remote control in your head and start feeling the music. Technically, at least from what I heard today, you're doing everything right. But you could loosen up a lot more. If you'll allow yourself to have some fun, you'll be a much better musician. I'll call Mr. Hammill and make some suggestions for your lessons. Or if you'd like, I'll set some time aside to work with you myself."

"Oh . . . well, sure, I'd like that."

"Good," she says. "We have a rehearsal at the school on Friday, so I'll be able to hear you play again before we work together. How is Saturday at three? There's a bit of a security problem getting into the school on weekends, but I'll be glad to come to your house if that's suitable."

"Yeah! Sure! That'll be perfect." I wonder how much I'll be able to practice between now and then. We say goodbye and hang up. I put on the Clayton Fillyau cassette – the 1962 live recording of "I Don't Mind" from the James Brown *Live at the Apollo* album – and I listen to the way Clayton lets the music skate around the space he leaves between the beats. As James Brown and his rhythm section navigate through the spooky harmonic changes to the song, I begin to grasp what Miss Blue just said to me. Clayton Fillyau's drumming is more than monster technique: it's emotion, it's spirituality, it's love. It has nothing to do with the head and everything to do with the heart, and maybe even the lower intestinal track. It's gut music, played by a gut player. In a way, it's magic. I've listened to this track a hundred times, but tonight I'm hearing a different song.

Maybe It's Spring

We organize the house for Olivia's visit like we're preparing for an audience with the Queen. At ten minutes before three, Mary One comes out of the guest bathroom and paces in circles near the front door. She's holding a wrapped gift in her tiny hands.

"What's in the package?" I ask. "Is it for Miss Blue?"

"Yes," she squeaks. "It's an autographed photo of Lady Day. One of my favorites, and I got me a double copy. Thought Miss Blue might like it."

Mary Two sniffs. She's wearing her oven mitts and her bouffant hair-do is higher than usual. It looks like she could be housing a family of woodpeckers in there.

"Your hair looks nice, Mary Two," I say.

"Thank you, Jane," she says. "I cranked it up this morning." She pats her head and sees the oven mitts. "Well fuck my old boots, I'm still wearing my mitts." She opens a console drawer and tosses the mitts inside.

"Mary Two," I say. "*Please, please, please* don't say *fuck my old boots* when Miss Blue gets here." I've gotten used to Mary Two's nervous outbursts, but this particular phrase is a little too much, even for me.

Dad joins the welcoming committee. Normally he glides around the house in a pair of hole-ridden slippers, but this afternoon he's wearing real shoes.

"So. Are we ready?" he asks.

"You know, I can handle this myself," I say. "Stop making such a big deal. Opening the door is within my repertoire."

"We know," says, Dad. "We just want Miss Blue to feel welcome. She's being very kind to you, Jane. The least we can do is properly introduce ourselves."

At precisely three o'clock, the "Chain of Fools" doorbell rings. Olivia Blue looks just as noble as she did on the day I met her. I'm mortified when Mary Two curtsies. Mary One presents the autographed photo.

"Thank you so much. I love Billie Holiday!" says Miss Blue as she hugs Mary One. Mary Two sniffs, again. "And Mary Two," she says, "I notice you've done something special to your hair. It looks lovely."

"Why thank you Miss Blue," says Mary Two, beaming. "I had it cranked this morning."

"My hair could use a good cranking," says Miss Blue. "You'll have to give me the name of your hairdresser." Mary Two swallows a smile, and looks at the floor. My dad clears his throat.

I introduce Dad and Miss Blue extends her hand.

"Please," she says, "call me Olivia."

"And I'm Sam," he says. I'm dealing with Olivia's coat, when a brief beat of silence causes me to turn around, just in time to see them gazing into each other's eyes. What's this? Mary One begins humming "Lover Man." Mary Two raises an eyebrow, but keeps a lid on the obscenities. *What's going on?* I look out the window, see Leo skipping up the front walk, and – *bam!* – I realize this has been Leo's strategy all along – a teacher for me, a companion for my father. It's Leo's style of one-stop shopping.

RHYTHM

I don't know where we're heading, but it seems that whenever Olivia Blue visits us she brings something beautiful with her. There's a crystal clear sensation that the earth is shifting, that the swampy sadness flooding our home might at last recede and trickle away through the thick walls. I don't care where it goes, as long as it's somewhere else.

* * *

Dearest Jane,

Hats off! Your dad tells me you've started playing with a band. Good for you! Your grandma would be so thrilled by your progress, and I know your mom would be, too. I'm not very musical, but I've been around you gals long enough to figure out that playing in a band makes things a lot more fun. This is huge step for you, and I couldn't be happier. Leo was using his noggin when he introduced you to Miss Blue. Smart lad, that Leo.

I remember when Helen organized her first band. She dragged a group of fifth grade girls home from school. The six of them had decided they would become a famous all-girl music group, and asked Helen to be in their band. What a disaster! She got them all set up in the living room, with percussion instruments and a little stage for anyone who wanted to sing. There was one girl, named Rachel, who played classical piano. Helen put on "Dancing Under Latin Skies," an old Tito Puente record, and told everyone to just play along.

Helen started playing her congas, and the rest of them just sat there gawking at her like she'd lost her mind. Rachel asked her for sheet music. The other kids stared at their feet and started mumbling reasons to leave. Your grandma saved the day by teaching them a few mambo steps and serving a plate of Cuban almond cookies. After they left Isabella told Helen that if she wanted to play with musicians who understood her kind of music, she was going to have to go out and find them. Helen and Isabella were like that, you know, they never waited for anyone or anything – a job, a paycheck, a promise. They got out there, worked hard, and found their own opportunities.

Sounds like you've discovered a swell group of chaps who really do know how to play the kind of music you love. Don't fret that you're the only girl. Boys and men surrounded your grandma and your mom and they thrived on it. You just get out there and have fun. Do your best, and you can't go wrong. That's exactly what I used to tell your mother.

Please give each of the Marys and your dad a hearty hug for me. And tell your pal Leo that I like the way he thinks.

Your grandma Isabella will kiss this letter before I mail it. We love you, very much.

Remember, you're my little heaven.
Love,
Grandpa Jack

* * *

Every Monday, Wednesday, and Friday, Dad drives me to Allegheny Gatehouse for rehearsal. Mary Two usually accompanies us, with a plate of cookies or muffins for the boys. I was pretty embarrassed the first time she charged into the music room with me – it's not every student musician who arrives at a rehearsal with a British nanny and a tray of baked goods – but I got over it when I saw the boys gobbling every last crumb. At each rehearsal, they stampede to greet Mary Two – big boys, men, really, scrambling to cop an extra cookie. They smile and tease Mary Two like she's a pin-up girl. Me, they pretty much ignore.

While we're setting up, Miss Blue usually trades a few words with Dad, and I eavesdrop as much as I can without being obvious. Dad has a big fat crush on her, and I can tell he's not quite sure what to do with the feeling. Miss Blue stays pretty cool, but André tells me she's been re-doing her make-up right before Dad and I arrive. I watch the two of them flirting, smiling, brushing elbows, trading goo-goo eyed looks they think no one else can see. When this happens, I don't know if I should be freaked-out or happy, so I pick up my sticks and start warming up, loudly.

Dad sits in the hallway during rehearsals, lounging on the floor, outlining chapters and brainstorming new ideas for his book. Mary Two, who brings her own collapsible stool, sits next to him, crocheting fragile lace doilies for the next Penn Academy Arts and Crafts Fair. While Miss Blue rehearses the band, Mary Two and Dad listen to us rock, thump and blast ourselves right up into orbit. Destination: Planet Funk.

On Thursday afternoons I have my weekly lesson with Mr. Hammill, who's psyched that I'm playing with a real band. Every two weeks, Miss Blue gives him a list of what I need to work on, what I need to learn. Technically, it's all in my range. Musically, I still have a long way to go. I understand it now; the difference between my robotic playing and the gutsy, soul-busting approach that marks the drumming of the really great players. I can hear it, I just can't get there. Not yet. But I will.

* * *

Six weeks into my probation period with the band, Miss Blue arrives at our house for one of our Saturday sessions. We usually begin with some breathing and relaxation exercises, and then I show her what I've been practicing. Today I'm seated in front of my drums, cross-legged on the floor, my back to the kick drum, working on filling up my entire chest cavity with air.

My eyes are closed. I inhale to a very slow count of eight. I still don't understand what deep breathing has to do with playing, but I like the way it relaxes me and gives me energy, all at once.

"Jane," says Miss Blue. "You must think about your mother quite often."

The air rushes out of my lungs. I crack open my eyes and look at one of the silver-framed pictures of Mom and me – in the hospital on the day I was born.

"Yeah," I say. "Yeah, I do. I try not to think about her, but I do."

"What do you think about?"

I close my eyes again. I'm not sure I can find the words.

"Just tell me as much as you'd like, Jane. I won't push."

"I think about how much I miss her, mostly."

"I'll bet. Can you be specific? What do you miss?"

"I don't know, she was more than a mom, she was a best friend and a teacher. She was funny and smart and pretty, and she could play music better than anyone in the world."

"What else Jane? What else was there about her that made her special?"

"That's not enough?"

"You're leaving out the most important thing."

"What? That she cared about our family? That she was brave and strong and used her talent and money to help other people?"

"Forget about other people. How did she help you?"

"She was the best teacher I ever had, even though she pretended not to be. I mean, she showed me how to play really complicated stuff – odd meters, even – when I was eight years old."

"For a moment, don't think about what she taught you. How did she feel about you?"

"She thought I had talent. She thought I looked good in red, bad in yellow, and that I should grow my hair long, practice my rudiments more often, and learn to bake a cake. She thought I had a mind of my own, weird taste in shoes, and a really messy room."

I'm crying now, and Miss Blue offers me a tissue.

"Thank you."

"You're welcome."

"She thought I had nice handwriting, that I didn't stand up straight enough, that my jokes were extra funny, that my ability to hide everything but my nose in a bubble bath was brilliant. She thought I was an excellent swimmer, lousy at math, and a good daughter to my father. She thought – "

"What Jane?"

"It sounds stupid."

"Say it Jane."

"She thought I was the best kid in the world. She was crazy about me."

"That's what I was looking for," says Miss Blue. "Your mother thought you were the best kid in the world."

"Why am I telling you all this?" I ask.

"You're not telling me," says Olivia. "You're telling yourself. You're ready. And you're finally telling yourself how much she loved you."

"What does this have to do with music?"

"Playing good music has everything to do with trust. And trusting yourself is the first step. Your mother loved you. Trust that. She's gone now, but that doesn't change the way she felt about you when she was alive. You'll carry that with you always, wherever you go."

Miss Blue touches my shoulder. "Let's start with 'I Got to Move,' " she says.

I stand up, feeling fragile and drained. The afternoon sun throws my shadow – bold, sturdy and larger-than-life – on the silk-covered wall behind the drums. I slide into place, and begin to play.

Surrender

Some memories should be covered with mud and left buried forever, or so I've thought until now. I've spent the last three years dodging questions from Leo, Dad, my grandparents and a bunch of psychiatrists and psychologists. All of them want me to talk about the night my mother died – as if recalling those hours might help me live the rest of my life. But they don't know what really happened in that nightclub. The very thought of talking about it makes me sick.

I don't want to lose her all over again.

Miss Blue, with her gentle probing, has convinced me that I need to remember. She tells me that crying is as natural as laughing, that anger is as worthy as happiness, that I'm allowed to be sad and pissed off, and that taking the long road back will, with time, help me move on. I can't understand how she knows these things, but she does.

I've learned to trust her.

It's three o'clock on a Saturday, our usual lesson time, and Miss Blue and I sit on the living room floor on huge embroidered pillows. I know that I'm ready to talk, and I know that Miss Blue is ready to listen.

"It's hard to go back." I pull at a tiny piece of lint clinging to the cushion. "The truth is, I never really left."

"Why don't you start by telling me about the events that led up to the fire?"

I unclench my fists, and begin.

"Okay. Okay. It – it was a pretty June day. A Thursday. Mom and Dad and I had planned a long weekend in New York, visiting my grandparents. School had just let out for the summer, and Mom was scheduled to tape the last Curly Dobson show of the season that weekend. Because she knew that I'd be free from school, she also booked a Thursday night gig at The Landing, a jazz club that had just opened at the South Street Seaport. Mom was playing percussion for José Valdez, the drummer and leader of the group. Dad had a meeting with his publisher that night, and Grandma Isabella and Grandpa Jack were attending a charity event at the Met. So it was just Mom and me, which suited me fine. I loved to go to gigs with her, especially small clubs where I could sit up close and really watch and listen. Plus I knew there was a chance I'd get to play, since José had let me sit in once before.

"Before the gig, we went to Jo Allen's for dinner, mid-town, which was Mom's favorite place. She said they had the best produce – fancy lettuce in a million shades of green, tomatoes as fresh as they come, perfectly steamed vegetables with sea salt and rosemary, the kind of healthy stuff she liked to eat before a concert. I liked the – you know – hamburgers and mashed potatoes.

"We almost always saw someone famous at Jo Allen's. That night, Al Pacino came in and sat practically right next to us. My mom talked to me about lots of stuff, but I wasn't focused on any of it, because I was trying to hear what Al was saying, so I could tell Leo when I got back to Pittsburgh. Leo had been begging Spanky to let him see *Scarface* cause he was such a huge Pacino fan. Anyway, we ate and then grabbed a cab down to the Seaport.

"The club was located in one of the red brick shopping centers built on the pier next to the East River. Everything seemed pretty new down there, except for the old Fulton Fish Market. When we stepped out of the cab I got sick from the fishy smell, I mean, I really felt like throwing up – like I was going to have to heave in a trash can or something. Mom said she wanted to take me home – that she would call a sub to cover the gig – but I started feeling better and I talked her out of it. That smell was so terrible."

My voice breaks and I feel like I'm losing my nerve.

"It's okay, Jane," says Miss Blue. "Memories of smells and sounds might trip you up, but keep going. You'll get through this, I promise."

I pull myself together. "We had to take an escalator to get up to the club – and I helped Mom with her equipment. She told me I needed to get used to lugging around heavy equipment – that part of being a drummer meant always traveling with a two-ton cymbal bag. Anyway, Mom carried one conga in a black leather case on her back, she pulled the other behind her on a trolley. I carried the bag of tricks, which held all the fun stuff she played when she wasn't playing the congas. She was wearing black boots and a sleeveless pink dress that had a silvery sheen to it. Her long hair was braided and she smelled like gardenias. I felt so proud to be with her, to be helping her. And just as I was thinking that, she told me that *she* was proud of me, and that she loved me."

I hold my breath, because I can't stand to say what comes next.

"Breathe, Jane," says Olivia.

"That moment, right outside the door to The Landing," I say, "that's the last moment I had alone with her. She held the door open for me with her free hand and said, 'Let's play our asses off tonight, shall we?'

I stop for a second. Miss Blue touches my arm.

I allow myself, just this once, to return. It's time.

* * *

Mom and I enter the club and the staff flits around us – waiters, bartenders, a hostess or two – all of them going crazy, trying to get the place ready for the evening. Mom hangs with the other musicians setting up onstage, and a waiter leads me back to the dressing room where snacks and bottled water are laid out for the performers. A few minutes later, the band straggles into the dressing room.

"Oh great," says Ziggy, the bass player. "Water. Don't they have any beer? And what's with the goddamn fuckin' ham sandwiches? Can't anyone in this business think of anything better to feed the musicians? If I see one more fuckin' ham sandwich, I'm gonna puke."

"At least these have pickles on them," says Wallace, the alto player, biting into one. "Do pickles qualify as vegetables?"

"Fuck the goddamn pickles," says Ziggy.

"Watch your mouth," says Ted, the pianist. "There's a kid here."

"Nothing she hasn't heard before," says Mom.

"Yeah, that's right," I say. "I've got a nanny who says the f-word all the time. But we love her anyway. She's one of the family."

"No shit?" says Ziggy. "A nanny who says fuck?"

"She's sort of a borderline Tourette's case," says Mom.

"You got a nanny with Tourette's?" says Wallace with his mouth full. "That's out, man. Whacked."

"You gonna play with us tonight, Janey?" Ziggy paces back and forth like a caged bear. He takes a twenty-dollar bill out of his pocket and starts to roll it into a long narrow tube.

"Jesus Christ, Ziggy. Not in front of the kid."

"Jane knows all about musicians and drugs," says Mom, glaring at Ziggy. "She also knows that coke will fry your brain."

Enough of this. I'm bored and I want the music to start.

"It's not nearly as bad as booze," says Ziggy. "Everyone knows that juicin' can kill you." He continues to play with the twenty-dollar bill, rolling it back and forth, back and forth, between his fingers. "Speaking of which, do you think we could get some fuckin' beer in here?"

"I'll play if José lets me," I say, trying to ignore the whole drug and alcohol conversation. I've heard this stuff on some of Mom's other gigs – especially from guys like Ziggy. "José is the leader tonight, right?"

"Yeah, at least he thinks he is."

José enters the room. "Of course I'm the leader and of course she's gonna play." He kisses me on the cheek. "How you doin' Janey? Still workin' on those Jab'o Starks grooves?"

"Yep," I say.

"She plays them better than you do, José," says Mom.

"What do you want Helen? I'm the Latin guy. Janey here is the funk guy."

"Gal," I say.

"Yeah, and don't forget it," says Mom.

"What are we gonna play tonight, Janey?" asks José.

"You guys do 'Tin Tin Deo,' right?" I say. "Maybe we could do a funky version of that?"

"What tempo you want?"

I look at my mom and she gives me a nod. I sing the melody to "Tin Tin Deo" and drum on the table with my hands.

"You got it, kiddo, 'Tin Tin Deo' it is."

"Hey, guess who I played with last night?" asks Wallace.

"Please don't tell me you were with what's her name again," says Ziggy. "You know, that Polish broad with the siren voice that's always just a tiny bit flat. Her hair looks like she got her head stuck in a fan."

"Aggggh, you mean Frederica," says Wallace. "And her voice ain't the only thing that's flat. Naw, I wasn't with her, although I wish I would've been. She always does something stupid to make the gig interesting, at least. Last time I worked with her she got all emotional singing 'The Waters of March,' in Portuguese, which was pretty bad – you know, a Polish chick singin' in Portuguese don't make it – but then she got all teary-eyed or something and backed up right into the bass player's bow. She goosed herself real good. Sorta took away from the drama of the song, you know?"

"Hey, I was on that gig," says Ziggy. "That was my bow she smashed into. I was pissed. Almost broke my damn bow."

"Oh shit – right – that was you. I forgot it was you on that gig," says Wallace.

"So who were you workin' with last night?"

"Rizzo."

"No shit. Rizzo? Is he still around? Playin' with him is like nailin' Jell-O to the wall."

"Please, please, please, don't start with the Rizzo stories," says Mom.

"Come on, Mom, I like the Rizzo stories," I say. Why does she always have to get in way?

"I'm goin' outside," says Ziggy, waving his rolled-up twenty like a wand. "You know, take care of business on my own," he says, nodding towards me. He opens the fire exit door onto the balcony overlooking the river and I can see the Brooklyn Bridge over his shoulder. He takes off one of his pointy black leather shoes and wedges it against the doorframe, so he can get back in.

"Yeah, hope it's not too windy out there," says Wallace. "And save a taste for me, okay?"

I look at my watch. Another fifty minutes until show time. My mom brushes my hair.

"Could you stop, please?" I grab the brush. "You're driving me nuts. It looks fine."

"This one braid is messy, Jane."

"Like anyone cares." I push her away. "Just leave me alone, okay?"

Mom puts the brush away. A waiter buzzes into the dressing room. "Gitano is my name," he says. "Everything okay here, my fellows?" He spots my mom. "Oh excuse me, signora, I don't know one of the band wives was here."

"I'm not a band wife," she says. "I'm the band." She pulls a ten-dollar bill out of her pocket and hands it to the waiter. "Look, Gitano," she says, "do you think you could get some beer in here for these guys, and maybe something warm for them to eat. We've got a long night ahead of us and I don't want them in a bad mood cause their stomachs are growling."

"No problem. Hey! You a beautiful lady." He snaps his fingers. "I bring somethin' hot. Pronto!"

"Thanks," she says and turns back to the guys. "All you have to do is ask." José sighs. Mom shrugs.

Awhile later, Ziggy returns from his coke perch on the fire escape, and the band talks through the set list, while slurping down steaming plates of pasta. Gitano, who seems to have fallen in love with my mother, lurks in the corner, staring at her. Ziggy doesn't eat, and bitches that the food has arrived too late – he says he doesn't like to eat right before the gig.

Outside the dressing room – in the club – I can hear the scraping sound of chairs being pushed back as people are seated. I listen to the clinking glasses, and the hushed buzz you only hear in New York City jazz clubs. It's so cool.

"Jane," says Mom, smiling at me as if she can read my mind. "Why don't you go out and get yourself settled. Gitano has saved you a seat at the press table, down front, right by the stage. If you want anything at all, let him know. José will call you up for your song. Remember to make sure the stool is the right height before you start. And keep your wrists relaxed."

"Okay, okay, okay," I say, rolling my eyes at her instructions. "I know what to do, Mom."

And I kiss her goodbye. I kiss her goodbye. I kiss her goodbye.

* * *

I'm squished at a table with four music critics and their dates. One of them – named Jared something – flashes a toothy smile, lights a cigarette, blows the smoke in my face, and turns away from me. I know this guy. He writes reviews for the New

York Daily Journal. In a stage whisper I could have heard in Brooklyn, he says to his date, "Looks like the hired help couldn't get a babysitter." My face turns red and I want to disappear. He yawns. "Who's playing tonight, anyway? I mean I know it's José Valdez, but I can never keep up with the rest of them. They all look alike."

"I think Ted Roblas is on piano," says the date, a girl named Linda who is sipping a drink that looks like a banana milkshake. "La-di-da. And Helen Bowman is sitting in on percussion. Just what we need. Like we don't see enough of her on that goddamn Curly Dobson show. Helen Bowman couldn't get arrested in this town if she didn't shake her ass and wear those obscene outfits."

"What?" says Jared. "I like the outfits."

"She's also got rich parents – Jack and Isabella Bowman," says Linda. "Probably bought her way into the gig."

I try to tune out the conversation because it really bugs me. No one ever talks about the way the male musicians look, or what kind of family money they have, but with my mom, these things always come up. Almost like they need an excuse for her talent, just because she's a woman. Mom says that maybe when I grow up things will be different.

Ten minutes later, the manager of the club races onstage.

"Good evening Ladies and Gentlemen! Welcome to The Landing, presenting New York's finest jazz to New York's finest audiences. Tonight we are honored to have the José Valdez Quintet, featuring the gorgeous Helen Bowman – of the Curly Dobson Show – on percussion, the amazing Wallace Rivera on alto, Ted Roblas on piano, and Ziggy Lewis on bass. Let's hear it for the band!"

The thick black velvet curtains part, and the musicians hustle onstage. I clap and hoot and do my truck driver's whistle and Mom waves at me from behind her congas. José begins with a stinging arrangement of "Manteca." We all feel the groove – even my nasty tablemates start bopping in time to the music.

I love this. You take five fearless players, set them free, and anything can happen, anything at all. Wallace closes his eyes as he starts his solo. He's a weight lifter, with a thick body and muscle-bound arms, but his music takes off and soars through the room like a falcon circling its prey. There's a long, open section in the middle of the song with just drums, percussion and sax, and Mom goes nuts on her congas. Then, on cue, there's a break, and José screams *Manteca!*

When the band returns to the head of the song, the crowd shouts and whistles – they're really getting into to it; stomping and clapping.

After the cheers die down for "Manteca," they go into José's arrangement of "Spain" – the Chick Corea tune. Ted starts with a rubato piano solo and – what an awesome feeling! – his playing beams me to a place where women in colorful lace dresses carry fans and click-clack their feet to Spanish rhythms. Later in the tune, as the fast-paced and bubbling tempo kicks in, Wallace plays the flute, and I imagine these same women, holding hands and skipping down village lanes, the song's rhythm mocking the tap of their high-heeled shoes on the cobblestones.

Cool. Listen to the way they play – improvising – composing on the spot! I love how they slide through musical transitions, hooked up tight on the ensemble sections, but supporting the solos by stepping back and making space for each other. Everyone has a turn. Sort of like a family.

Halfway through the first set, after the band tears though Ted's frantic arrangement of Chick Corea's "Captain Marvel," José gets up from the drums and introduces me.

"Ladies and Gentlemen, we have a surprise for you to-night; a nice kid who just happens to be an excellent drummer. The little lady has already found her own style, and it's about as funky as it gets. So let's give it up for Jane Bowman, Helen Bowman's daughter!"

Wallace Rivera reaches down with one beefy arm and lifts me up to the stage. The lights are warm, with pink and orange gels that make my skin look like butterscotch. It's weird for me when people clap before I've done anything, but I smile and wave like Mom taught me, and make my way over to José's drum set. It's a small set – just like the one I play at home – but with an extra-suspended tom-tom, which I kind of like.

"You wanna count off, Janey?" says Ted from the piano.

"Uh, wait a minute." I adjust the stool. The crowd laughs. The cymbals are high, but I'm pretty tall for my age, and José is pretty short, so I can make it work.

We play "Tin Tin Deo," and the music churns in a solid medium-tempo funk groove. I'm nervous, but I stay focused, trying to split my attention between what I'm playing and what I'm hearing. It's tricky, the lights are hot, and I'm sweating. Ziggy's bass line locks into my groove, and I begin to relax. There's a rhythm break in the middle of the song, and Mom and I play together, strong and swinging, reaching that place where the beat of the music is the only thing that matters. I concentrate really hard, but at the same time I pretend that each drum is a different color and every hit is another brushstroke on the canvas I'm sharing with Mom. The bass drum is purple, the snare daffodil-yellow, the floor tom a clear cobalt blue, the suspended tom a hot shade of red. The cymbals are like spotlights – shiny silver – lighting up my groove. Mom plays along, following my outline and filling it in with her own colors. By the time we've finished the song, we've painted a crooked-edged rainbow, and even though it's not perfect, it's right. For a moment, the picture hangs in the air in front of me, then fizzles and fades as the applause peaks.

As Wallace helps me down from the stage, the music keeps playing, throbbing, dancing through my brain. This. This is want I want to do. Forever. I turn to face Mom. She blows a kiss in my direction.

I go to my table as the band starts the last tune of the set, but my seat has been taken by some bozo from the bar who wants to sit closer to the stage. Rather than cause a ruckus, Gitano gives me the man's place at the bar in the back of the club. Then he hands me a dish of strawberry ice cream. "Girly! You play real funky," he says. "And you're beautiful too, just like your mama."

"Thank you!" I say, and I eat my ice cream. I want this feeling to last forever.

A man sitting next to me, a fat guy with taped glasses and a greasy-looking beard, says to no one in particular, "Do you smell smoke?" Of course I smell smoke. Practically everyone in the place is smoking. The people sitting on my left are puffing on Benson and Hedges Lights. The package is pretty, even though I hate the stink.

"I smell smoke, there's something burning," the guy says again, squirming in his seat. The band is playing a groovy mambo, but his voice cuts through the music. The customers sitting at the bar sniff and look over their shoulders, trying to find the source.

"Maybe it's your cigarette," I say, and laugh.

"It's not that," he hisses at me. "It's an electrical smell." His nose twitches and his eyes dart back and forth, as if a bad smell were something he could see. The musicians, oblivious, continue to play. As Wallace digs into his solo, I turn to look for Gitano – I'm almost finished with my ice cream and I'd like something to drink. I wonder if they have root beer. But Gitano is on the far side of the club, by the service bar, huddled with several waiters and a manager. They look worried.

I rock my spoon back and forth in time to the music and watch the ice cream slide around. It's funny how the last little scoop always tastes the best – a half-melted, half-frozen, creamy-dreamy bite. I listen to the pulse of my mother's congas. She sounds like a groovy Latino locomotive, chugging her way through a perfect Manhattan night.

Music and strawberry ice cream – it doesn't get much better than this.

But something's not right. A horrible whining noise fills the club, growing louder and louder with each split second. The band stops playing. A waiter leaps over the bar, almost knocking me off the stool. I spin around and see orange flames framing the stage like a strange piece of performance art. A thick column of pewter-colored smoke streams from the little window above the dressing room door.

The players – unaware of the danger behind them – stare at the audience with puzzled looks. My mother swats at the burning embers tumbling onto her congas, as smoldering scraps of fabric land in her hair. She scans the audience, looking for me. Her eyes travel to the press table, but I'm not there. Panic consumes the room. The crowd pushes towards the exit and blocks my view of the stage.

"Mommy!" I cry. "I'm here! Over here, Mommy!" There's a sickening gush of sound, then a deafening thud – like wind slamming a door shut.

"Mommy! Over here!"

My words are smothered by shouts and a blast of fire and smoke.

People thrash against each other as they head toward the exit. They push past me, screaming and climbing over tables and chairs as they fight to reach the door, just beyond the bar area, ten feet from where I'm sitting. My eyes sting, and when I stand on my toes to search for my mother, the fat guy – scrambling for the exit – knocks me to the floor. As I crawl to the back row of tables, someone stomps on my right hand and a stabbing pain shoots up my arm. I'm dizzy and I feel like I might throw up, but I want to go to Mom, so I hoist myself to my feet and struggle through the smoke towards the stage. But I'm moving against the surge of the crowd and I'm shoved back towards the door.

"Grab the kid!" shouts a woman as she rushes for the door. "Someone grab that girl and get her out!" A man snags my elbow, but I duck away from him and squat next to a cigarette machine where no one sees me. I can't leave. I've got to reach the stage and find my mom.

It's hard to breathe; the air smells and tastes metallic and dirty – like tarnished silver – and each new breath burns more than the last. Once more I fight my way back towards the stage. A huge woman jostles me and jabs her elbow into my throat. I crash to the floor, but manage to drag myself under a table so that the crowd doesn't trample me.

It's hot, I can't see much, I can hardly breathe, but I can hear people shrieking. Crouching under the table, I hold an old napkin to my mouth and rub my throbbing eyes. I think I spot the tuxedo-ed legs of one of the waiters.

"The musicians!" I hear him shout. "What about the musicians?"

"You gotta help them," someone wheezes.

"No," another choking voice replies. "Stage collapsed – just get out – save your own ass."

My heart breaks into a thousand pieces and I roll into a ball on the floor. A few minutes later, the sound of passing feet stops and the screams fade. I'm so dizzy. I dream I hear my mother's voice calling out to me over and over and over again: *"Jane, where are you? Jane, please answer me. Jane, please be okay. Please be okay. Jane, I love you. Please be okay."*

Another blast rips through the club and covers up the sound of her voice. I'm alone with a table leg, clinging to it, pretending it's my mother's arm. "Mommy, Mommy, Mommy" I cry. "Hold me, Mommy. I'm so scared."

A voice from above says, "It's okay, sweetie. We'll get you out. It's okay."

I feel someone grabbing my legs, pulling me out from under the table. He lifts me up and carries me outside. I gulp at the cool air like a starving dog. I crack open my burning eyes and see a man in yellow helmet staring down at me.

"Hang on sweetie, we've got a doctor coming. You'll be okay. Don't try to talk," he says, patting my face with his gloved hand. "Anybody know this kid?" he shouts.

"Janey? Oh thank you Jesus," says José.

José? He's fine? Everything will be okay – I just need Mom. Please, someone get Mom.

"You know her?" says the firefighter to José, as he places his coat over my trembling body.

"Yeah, she's Helen Bowman's daughter."

"Who's Helen Bowman?" he asks. "Help me out here."

"She's one of the musicians," says Jose.

I open my mouth to yell, "The musicians! Get the musicians!" but my throat is parched and no sound comes out. I struggle to sit up, but I can't.

"We got out through the dressing-room fire escape door," says José, talking as quickly as he can. "The fire swept around the stage so fast. Helen wanted to go into the house to find Janey but there were flames between the audience and us. I dragged her back to the fire door. Wait. Hey Ziggy!!! Wallace! Ted! Someone find Helen. She's going crazy looking for Janey."

"Oh my God," says Ziggy. "Oh my God."

"What?" says José.

"Helen went back in. When she couldn't find Janey out here, she ran around to the front and back into the club. It was before the fire department got here. I tried to stop her but I couldn't. I'm sorry. I tried to stop her, I really tried."

Mommy! I fight to sit up – I have to go find her – but José won't let me move. Scalding tears roll down my chilled face and neck, and run under my collar. He wipes my face with his fingers. When he takes his hand away, it's covered with soot.

"Here Janey," says José, reaching for the drumstick wedged in his back pocket. "Instinct made me take my sticks with me on the way out. You hold onto this, okay? And don't give up. Don't give up. We'll find her." Jose places the stick in my hand and wraps his fingers around mine.

"You believe in God, Janey?" he asks, his broken voice close to my ear.

"No," I whisper.

"Neither do I," he says. "But let's pray, anyway."

The firefighter picks up his radio. He moves away from us, but even with all the chaos on the pier, I can make out his words. "Base to Unit Three, come in!" he shouts into the speaker. "We got a female adult who went back into the club before we got here. She went through the front entrance, lookin' for her kid. Anyone get her out? Over."

"Yeah, we found her." The radio crackles with static. "10-55. Repeat: 10-55. We found her in the backstage area. Looks like she's the only one. Over."

"What the fuck is 10-55?" yells José.

"I'm sorry," says the firefighter to José. "She didn't make it." He looks down at me and lowers his voice. "I'm really sorry, sweetie. She shouldn't have gone back into that fire. I'm sorry."

I squint at the hungry flames leaping into the empty night. From a distance, I hear another explosion. José huddles closer – even though the blast, and the ones that follow, seem soft and harmless. Covered by coats and blankets, I lie on the wooden pier, slowly inhaling the June sky, watching the fire sink into the gloom. My burning eyes track the taillights of a jet traveling through the darkness. I wish it could swoop down and carry me far away, into the caring arms of a heaven I don't believe in. My tears stop. I cover my ears and squeeze my eyes shut, hoping for blacked-out silence, trying to block out the truth.

She had come back into the club to rescue me. But I hid from her. Under a table. Her voice echoes through my head, calling my name, over and over, daring me to respond.

"Jane, where are you? Jane, please answer me. Jane, please be okay. Please be okay. Jane, I love you. Please be okay."

I open my mouth to scream. But I'm the only one who hears.

* * *

They take me to NYU Medical Center where I'm treated for smoke inhalation and shock. My dad and grandparents arrive an hour later. I can't talk, I can only cry. Grandpa Jack, still wearing his tuxedo, buries his head in my bed covers and sobs. Isabella hovers by the window, watching the lights on Second Avenue, her chiffon covered shoulders shaking as she tries to pull herself together. Daddy holds my hand, and stares at a worn spot on the wall.

The nurse injects me with some sort of tranquilizer, and I drift off, my empty dreams a blessing. The next morning, awakened by the dawnish glow of a grayish day, I crack open my eyes and see my grandparents and Daddy struggling to sleep in skinny cots that have been set up in my room. When they realize I'm awake, they spring out of bed and try to smooth the wrinkles from their formal evening clothes. Then they begin to cry again.

The dark smell of smoke is everywhere, still – in my hair, on my skin, in the fabric of my nightgown.

José, Ziggy, Ted, and Wallace visit me. They line up by my bed, dressed in fresh outfits, but looking pale and dirty, like they haven't been able to shower away the grime. The drumstick that José had given me is propped in a water pitcher next to my bed.

"Here," he says, handing me the matching stick. "When you start to feel better, you'll need something to keep yourself busy." He pulls a brand new practice pad out of a plastic Manny's Instrument Shop bag. "I bought this for you cause I didn't know what else to do." We look at each other. "Music will rescue you, Janey. Helen used to say that to me all the time."

José turns away and joins Isabella by the window.

Ted and Wallace hug me, and I allow them to cry, just for a moment, onto my white-gowned shoulder. I wonder, for a split second, if this will be my job will be from now on – to remind everyone of Mom and the way she died. I push Ted and Wallace away, and face the wall.

Ziggy leans over my bed. "I'm so sorry, Janey. I'm so sorry. This is the worst thing that could happen to a kid. Your mother loved you more than anything, and I know you loved her too. You're going to miss her so fuckin' much."

I stroke Ziggy's hair and nod. Finally, I think. Finally some-one gets it.

* * *

Here I am, three years later, in Miss Blue's strong embrace, my head resting against her shoulder. I feel peaceful and calm. Sad, but calm.

"It was my fault that she died," I whisper. "I hid under a table and she died. She came back to find me and she couldn't, and that's why she died."

"The fire killed her Jane. You didn't."

"But . . ."

"You were trying to help your Mom. You thought she was in danger. You wanted to get to the stage to help her. To rescue her. Your actions were heroic."

"My actions were stupid."

"No, Jane. Heroic. You were trying to help your mom, just like she was trying to help you when she ran back into the club. You were both heroes that night. One of you lived, and one of you died. It's not a good ending for either one of you, but that's the way it is. No one is at fault. Not your mother, and certainly not you – a twelve-year old girl who wanted to hide because she thought she had lost everything."

One perfect teardrop travels the length of Miss Blue's face. She turns away from me. "A mother and daughter trying to rescue each other," she says. "There's no greater love."

There's no greater love.

As I breathe in the cool air around me, I start to forgive myself. It has taken three years, but the smoke begins to clear. My life has been blessed; by my mother, by Olivia Blue, by music. The rest is up to me.

* * *

Faulty wiring.

Three and a half years after the fire, and two weeks after my breakthrough session with Olivia, an official report arrives from the investigative unit of the New York City Fire Department: "The fire was caused by an unintentional electrical discharge, characterized by low and erratic current, that ignited combustible materials." My mother lost her life because an electrical contractor – who is nowhere to be found – refused to pay the hundred dollars extra it would have cost to insulate the wires buried in the walls.

Body and Soul

Love is inconvenient,
It's a scene I should avoid,
I've been trampled down by romance,
I've been hurt, I've been annoyed,
Please give me a reason to jump deep into the void,
Convince me I should fall in love with you.

"Hey you, there! Canary!" yells Mary Two as she pounds on the guest bathroom door. "Could you learn some other songs? Miss Blue is arriving any second now."

"Forget it," shouts Mary One from the other side of the door. "I'll sing what I want to. And I done told you a million times, I ain't singin' that *Superstar* crap. The only tunes worth singin' come from Lady Day herself." Mary One whips open the door. "And if that's not good enough, then you just plain don't know what's good." She slams the door shut and continues singing.

"Fuckin' knees up Mother Brown," says Mary Two.

"And stop saying fuck!" says Mary One, before she resumes singing.

"Bollocks!" says Mary Two. "What will we ever do with her?"

"Stop trying to change her," I say.

Before Mary Two can respond, the "Chain of Fools" doorbell rings and we all rush to answer it. Olivia Blue visits us a lot these days. It's official. She and Dad have started dating.

Olivia and I still have our private sessions together on Saturday afternoons, but several times a week she shows up here for dinner with us, then she and Dad go to the movies or an art exhibit. Or sometimes they hang out in his study on the third floor and I can hear them, in the distance, laughing and talking until late at night. I had forgotten what it was like to have a happy father. Maybe I should be worried that Olivia might try to take my mother's place, but it's not like that, not at all. My memories of Mom are stronger than ever – having Olivia around seems to help us remember Mom even more, in a good way.

The Allegheny Gatehouse Band has elected to keep me on as the permanent drummer in their group. It took them six agonizing months to make up their minds, but during that time, with Olivia's emotional support and Mr. Hammill's technical training; I've become a much better drummer. I practice by myself for hours and hours every day, except on days when the Gatehouse Band rehearses. When I'm not practicing, I'm listening.

Leo is on cloud nine. We've made a lot of progress around here, and he takes full credit for orchestrating the entire plan, as well he should. Every so often he comes to a Gatehouse rehearsal with me. Truth be told, I think he has a crush on Octavious, the backup singer and rapper. And I'm pretty sure Octavious feels the same way about him. I worry about Leo sometimes. His mom Spanky is the coolest of the society ladies, but I still can't imagine her explaining to the Binky Pendletons of this world that her son is gay and is having a romantic relationship with a reform school student-rapper named Octavious. But then again, maybe I don't give Spanky enough credit. Mom always said that people are cool until proven otherwise.

RHYTHM

I don't know if love is in the air or what, but André the piano player keeps staring at me. Lately he has been rolling up his sleeves when he plays so that I can see his very impressive muscles. Leo says he has biceps like grapefruits. Turns out that André has Cuban blood, which anyone with an ounce of musical sense would realize if they heard him play his cool-ass salsa-funk fusion. He has talent, that's for sure. Plus he's very easy on the eye. At rehearsals, I catch myself looking at him more than I need to. Sometimes he looks at me sideways and smiles, just a little, and I feel like everything inside me is melting, and that, if I'm not careful, I might turn into a puddle right there on Miss Blue's music room floor. To distract myself, I make sure to hit the snare drum a little harder on the backbeat. Usually that straightens me out right away, although lately it seems to just turn me on more. I love the melting feeling, but – as Mary One says – it's the kind of thing that can get a girl into a heap o' trouble.

My body looks different these days, too. I have breasts, and a butt, and it seems like they're getting bigger by the hour. Exactly one year ago I was skinny and as straight up and down as any of the guys in my band, but now I've developed Grandma Isabella's bumps and curves. I stand in front of my bedroom mirror, naked, and wonder if Martians have invaded my body. But then I think about André and the way he looks at me and I realize that the changes can't be all bad. I imagine myself in one of Isabella's tight red dresses. I close my eyes and feel the rough sequined fabric clinging to my skin. I'm transported to Miami, leading a Conga Line onto the terrace overlooking the beach – with a hundred helpless men following me. André is at the front of the line, rubbing his hands on my hips and my ass, pressing himself against me. When I turn to him he rips away the straps of my dress and begins kissing me.

High on my own fantasies, I begin melting again, everything inside me dissolving, pooling, dripping. I fall to my knees and beg him to taste me, to sip me, to drink me, all of me. Until, at last, I disappear.

* * *

On the night of my first concert with the Gatehouse Band, I find myself alone in the equipment room with André. We'll be performing tonight in the school auditorium, and we're expecting a big crowd that includes a KDKA news crew, the Pittsburgh Post-Gazette, and a reporter from Psychology Today who is doing a profile of Miss Blue and her particular style of teaching music to teenagers in trouble. The other kids have already gone onstage to start a sound check, and Miss Blue has asked André and me to search for some extra music-stand lights in the back room. Her eyes follow me as I leave the stage. She knows.

"So, you nervous?" he asks. His back is to me and his dark blue jacket stretches across his upper torso. He must lift weights when he's not practicing the piano. Man, look at that. I can barely think.

"Huh? No. Yeah. Well, a little. You mean about the concert, right?" I've got my hair braided down my back so it won't bother me while I'm playing, but out of habit I brush a ghost strand from my eyes.

"What else you got to be nervous about?" He rummages through a crate of tangled cables and cords. "Your life is about as perfect as it gets, isn't it?"

"Lately, yeah," I'm not sure where he's heading with this. I feel funny standing here in my Gatehouse uniform. Miss Blue has insisted that I dress like the boys, which doesn't bother me too much. I just wish the uniform were more casual. She let me off the hook with the tie, at least. And I'm allowed to wear my Adidas sneakers. They're the only shoes I own that feel right when I play. They're red, with white stripes.

"You're rich, you've got talent, you're hot looking." He grins at me. My face heats up. I look down at my blue blazer and button-down white oxford shirt. I'm so turned on I can hardly stand up straight.

"Too bad about your – "

"What?" All of the sexy feelings dry up, cause I sense what he is about to say. "What?"

"About, you know," he says.

"No, I don't know." I might as well make this awkward for him.

"Your mom," he says.

"Oh, that. About my mom being dead, you mean?"

"Yeah, about your mom being dead. It's too bad. I'm sorry. Really."

"Yeah, it is too bad, isn't it?" I'm shocked that I'm staying so cool. "But I'm okay now. Or at least okay enough to function. It was pretty bad for a while, but Miss Blue helped me deal. It's hard to explain. You have no idea what it's like to lose your mom."

"I lost my mom, too," he says.

"You did?"

"Well, yeah. I mean pretty much everyone in the band only has one parent, if they have any parent at all. Didn't you ever think about that? Why do you think we're at this school? Most of the guys don't have dads. I don't have a mom. Or much of a dad, either."

"What happened?" I ask, ashamed of myself. I thought I was the only one. I should have known.

"My mom o.d.-ed on heroin. My dad's in jail, but he might be out by now – I don't give a fuck. Pretty typical in my neighborhood. Don't mean shit. Not like a nightclub fire – I mean, that's some shit straight outta some Hollywood action movie or something."

I gasp. *"What?"*

"Sorry," he says. "I'm probably not supposed to talk about the fire, but everyone does. Leo told Octavious and Octavious told the rest of us. We even went to the library and found the old newspaper articles about the accident. It's sort of strange; it makes you more like one of us. Until we found out, we thought you were just a talented little princess from the rich-folk part of town. You know, one of those kids who gets everything she wants. One of those kids who takes everything for granted."

"One of those kids who just assumes that both parents will always be there for her," I say. "You know. To tuck her in at night."

"To pick him up after basketball practice."

"To tell her a goofy story at bedtime."

"To heat up a bowl of soup."

"To plan a vacation in a far-away place."

"To sit on a porch step and tell bad jokes."

"To listen."

"To show up."

"Right," I say. "To show up. Showing up is everything. So now what? Because I have a dead mother I fit in? I'm *allowed* to join the club?"

"Well sort of, yeah."

"That's low, André."

"I mean musically you always fit in," he says, "but now everything else fits, too." He is getting closer and closer to me. Oh man, I can see the veins in his wrists, and I smell something lemony – is that cologne, or soap? I think I like it. I want to slap him and I want to taste him, I can't decide which. I make up my mind and I reach out and place my hand on his stomach. The tips of my fingers land between the folds of his starched white shirt and touch his bare skin. His stomach muscles tighten, and then quickly, he grabs the braid on the back of my head and pulls me to him, kissing me, hard. I could do this for a very long time, but he stops, smoothes my hair, and clears his throat.

"We'd better get a couple of music stand lights out to Miss Blue," he says, "or she'll be wondering what's going on back here."

"Yeah, you're right," I say. "Wait. Let me fix your tie."

He turns to me. I grab his tie, press myself against him, and whisper in his ear. "More, I want more."

He smiles at me. "You got it, girl," he says, and struts away empty-handed, leaving me alone to continue searching for the lights. I hug myself and laugh. Man, what a feeling.

* * *

Ladies and Gentlemen, put your hands together for the funkiest group of kids in Pittsburgh, Pennsylvania. Here they are, The Allegheny Gatehouse Band, featuring Jane Bowman on drums!

Wow! I didn't expect to hear my name announced. Suddenly, my stomach flutters and I wonder if I'm making a huge mistake.

This is the first time I've played in public since the fire, and I've been worried about having some kind of weird flashback or anxiety attack or something. But Olivia has coached me to do my breathing exercises, to focus on playing the drums, and to stay in the moment. She has assured me that if I do these three simple things, I'll be okay.

Breathe.

Focus.

Stay in the moment.

We start the concert by ripping into a piece of André's called "Bad Girl." I feel a little hesitant at first, but then – about halfway through the second chorus, it happens. For the first time in three years, I get inside the music, really inside, and the colors begin to return. Tonight, the shades of my drums are concentrated and forceful – hot reds jumbled with explosive pinks, airborne flashes of gold and copper. I listen as the band responds to my groove. The crash of the ride cymbal turns me on and makes me crave second portions of everything.

More. I want more. More music, more André. More.

After the show ends and the audience leaves, we pose for a Post-Gazette photographer. I stay in my place and the boys gather around my drums for the picture, with Olivia Blue on our left. Leo and the Marys remain in their seats in the first row of the now empty auditorium. Dad waits in the aisle, holding a huge bouquet of roses for Olivia. Mary One's little legs stick straight out from her upholstered chair and her eyes are half closed, like she's recalling a happy dream. Mary Two, her hair cranked impossibly high and dressed in her best Margaret Thatcher suit, waves at us from her seat in the first row.

"What did you think, Mary Two?" shouts André from the stage. He's probably hoping she brought a tin of macaroons.

"You were great, you fuckin' were, alright!" yells Mary Two. The photographer raises his eyebrows, clears his throat, and adjusts his tripod.

"Come on you guys, smile!" shouts Leo. "What are you, a funk band or an oil painting?"

"Wait!" says Dad. And he bounds up onto the stage, his long legs carrying him in three giant steps to Olivia's side. He thrusts the flowers into her arms and she kisses him on the cheek. He turns to me, gives me a quick thumbs-up and leaps back down. André, from out of nowhere, produces one long stemmed red rose, and places it on my snare drum.

"It's from all of us," he says. "Welcome to the Gatehouse Band."

This. I have this moment. I accept it, I honor it, I tuck it away in my mind's treasure chest of prizes and rewards. I'm not looking ahead or looking back. I'm here, and aware, and thankful that this memory will never abandon me. I take in the wounded and shining faces around me, and it occurs to me that this is the one gift of a broken childhood. We learn that most things – things that count – can be taken away, so we cling with a passion to the things that cannot. I catch Miss Blue staring at me, her eyes luminous and wide. She nods and smiles. She gets it.

André picks up one of my sticks and pokes me in the ribs. I fling my arms out to the side and scream with laughter. At exactly this moment, the photographer takes our picture.

PART II: 1989

Sweet Magnolia

Doom-boom! Doom-boom! Doom-boom! Doom-boom! The out-of-tune timpani thunder as the Penn Academy Class of 1989 marches down the red-carpeted center aisle of the school auditorium. The student orchestra plods through a dramatic version of "Pomp and Circumstance" like they're playing for the opening ceremony of the Olympics. I wonder why no one in the music department can figure out how to tune the timpani. This arrangement of "Pomp and Circumstance" is written in the key of G, but the timpani are tuned to an A flat and a D flat. It's excruciating, but there's not much I can do – short of running onstage and tackling Chantal Finkbinder, the timpani player who insists on playing with crossed ankles. "Why does she stand that way?" asks Leo. "It really makes her look like she's got to pee."

I hold onto my mortarboard to keep it from sliding off my head, and try not to listen to the music. Mr. Dilernia, who conducts the orchestra by waving his arms like a tortured octopus, has big sweat rings in the pits of his tan jacket. This trip down the aisle seems cinematic; almost a slow motion rewind of my past. Many of the shepherds of my childhood are here – all of my teachers, my family, and the parents of my classmates – sitting with straight backs, forced smiles, and expectant faces. I wonder what Mom would have made of this. I'd been thinking about her earlier this morning when I was trying to braid my hair in a way that didn't look goofy with the mortarboard. She would have known what to do; she was always good with hair. I chase away the sad thoughts and keep marching, because really, there's nothing else to do.

On our single-file journey through the packed auditorium, we pass Mrs. Dick, our cookie-faced first grade teacher, sitting with her husband Richard. Dad, my Pittsburgh grandparents, the Marys, André, and Olivia sit next to Spanky Wainwright and her third husband Pudge, and right on cue, all eight of them wave at me as I pass their row of chairs. André, who is now a University of Pittsburgh college guy, leans into the aisle and squeezes my hand. Both Marys dab at their eyes, and I wonder why in the world everyone seems to be so teary. This is pretty much the happiest day of my life. Finally, no more Penn Academy! Leo and I feel like dorks in our dark purple caps and gowns, but everyone keeps telling us we look very grown up and that we should be proud of ourselves. According to Mr. Clement Tucker – our commencement speaker and Chairman of the Board of Silvercon International – we are the future of international finance.

"As long as our parents don't cut us off," says Leo.

I've been treading water for the last three years at Penn, compiling enough credits to graduate, while doing the minimum amount of work to pass. All I care about is music – practicing, rehearsing and performing with the Gatehouse Band, practicing some more. There isn't much time left for anything else, except for the occasional grope in the corner with André. I've aced all my creative writing courses, and I've tried to do well in literature classes, because Mom always said that a study of the classics is crucial for anyone in the performing arts. But I've had to force myself to pay attention to Chaucer and T.S. Eliot when my brain is full of Clyde Stubblefield and Steve Gadd grooves. Math is even worse. There's this rumor going around that drummers are good at math, because rhythm is math, in a certain way. This theory doesn't apply to me. I mean, obviously I can count to four. And I can isolate my feet from my hands and play fractions of different time signatures with four appendages at once, but I still can't figure out what this has to do with long division and probability formulas. A groove takes place in your gut – you can analyze it 'til you're dizzy, but ultimately you have to feel it. Math, on the other hand, is purely a head-trip. About the only thing I've learned in math class is how to cheat on tests. Leo is a math wizard and he invented a special cheater's Morse Code to get me through exams. That's Leo, always looking out for me.

After posing for pictures, we chuck our mortarboards into the school athletic field. Leo and I say good-bye to each other, make plans to meet the next day, and leave with our families for lunch. Spanky and Pudge have booked a table at the Duquesne Club, and my family will be going to Grandma Millicent's and Grandpa Vernon's for an extravagant roast turkey noontime dinner. As I walk to the waiting car, Mary One on my left, Mary Two on my right – each of them clutching one of my elbows – I remember that neither one of them ever graduated from high school. For about the millionth time in the last three years, I remind myself that I'm lucky, in a way. Lucky me. Lucky me. Lucky, ducky, lucky me.

Dad and Olivia drive off in his ancient Mercedes convertible, and I climb into the old wood-paneled family station wagon with André and the Marys. Although the backseat of the car is the size of a rowboat, André squeezes right next to me, puts his arm around my shoulder, and whispers something about putting his head under my purple gown and having a little graduation party of his own.

Mary One hums a chorus of "I Cover the Waterfront."

May Two, who is driving, glares at us from the rearview mirror and says, "No nasty-nasty in the car, you two. Let's not ruin your graduation day. I still have tears in my eyes from that ceremony. Fuckin' brilliant, it was."

I push André away gently, and say, "Later." We've been doing the nasty-nasty for two years now. Everyone knows it, but Mary Two sets limits about what she's willing to witness firsthand. Handholding is okay, but that's about it.

We pull into the huge circular driveway leading to Grandma Millicent's Fox Chapel house, park next to her enormous rose garden, and tumble out of the car. Our house in Sewickley Heights is big, but this place borders on palatial. It's almost silly, really. We have drinks in the parlor, and then head into the dining room. Grandma Millicent has set her table with cream-colored Irish linen, Wedgwood china, and Waterford stemware. A huge crystal vase holds branches of Magnolia blossoms from one of the trees in the back garden. All this fancy stuff is nice, but basically we're happy just to eat at a table with a smooth surface – no spilled beverages, no flying lamb chops, no sliding saucers threatening to crash land on the Persian carpet. The Marys, seated next to each other, look on with curiosity and a touch of envy as Tawny Suttridge, Grandma's cook for the last twenty years, serves a perfectly prepared meal of all my favorites: turkey, mashed potatoes, green beans, and stuffing. I love this; it's like Thanksgiving in May. I spoon gravy onto the creamy mountain of potatoes in front of me, and wonder where I'll be next year at this time.

"So, Jane, darling," says Grandma Millicent, "Do tell us your plans for the future. We know you've decided to put off college for a year, but whatever will you do with your time?" Grandma Millicent is wearing a sugary-pink tweed suit. She looks like she belongs on top of a fancy bakery cake.

"Mother," says Dad, answering for me when he sees my mouth is full of potatoes. "We've already discussed this. Jane wants time to practice the drums. She'll continue to play with the Gatehouse band, as long as they'll keep her on."

"I don't think that will be a problem," says Olivia, who is sitting on the other side of André. This is the first thing she has said all afternoon. I wonder why she's so quiet – something must be up. Earlier today, when I walked into Dad's office, she looked troubled. The phone rang. She answered, and then quickly replaced the receiver.

"Who was it?" I had asked.

"No one," she said. "Someone is calling and hanging up as soon as they hear my voice. That's the third time today."

I didn't think much of it until now.

"You okay?" I ask, under my breath. Olivia shrugs.

"Well." I return to my grandmother's question. "I'd like to play as much as possible in the next year – with the Gatehouse band, but also with some other groups. I'm thinking a lot about New York City – about spending more time there to check out the scene. Leo is still waiting to hear about being accepted into the architecture program at NYU, so we have this fantasy of moving to New York together. You know, using our apartment at Grandma Isabella's house."

There is a loud gasp from the other side of the table.

"Jesus, Mary, and Joseph!" shouts Mary Two. "What does André have to say about that? You livin' in sin with Leo – a strapping young hunk of man if ever I saw one!"

I hope Leo's ears are burning at the Duquesne Club.

"I'm cool, Miss Mary Two," says André. "Leo and Jane are just good friends. Nothing to be jealous about. I don't believe in that jealousy sh – stuff."

Everyone at the table knows that Leo isn't interested in girls, but Mary Two refuses to give up on his heterosexual potential.

"Well, you may regret saying that, young man!" says Mary Two. "Because one of these days Leo is bound to make his move."

I'm positive André is about to say something about Leo's boyfriend Octavious, so I kick him under the table. Olivia kicks him, too. André's winks at me and says, "How about that Pirates game last week?"

Dad makes a short speech about the philosophical side of baseball, the plates are cleared, lemon meringue pie is served, and we move to the terrace for coffee and tea. A light wind gusts through the magnolia trees surrounding the patio area, and the ripened blossoms, pale pink and white, swell with the weight of the breeze. One petal at a time they float to the warm ground, marking the end of one season, and the start of the next.

Mary One wanders through the garden, gathering the fallen petals and placing them in a small basket. When her basket is full, she presents it to Olivia.

"For you," says Mary One.

Olivia holds the basket on her lap for a moment before running her long ebony fingers through the silken petals.

"Thank you," she says. "Thank you."

Speak Low

"You might as well get comfortable," says Olivia Blue. "What I want to tell you will take awhile."

Olivia hasn't been herself since my graduation last week. She seems distracted, and sort of sad. I'm bursting with curiosity over what she's about to tell us, even though I'm afraid it might be something terrible. Dad and I settle into the old red velvet sofa in his office. Olivia sits across from us in an overstuffed brocade chair. Her hair, which she normally wears coiled on top of her head, is loose and flowing down her back. She's thirty-nine years old, but this evening she looks like a teenager. As she weaves her fingers together, she bows her head into her hands. She's not praying, at least I don't think so, but she's doing something that looks a lot like it.

"Olivia," says Dad. "I love you. Jane loves you. There's nothing you can tell us that will change that."

"I know," she says. "This concerns the way I feel about myself and the mistakes that I've made. Big ones. I don't talk much about my past, but it's time. You're my family now, and we need to be honest with each other. You and Jane have been very honest with me. It's time for me to reciprocate."

Olivia takes a deep breath.

"You see, I once had a daughter. She would have been eighteen last month."

Speechless, Dad and I wait for her to continue. Olivia Blue leans back in her chair, closes her eyes for an instant, and begins to tell us her story. Dad and I listen, because when you really love someone, it's the thing you do best.

* * *

On a rainy spring morning in 1950, a baby girl – wrapped in a blue blanket – was found in a shoebox next to the emergency entrance of Lenox Hill Hospital in New York City. A note pinned to the blanket, written in crayon and smeared by the rain, said, "My name is Olivia. Please take care of me."

After she was whisked to the nursery, dressed in dry clothing, examined by doctors and deemed healthy, baby Olivia – who was given the last name "Blue" because of the blanket wrapped around her – was sent to a Catholic orphanage in the Bronx. For years the good Sisters of the Bleeding Heart tried to place Olivia in a real family, but she was never chosen. The girls with peachy complexions and blonde curls landed in the caring arms of well-meaning adults with proper homes. Girls like Olivia grew up in the orphanage.

"Not to worry," said Sister Mary Katherine, who was fond of Olivia. "We'll give you a proper home. Right here."

Olivia attended church every morning, studied her catechism, prayed to a benevolent God, worked hard at school, and played the piano whenever she got the chance. There was an old upright piano in the recreation room, and Sister Mary Katherine – impressed by Olivia's musicality – gave Olivia permission to practice it whenever she liked, even late at night, when the other girls were tucked into bed. Olivia began serious piano lessons at age nine, paid for by a mysterious source that Olivia suspected had something to do with the offering plate at the local church. Mrs. O'Malley, the piano teacher, was paid in quarters and dimes at the end of every lesson.

Playing the piano gave Olivia a sense of purpose. She gathered a dozen of her orphanage classmates, and convinced them to sing in a choir. Olivia listened to gospel records smuggled into the orphanage by Sister Mary Katherine, who did everything she could to find musical role models for Olivia. She listened for hours at a time to these recordings and began to transcribe arrangements for the girls in the choir. These were girls who, like her, had not been chosen for adoption. They were girls of color, girls with disabilities, or girls who had been brought to the orphanage after they were too old to be adopted. Music was a way to create, a way to explore their feelings, a way to belong.

To belong.

Olivia was well educated, well dressed, and well fed by the Sisters of the Bleeding Heart. By her sixteenth birthday, she had perfect table manners, was passably fluent in French, had a working knowledge of Latin, and was performing classical piano recitals and concerts sponsored by the church. She also began to compose and arrange songs influenced by her collection of gospel recordings. She learned to improvise, excited that the harmonic structures she had learned could lead to the creative freedom she craved.

At seventeen, Olivia received a full scholarship to the Juilliard School of Music. Sister Mary Katherine helped Olivia pack her boxes of sheet music and record albums, and her one small suitcase of clothes – a collection of cashmere sweaters and pleated skirts donated by the Junior League of Riverdale. They drove together – in the old orphanage van – to her student apartment in Manhattan.

"Look Olivia, isn't this glorious?" said Sister Mary Katherine, sweeping a robed arm out behind her. "A room to yourself! Your first real home."

Olivia, who would have been happy to spend the rest of her life giving casual concerts and conducting the choir at the orphanage, didn't think it was glorious at all. She peered into the tiny room. There was just enough space for a single bed, a scratched wooden chest of drawers, and an old metal desk squeezed into the corner. The room seemed enormous to her.

"Sister Mary Katherine," she said, trying to be brave, her voice breaking. "I don't know how to say goodbye. You've been so nice to me. I'll try, I really will, to do a good job at school. I know how lucky I am to have this chance. But, I'll really miss you. And the other sisters, too. But mostly you. I hope that maybe I can come and visit you. Not right away. Someday." Olivia knew that her corner of the four-bed room at the orphanage had already been assigned to an eight-year old girl. Olivia would never be able to go back. Not really. Home, it seemed to her, shouldn't be a place of no return.

"Remember who you are, Olivia Blue," said Sister Mary Katherine. "You're a young woman with talent, intelligence, and the ability to make a difference in the lives of others. Never allow those things to be taken away from you." She paused and reached into her Sisters of the Bleeding Heart tote bag. "Here, I've saved this for you all these years. Not that you need it, now." With shiny eyes and a sad smile, Sister Mary Katherine handed Olivia the blue blanket she had been wrapped in as a baby.

"God bless you, Olivia." she said, patting Olivia's shoulder, turning on the heels of her sturdy black shoes and walking away.

"And you, too, Sister." Watching Sister disappear down the staircase, Olivia felt herself becoming small and insignificant, shrinking to almost nothing.

Olivia held the blue blanket against her cheek and wondered how in the world a scrap of fabric, so worn and thin, had ever protected a newborn child from the wind and rain.

* * *

At Juilliard, Olivia entered a competitive atmosphere where music seemed to be ruled by technical expertise and theoretical knowledge. She had studied those things, but was nowhere near the level of the other young men and women in the piano and composition departments, her two areas of focus. As much as she practiced, as much as she wrote, nothing she accomplished ever compared to the flashy work of her fellow students. She longed for support from her colleagues, praise from the faculty, or just a smidgeon of joy to the whole process.

Olivia found it difficult to socialize with the other college students, who floated around each other in isolated bubbles. Then she met Joseph, a violin major with pasty skin, a rich family, and a huge apartment on Riverside Drive. When Joseph first approached Olivia – outside Lincoln Center on a cold February morning – she was so shocked that a fellow student had spoken to her that she felt frozen to the pavement, unable to reply, as if she had lost the ability to conduct a casual conversation with another human being.

"Excuse me?" she finally said, looking him straight in the eye.

"Would you like to have coffee?" said Joseph. "Or lunch?"

"Coffee is fine, I'm on a pretty tight budget."

"It's on me. Come on, I know a cool place on Columbus. Let's go for lunch. Do you like Chinese?"

"Yes. I mean – I think so. I mean, I don't really know . . .but I'll go with you."

"Good." He glanced over his shoulder and tugged his hat over his ears.

Olivia wrapped her winter coat around her, and off they went, leaning into the wind. Three hours later, she was in Joseph's apartment, naked on his bed, and high on cocaine. Just like that. She shoved all thoughts of Sister Mary Katherine, the choir, her music, and her studies, into the back corners of her mind. She knew she was doing things that would send her straight to hell, but she didn't care. All she cared about was being liked. And it seemed that Joseph liked her. A lot.

"You look like an African princess," Joseph said, licking and pawing at her. Olivia lay back on the bed, feeling warm and keenly interested in everything around her: the blemishes erupting on Joseph's back, the wail of the sirens outside his bedroom window, the pleasantly bitter taste of the coke trickling down her throat, the pressure of the silk ropes circling her wrists, the stinging pain of him ramming inside her, the smell of her sweat blending with the odor of stale cigarette smoke, the bland yellow color of the scraped bedroom wall as her head slammed against it, the numbness settling around her and chilling her fingertips, the melodies of little girls singing *I belong*, the cry of her own voice saying *thank you, thank you, thank you.*

* * *

Olivia returned to Joseph's apartment often. She liked it there – the freedom from school, the attention, the coke, the sex. She kept going back and staying for longer periods of time, until finally – she just never left. She quit school and moved in with Joseph, where she had a steady supply of cocaine, Valium to help her sleep, television to keep her company while Joseph was off at school, and endless hours of sex to keep her occupied when he was at home. There was no piano at Joseph's apartment. Every so often – when Olivia felt sad about the lack of music in her life – she would beg Joseph to rent or buy a piano. But he refused. There was a stereo in the living room, but shortly after she moved in with him, he threw away her collection of gospel records.

"That's not real music," he said. "It's trash."

Joseph did the shopping, paid the bills, took care of the laundry and dry cleaning, and made sure that Olivia had enough drugs to keep her quiet. Her only contact with the outside world was with an Irish maid, who showed up twice a week to tidy the apartment. The maid was given orders never to talk to Olivia, and Olivia was too stoned to care.

A year passed, and Olivia's drug addiction began to affect her appearance. Joseph's interest in her waned as her body caved in on itself, as if she were starving. When Joseph became obsessed with a seventeen-year old cello player, he told Olivia to leave.

"But I can't. I have nowhere to go."

"I don't give a shit."

"But . . ."

"But what? This is my place, and you can't stay. I make the decisions around here."

"I know, but what am I supposed to do? Where am I supposed to go?"

"I really don't care. Go back to that fuckin' Sister whatever her name is. Maybe she'll take you in again. Or go shack up with someone else. Go spend someone else's money on your sorry-ass drug habit."

"But you're the one who gave me the drugs."

"You're the bitch who took them. You're the stupid bitch who got addicted."

"I'll quit. I'll clean up. Please Joseph, I'll do anything to stay. Please."

"No. You're out of here. Now."

"You can't just throw me out on the street."

"Watch me," said Joseph, as he pitched Olivia's drawer of sweaters and skirts, most of which she hadn't worn for a year, into Sister Mary Katherine's old suitcase.

Before he slammed the suitcase shut, Olivia said, "Wait!" She reached under the pillow on her side of the bed, pulled out her worn blue baby blanket, and tossed it onto the pile.

"Here," said Joseph. "You'll need this to tide you over." He handed her a vial of white powder and a large bottle of ten milligram Valium.

Olivia, standing in the hallway outside of the apartment, grabbed the drugs and stuffed them into the pockets of her coat. "Thank you," she said. "Thank you."

"You know, you're such a whore," said Joseph, slamming the door.

* * *

Two weeks later, outside of the Edison hotel on West 46th Street, a security guard found Olivia unconscious and crumpled in a heap on top of her suitcase. She was rushed to St. Claire

Hospital where it was determined that she had been beaten, raped, and most likely pushed out of a moving car in front of the hotel entrance. The doctors also discovered that she was in the middle of Valium withdrawal, and wrote orders to place her in a detoxification and rehabilitation program when she recovered from her physical injuries.

As the drugs seeped out of her system, they were replaced by another kind of poison – shame. The bruises and cuts faded away, but appalling memories of the last year penetrated Olivia's awareness and held her hostage to her own remorse.

When Bruce Whitman, a deacon at the Mount Laurel Fundamentalist Church of Christ, visited Olivia, he arrived with two women – both of whom belonged to the same congregation. Bruce asked Olivia if she was a woman of faith, and she said yes. They held hands and prayed together.

Olivia, who had been scooped up as a baby and rescued by the Sisters of the Bleeding Heart, hoped the Fundamentalists would do the same for her this time around. Aching to be forgiven for the sins of the last year, she welcomed Bruce's visits, even when he began to call on her by himself. He asked Olivia to join his church, making it clear to her – as he rested his fleshy hand on her shoulder, her wrist, her thigh – that she would be welcomed with open arms, loved and accepted by the members of his congregation, and nurtured both physically and spiritually. His church would support her and give her a place to live until she could get back on her feet.

When he kissed her the first time, she felt disgust and a familiar longing for something she couldn't name.

"I love you," he said. "I love how the bright light of God comes from deep inside you. Our Lord and savior Jesus Christ has brought us together for a reason. We've been put on this earth to worship Him through our love. Come with me Olivia, and we'll walk through the garden of life together as good Christians, for only we are protected by the loving eyes of our God."

Even with Olivia's eroded sense of dignity, she knew that Bruce was conning her, spouting carefully rehearsed words that he had used on other women, trying to get a piece of something forbidden by making vague promises he wouldn't keep. But because she had nowhere to go, nothing to lose, and no one to whom she could confess the depth of her shame, she allowed him to preach. She allowed him to touch her. She allowed his hot breath and steamy rhetoric to travel the length of her weary body. As he backed her into a hospital utility closet and stripped away her robe and nightdress, she pretended to believe his twisted promises of salvation. Bruce's self-righteous proselytizing sickened Olivia, but she played his game. She told him he was an angel, a savior sent to her by a God who understood her need to be rescued.

She agreed to join his church. Olivia Blue would reinvent herself. She would stay away from drugs, marry Bruce, and try to forget everything about her past. She would become a blank slate, a good Mount Laurel Fundamentalist Christian woman, and hope that faith might save her from the streets. She was too worn out to consider any other option.

* * *

"We welcome any woman who accepts the Lord Jesus Christ into her life," the church members said to each other in voices oozing with fellowship. Five years earlier they had turned down a man of color who had attempted to join the church. But Olivia was different. She was now a Whitman, a name that had clout in the church community.

Bruce and Olivia lived in Upper Mount Laurel, New Jersey, in a restored Victorian house with a beautiful garden and a swimming pool. Bruce's father, real estate king Ted Whitman, had made his fortune developing strip mall properties and industrial parks. Fredericka, Bruce's mother, was a shopaholic and a slumlord – she owned hundreds of run down apartments in the Teaneck area. Bruce, a professional son, spent most of his time at the church, the golf course, and the sex shops on 42nd Street in Manhattan.

The Whitman family – the church's biggest contributors – financed the Board of Directors annual missionary trips to Third World countries and paid for the newly constructed fellowship hall that housed most of the church's social events. The church members invited Olivia to dinners, lunches, ice cream socials, weddings, baby showers, funerals, and fundraisers. She became skilled at conversing with privileged people, and learned to endure their stifling and close-minded values in exchange for their feigned acceptance of her. She figured out how to dress like them, how to decorate her home, how to arrange a perfect silk-flower centerpiece, how to avoid confrontation by looking the other way, and how to plan a menu for any occasion. Since the church members didn't drink – or at least claimed they didn't – every event revolved around some form of lard-heavy food, served with great ceremony on tables with coordinated table linens and theme-appropriate decorations. Olivia found this both exhausting and puzzling. But she kept quiet and learned to bake.

She fantasized about leaving him, about finding a place to live where she could rediscover her music. Working toward her dream, she skimmed money from her household allowance and squirreled away the loose bills and change that Bruce left in the pockets of his clothes before they went to the laundry. She didn't know when she'd have enough money – or nerve – to leave, she just knew that she would, someday.

Olivia's sexual relationship with Bruce was lonely and humiliating – but determined to keep him from discovering her plan to leave – she worked hard to keep him content. She dressed up in the degrading outfits he provided and played along with his warped fantasies. Once he forced her to shave her entire body, including her head – while he watched – because he said God would have wanted her that way. He bought her a good wig to wear to church functions, but at home, in the bedroom, he wanted her bald.

A year into their marriage, Bruce began hiring a blond prostitute named Jenna. Once, during one of their meetings, Olivia looked directly into the girl's pale face, and saw something she recognized – defeat, boredom, and a plea for help. Olivia averted her eyes and pressed her cheek against the woman's bare breast.

If I could save you, she thought, *I'd save myself.*

Following the sessions with Jenna, Bruce would drag Olivia from the bed and force her to her knees, insisting that she pray to the Lord for forgiveness. It was during these times that Olivia Blue – pride and joy of the good Sisters of the Bleeding Heart, ace student of religious studies, childhood champion of Bible trivia, believer in the benevolence of a loving God – wondered if there was a God at all. But she kept praying, just in case.

She took birth control pills, but later, after she discovered she was pregnant, learned that Bruce – with the doctor's help – had substituted the pills with placebos. As her stomach swelled, the church ladies buzzed around her, offering advice, and inviting her to prayer breakfasts and showers to celebrate the pending arrival of the newest Whitman. Behind her back, they gossiped about what color the baby would be. Since Bruce was as pale as Olivia was dark, anything was possible.

While all of this was going on, Bruce's sexual demands increased. Jenna began to arrive with one, sometimes two other women. Olivia endured the sessions by willing herself into a state of blankness. But one night, when Bruce and Jenna brought home a male prostitute, Olivia found herself unable to comply with Bruce's commands. Hovering somewhere outside of herself, she looked down and saw what she had become — a broken woman behaving like an animal, writhing on an expensive plush-carpet, bald and pregnant, with two naked men and a strung-out woman hovering over her; smearing their sweat and secretions over the smooth surface of her distended belly.

She struggled to her feet and screamed, "No! No more. No!"

Bruce dragged her into the bathroom and hit her so hard that she fell backwards into the shower, cutting her head on the metal rim of the door. Then he began kicking her.

Jenna and her co-worker, who sensed danger, decided to leave. But before they scrambled out the door, Jenna picked up the kitchen phone extension and dialed 911, a phone call that most likely saved Olivia's life.

* * *

"I don't know what happened officer," said Bruce to the two policemen standing in the foyer of the Whitman home. "She fell in the shower and cut her head. You know, she has a history of drug abuse, maybe she was high or something."

Olivia, wearing a bathrobe and holding a towel to her bleeding head, walked into the foyer. She said, in a voice both quiet and firm, "That's not true."

"Would you like to press charges, Ma'am?" asked one of the policemen, whose last name was Williams.

"Yes," said Olivia, avoiding Bruce's eyes by looking straight ahead. "And I need a doctor, immediately. I'm eight months pregnant."

"How many weeks exactly, Ma'am?"

"Thirty-two," said Olivia.

"Call an ambulance," said Officer Williams to his partner, as he began to read Bruce his rights.

"You'll pay for this you fucking nigger bitch," said Bruce as the policeman cuffed him.

"I usually do," said Olivia, still not looking at him. "But not this time." After Bruce had been escorted to the squad car, she turned to Officer Williams and said, "Please help me. I need to get out of this house and find a safe place for my baby and me."

"Take my advice lady," he said. "Run as fast and as far as you can. I know the Whitman family. They buy their way out of everything. That religious stuff they hide behind is pure bullshit. Your husband likes to beat up women – I've arrested him before, and it's usually for things a lot nastier than what he did to you. His father is just as bad. Ever take a good look at your mother-in-law? Her face has been cut so many times it looks like a roadmap, even after all the plastic surgery. You wanna end up like her? In my opinion, these hitters, they never change. Mostly they just get worse. At the hospital they'll have a social worker who can advise you about where to go."

"But I've got nothing. No family, no job, no money. Nothing."

"You have your life. And the life of your baby. Come on Mrs. Whitman, that's not nothing."

Overwhelmed by the policeman's kindness, Olivia began to cry.

"At some point," he said, "you're gonna have to come to the station to press formal charges, but we'll wait until after the doctors get a good look at you. We wanna make sure the baby is okay. How are you feeling?"

Before she could answer, Olivia vomited into the umbrella stand by the front door. Officer Williams caught her just before she collapsed onto the cold marble floor. Ten minutes later, the ambulance arrived.

* * *

Olivia stayed in the hospital for four weeks, until her baby was born. With the help of a social worker from an organization called SAFE, she filed formal charges against Bruce. The court issued a restraining order that prevented him from coming anywhere near her or the baby. SAFE, dedicated to the protection of women and children in abusive relationships, promised to find a secure home for Olivia once she was released from the hospital, and provided her with a lawyer to deal with divorce proceedings.

Bruce, irate and vengeful, hired Dean Lavernge – the most successful divorce attorney in Mount Laurel – to represent him. Bruce's parents squelched the nasty rumors circulating through the church community by concocting stories about Olivia's extra-marital escapades and drug abuse. They sneaked into the hospital to look at their grandchild and check out her skin color. Satisfied that she was light-skinned enough, they ordered Dean Lavernge to sue for permanent custody of the child.

Born at thirty-six weeks, Olivia's baby girl was small, but healthy. She named her Kate, after Sister Mary Katherine. Olivia had feared she wouldn't bond easily with her daughter, but her worries disappeared when she looked into Kate's dark eyes. Olivia's anguish over her own uncertain future was replaced by a desire to give her child a decent life, a decent home, a sense of belonging.

To belong.

Olivia cradled her baby in her arms, and for the first time in several years, began to sing.

* * *

Olivia's SAFE-appointed attorney was a hard working lawyer name Karen Geisler. During the trial to determine custody, the law prevented Karen from mentioning the restraining order and charges of abuse brought against Bruce, even though he had pleaded guilty and had supposedly gone into anger-management counseling to avoid a jail term. Numerous witnesses, probably bribed by the Whitmans, were paraded forth to testify that Olivia was a drug user, a sex addict, and an unfit mother. Jenna the prostitute, wearing a dark blue conservative suit and a blouse with a drooping bow attached to the collar, showed up to testify how Olivia had propositioned her. Then, several church members took the stand to swear that Olivia had routinely attended church functions stoned, drunk, or both. Karen Geisler fought as hard as she could, until Bruce's lawyer showed up with surprise evidence. Secretly, Bruce had arranged to have photos taken of Olivia with Jenna. In one of the pictures, Jenna – her eyes closed – was tied to the four-poster bed. Olivia, her bald head resting on Jenna's naked chest, her face to the camera, looked to be in the throes of passion. Another picture showed Olivia pregnant and flat on her back, with the male prostitute on top of her. Bruce was nowhere to be seen in the photos. Jenna testified that Olivia had drugged her, the male prostitute testified that he had been paid by Olivia to have sex with her. Both of them swore that Bruce was not involved in any of the trysts.

Her back rigid, her fists clenched, Olivia sat in the court-room with her hands folded, her head bowed. She knew what was coming. Bruce was awarded permanent custody of Kate. Olivia would be allowed to visit her one day a week, and only with supervision. Baby Kate, who had remained with a volunteer from SAFE in the corridor of the courthouse building, was bundled up, handed over to the Whitmans and whisked away before Olivia could say good-bye.

* * *

"I'm sorry," said Karen Geisler. "I'm so sorry, Olivia. We can appeal, but with those photos, I doubt we'll get anywhere. The photos are really bad, you understand that, don't you?"

"He – he – he forced me to do those things. He was there."

"I know Olivia. I believe you. But we don't have photographic evidence of his participation, do we? He not only has the photos, he has two witnesses willing to swear he wasn't there. I *know* you didn't want to do those things, but even if I can get the judge to believe that, he'll still want to know why you didn't say no and run away."

"Because I was trapped. Or I thought I was trapped. Look, before I met Bruce I lived on the street for weeks. I didn't want to end up there again, so I went along with him, thinking that if I cooperated, I could eventually save enough money to get out. I didn't know about SAFE, back then, I didn't know there were people willing to help me. I didn't know."

As Olivia packed her daughter's toys and clothes into the plastic garbage bags that were supposed to be picked up by the Whitman driver later that day – but never were – she considered her options. She knew that the Whitmans would fill Kate's head with poisonous thoughts and horrible lies about her. Olivia knew that the stories and gossip would alienate her child, that her presence in Kate's life would cause much anguish and embarrassment for her. But she also knew that by abandoning her child completely, she would be dooming Kate to an uncertain future with an abusive father, abusive grandparents, and a church full of self-righteous zealots who would find it convenient to look the other way – even if they suspected an innocent child was being harmed.

When the judge, who seemed to be personally offended by Olivia's purported behavior, ordered her to return to church every Sunday – the Mount Laurel Fundamentalist Church of Christ – for her one-day-a-week supervised visit with Kate, Olivia's resolve to play a role in her daughter's life began to weaken.

"What does he want?" she asked Karen Geisler.

"What does he really want? Deep down inside, he wants to beat you until you die," she said. "That would be his first choice. Plan B? He wants you out of his life so he can find a new victim. He wants you out of town. Gone forever."

"You think I should, what? Just leave?"

"I can only tell you Olivia, that he's an extremely dangerous man. Abusive men continue to abuse. Look, unless there's an intense willingness on the part of the abuser to heal himself, he will never ever change. Bruce hasn't indicated any willingness at all. Those court-ordered anger-management sessions? I'm willing to bet he never attended a single one. The judge allowed Bruce to select his own counselor. He probably paid one of his cronies from the church to file that glowing report. Anyway, my point is that he's likely to come after you, especially if you stay in town. We're dealing with a thirty-seven year-old man who has never been held accountable for his actions – his parents have always bailed him out. It's my opinion that your only option is to protect yourself. The court has awarded him custody of Kate and we can't do a damn thing about that."

"I could take her. I could take her and leave."

"You mean kidnapping?"

"Yes."

"He'll find you, then you'll both be in danger. Are you listening to what I'm saying, Olivia? Guys like this don't give up. Plus the Whitmans have the financial resources to track you down wherever you go. Forget about taking Kate and running, Olivia, it won't work. I'm so sorry. Really, I am. SAFE can help you with money, but we have to stay within the boundaries of law, even though sometimes the law seems more intent on helping the abuser than the abused."

"What would you do in my shoes?"

"Olivia, I've been in your shoes. That's why I'm doing this work. Protect yourself. Then maybe, someday, you'll be able to rescue your child."

"So. I should just leave? How? And how do you know he won't still come after me?"

"I don't know. Men like this tend to – well, like I said, they don't go away. You never know what might set Bruce off. Look, we'll make sure he signs a big stack of threatening legal documents – not that they'll do any good, but I can guarantee you he's terrified of jail, so he'll go along with us, at least for the time being. We'll keep the restraining order in place. And we'll also make sure he gives you a lot of money to get out of town. I'm guessing his family will settle with you for a nice sum if it means the church gossip-mill will stop running overtime. My gut feeling is that the Whitmans are humiliated – just a little – by this whole situation. But listen to me, Olivia. You'll never really be rid of Bruce. Psychologically, I mean. He'll haunt you for the rest of your life."

"And what about Kate?"

"Nothing to do but pray."

"What? How can you even say that?"

"I'm sorry. I – I'm sorry. Look, for a lot of abused women faith helps get them through."

"Faith has gotten me nowhere. I've been praying my whole life, and look what has happened."

"I can ask SAFE to put Kate's name on the *please inform* list. That way we'll be able to keep track of any unusual medical problems, emergency room reports, that kind of thing. I've got an inside track to school reports of children who are suspected of being abused."

"I can't – This can't be happening."

"You can cry, Olivia. It's okay to cry. This is about as bad as it gets. But look, I'm gonna nail that mother-fucker for as much money as I can. You'll have a fresh start. And then, if we get really lucky, maybe you'll be reunited with Kate someday. I'm sorry to pin all of your hope on one small possibility, but it's all we've got."

As Olivia smoothed, folded, and tucked away the baby clothes that her daughter would never wear again, she wondered if her own mother had suffered the same crushing heartbreak on the day she had left Olivia in a shoebox on the freezing pavement – wrapped in a blue blanket that had protected her from nothing at all.

* * *

While Olivia waited for the financial settlement from the Whitmans, the SAFE staff moved her to another house, one with a piano. Olivia stared at it for hours, and then, because she didn't know what else to do, she slid onto the bench. Her fingers stiff and hesitant, she began to play. Once she started, she couldn't stop. As her tears dropped onto the ivory keys, sensations and memories began to surge through her and into the music. First came sadness for what she had lost – her music, the touch of Sister Mary Katherine's bony hands on her shoulders, the companionship of her orphanage friends, the unexpected love she had felt for Kate. Then, with no warning, her hands began to shake, and the rage that had seethed in her for three years worked its way into angry blocks of chords, the dissonance pounding against her ears, her heart, her spirit. For almost two hours she played this way, until the waves of her wrath diminished and were replaced – gradually – by gentle swells of emotion that matched the rhythm of the lullaby she had once sung to Kate. She kept playing, and playing, and playing, until finally, there was nothing left inside her but empty space, hollow and echoing and liberating.

The Whitmans paid off Olivia the same way they bought favors from everyone else. They gave her a lump sum of one million dollars. In return, Olivia agreed to stay away from Kate. She also agreed to leave town. Olivia Blue Whitman – the twenty-two year old former orphan, former drug addict, former Christian, former victim of sexual and physical abuse, and former mother – bought herself a new life, based on an old dream. She purchased a respectable suitcase, a passable wardrobe, and an airline ticket to Pittsburgh, where she rented an apartment and enrolled in the Music Therapy program at Duquesne University.

On Olivia's first day at Duquesne, she stepped through the double doors of the music building and looked down the long stretch of hallway that led to practice cubicles and classrooms. As she began to walk she listened to the muted sounds of young people making music; the fanfare of a trumpet, the cautious vocalizing of a soprano, the mournful passage of a cellist, the burning swing-tempo of a jazz group trying to imitate Oscar Peterson's trio, the silvery trill of a flute player racing up and down an impossible passage, the spine-tingling screech of a violinist stretching for a note he would never reach. The sounds were no different from those she had experienced at Juilliard, but this time, she heard vulnerability and yearning – young people with one foot in adulthood – attempting to tame life's chaos by conquering the tricky musical passages assigned to them by their teachers. She heard grit and perseverance. She heard the sounds of hope – not the smooth-edged hope of easy optimism, but hard-earned hope, the kind that comes from determination and courage, brittle and jagged and beautiful, like the satisfying crunch of heavy boots stomping on pieces of shattered glass.

RHYTHM

Music is an art that cannot be mastered, she had written in her application essay to Duquesne, *a means without an end, and a complicated yet kind process that helps us cope with the simplicity and cruelty of life. My goal is to teach young people to protect and heal themselves through the study of music, to teach them that music can offer a path to self-dignity.*

She would succeed in teaching music to others, and in doing so, she would start to believe in herself.

* * *

I exhale, slowly. Dad and I crumple into the sofa cushions. I cover my face with my hands and cry. I cry for Olivia, I cry for her lost daughter, and I cry for my lost mother and myself. Now I get it. In a flash I understand how Olivia has helped me climb out of my slippery-walled pit of sorrow, and how she has helped so many of the Gatehouse boys do the same. As I'm thinking over the miracle of her presence in my life, Dad leaps from the sofa and grabs Olivia's hand. She looks up at him, the hard angles of her cheekbones reflecting the speckled June light streaming through the window.

"You belong, Olivia. You belong here, in our family." Dad's voice cracks as he strains to hold back his tears. He kneels next to her chair. She touches his face.

Out of the corner of my eye, I catch a glimpse of one of the silver-framed photos of Mom. In the picture, she's pointing to the sky and laughing, her hair tied back with a fluffy orange scarf that blows in the wind. I long for her approval and for a fleeting moment I swear the image in the frame nods at me, not just once, but twice, as if one nod is meant for me, the other for Dad.

I kiss Dad and Olivia goodbye, and leave the two of them alone to discuss Olivia's story. I know Dad has unanswered questions – so do I – but it's clear to me that he has an unfailing love for her.

I tiptoe down the staircase and out into Mary Two's formal English rose garden, afraid to interrupt the perfect balance of silence and anticipation hanging in the early summer air. Drunken clouds shaped like dinosaurs and lambs stagger through the indigo sky, and a pale yellow butterfly lands on the back of my index finger. The translucent wings stop fluttering just long enough for it to realize it should fly away while it can.

Mom gave me the end of her life, Olivia has given me the beginning of hers. I squeeze my teenage backside into the old wooden swing in the garden – the one Mom used to push me in when I was a kid – and begin to swing, back and forth, back and forth, soaring higher and higher, pumping my legs just the way she taught me. From these dangerous heights, the ugliness of Olivia's story fades into a blur of green and blue. I shove the flashes of doubt and fear far away, back behind the clouds, and pretend I can fly.

I wonder if I'll get to be a bridesmaid.

Blushing Moon

A lot of aisle marching is taking place this season. First graduation, now the wedding. It's funny – we spend so much time spinning in messy little circles, but for benchmark occasions, we stop whirling, recover from the dizziness, focus on what we want, and march, in a tidy line, up one aisle and down another.

Olivia asked me to choose the color of the bridesmaid dresses and I picked red, since it's always been my best color. Olivia, the Marys, and I went to the fancy bridal department of the Joseph Horne Company in downtown Pittsburgh, and were snubbed by a snotty saleslady. She took one look at the four of us, and immediately pretended to be busy rearranging her display of lace gloves. But Olivia stood there and stared her down until she helped us. The saleslady, who fell all over herself once she recognized the Bowman name, said – with one of those fake frozen smiles – that in the entire history of the Joseph Horne bridal department there had never been a single instance of the bridal party requesting red dresses. She tried to convince us to go for aqua, but we refused. She filled out the order form and we made appointments for fittings.

My dress has tiny straps and a long tight skirt with some sort of stretchy stuff in it. André will probably have a heart attack when he sees it, cause it makes my butt look even curvier than it is. Junk in the trunk, he likes to say. Mary One and Mary Two are also wearing red dresses, but with different styles. Mary One's dress has a huge chiffon skirt, trimmed with sequined bumblebees, and Mary Two's outfit has a long tailored jacket and a fishtailed skirt. Plus, she's wearing one of those royal wedding hats – a wide brimmed red straw number with a big puffy veil. Leo says that the three of us look like some sort of mismatched fire brigade, but what does he know.

Grandma Millicent offered her formal living room for the wedding, and Dad and Olivia jumped at the chance. It's more of a ballroom really, and there's enough space for a large crowd. For today, Grandma's furniture has been cleared and neat rows of taffeta-covered chairs line both sides of a long aisle. Octavious and Leo, dressed in dark blue suits with red rose buds in their lapels, practically blind me with their movie-star good looks as they greet guests and escort them to their seats.

"Friend of the bride, or friend of the groom?" they ask, over and over. I wonder what happens if you can't make up your mind.

I see through a crack in the dining room door that Olivia's side is overflowing and that Dad's side is half empty. I also notice that the room is full of men and boys, most of them arriving unaccompanied. Wow.

"Hey Olivia, it's a packed house and we still have fifteen minutes before show time. How many people did you invite?"

"Let me think. Sam's list had about thirty people on it and mine had about the same. Then there were some last-minute invitations. I'd say total about 85."

"It looks like they all brought friends and relatives."

"Really?"

"Look for yourself."

"Oh my God," she says, peeking into the room. "They're my old students. I haven't seen some of these boys for years. Look!

There's Louis Shore! I can't believe he's voluntarily wearing a tie. Oh, oh, oh – Ralph Haverman is out there next to Manny Lazzaro and Stinky Grimm."

"Stinky?"

"Don't ask."

"We have way too many people. I hope no one calls the police."

Mary Two, who is repairing her scarlet lipstick for the fifth time, stops preening long enough to look at the crowd. "Jesus m'beads! Look at all those fuckin' people."

"There are no more chairs," I say. "SRO, Olivia."

"I can't believe all these young men have come," she says. "Some of them live really far away."

"I'll be buggered," says Mary Two. "How did they know?"

"Oh!" says Olivia.

"What?" I say.

"It's Franklin! All the way from Boston!"

"Franklin? *Franklin the drummer?"* I say. Uh-oh. I still get nervous whenever I hear his name.

"The one and only, and he's talking to Leo." She leaps away from the door like a nine-year old. "They're coming back here," she says. "What do I do?"

"Hide behind the china closet!" says Mary Two, pushing Olivia to the other side of the room. "It's bad fuckin' luck if they see you before the ceremony."

"I think that rule just applies to the groom, Mary Two," I say, as I open the door enough to let Franklin inside. He and Olivia stare at each for a moment.

"Hello, Miss Blue." He's as close to tears as a guy can get without actually crying. "Congratulations. Wow. You look just beautiful."

"Oh Franklin," she says. "How did you know to come? I didn't invite you. I mean I would have, but I didn't want you to go to any trouble and – "

"Your husband-to-be invited me and sent me an airline ticket. Mr. Bowman asked if I would walk down the aisle with you and give you away, you know, sort of as a representative of the Gateway Band. We're all here, Miss Blue, just about all of your band students."

Holy cow, I think. Dad did this. He invited Olivia's students as a surprise to her. At this instant, I love my father more than ever. I peek into the living room and see Octavious opening the huge glass doors to the conservatory. Waiters appear out of nowhere with more of the taffeta-covered chairs.

Leo, playing stage manager for the day, sticks his head in the door. "You ready back there?" he says. "I'll cue the band to start the overture. Five minutes to show time, Ladies and Gentlemen, five minutes."

"Leo," I whisper. "Did you know about this? That all of these people would be coming?"

"Are you kidding?" He looks in the gilded mirror hanging on the dining-room wall and slicks back his long golden hair. "I helped your dad plan it."

Typical Leo.

"Where are my manners?" says Olivia. "Jane, please meet Franklin Boswell! Your predecessor in the Gatehouse Band!"

Franklin Boswell has dark brown satiny skin, a perfect blend of cookie and bird-face, and has the longest eyelashes I've ever seen. "Hi," I say, "I mean, how do you do?"

He laughs. "I'm fine. I hear you're tearin' it up over there with Gatehouse boys. Glad to hear the drum chair is in hard-hitting' hands."

"Thanks." My knees feel weak.

"Careful there Miss Jane," says Mary Two. "June is bustin' out all over."

I look down and see that my boobs are about to pop out of the top of my dress. Mortified, I turn away from Franklin and make some minor adjustments. André, playing my grandmother's 1923 Steinway art-case grand piano, begins a rhythm and blues version of the old standard "Second Time Around," accompanied by Carlos on electric bass and David on alto sax. Octavious goes to the front and begins to sing.

God, this band is groovin'. They slip into a funky version of "All the Things You Are." I turn back to talk to Franklin again, but he's leaning over and whispering in Olivia's ear. Oh my. He looks as good from the back as he does from the front.

I sneak another peek out front and see the backs of the guests' heads bobbing up and down in time to the music. Even Grandma Millicent, who had seemed a bit shocked when Dad announced his engagement to Olivia, bounces in her front row seat. She sits between Grandpa Vernon and dear old Grandpa Jack. Jack has left Grandma Isabella in the care of her nurse. It must have been hard for him to be without her, even for a few days, but he wanted to show his support for Sam and Olivia. Sometimes I think Grandpa Jack is the bravest man in the world.

Mary One hands me my bouquet of red and pink roses and André and his band begin playing a very funky "Here Comes the Bride." Dad waits at the other end of the aisle, looking wired, happy, and maybe just a little bit afraid. Sort of like me.

Leo throws open the big mahogany doors leading into the living room, and I step through the threshold. The band would sound better with me playing, but even without a drummer, André rocks along at a tempo that manages to be both sexy and powerful. The music builds. I think about Mom and I'm sad and joyful all at once. I look over at André and he smiles at me. Then, as the guests rise to pay tribute to the bride, Olivia enters through the big wooden doors. Ribbons of sunlight shine on the uncluttered path leading to my father. She walks down the aisle, with Franklin holding her arm. She turns to face Dad.

The judge asks, "Who gives this woman in marriage?"

Franklin clears his throat and says, "I do, your honor, Franklin Boswell, her former student."

"And what," says the judge, "did this lovely woman teach you?"

"Everything," says Franklin. "But mostly, how to play the drums."

"Hey!" shouts a voice from the back. "I give this woman in marriage, too."

"And who are you?"

"Louis Shore, first trumpet."

"Me, too" says a familiar voice. "André Kenyon, keyboards."

"Carlos Vierra, bass."

"David Herman, alto sax."

"Manny Lazzaro, vocals."

"Stinky Grimm, lead trombone."

And so it continues, with each of Olivia Blue's former students – dozens of them – standing up, going to the front of the room, and giving away the bride.

I know what I have to do. When the guys finish, I make sure the top of my dress is in place, step forward, and join the crowd of boys and men huddled around Olivia.

"Jane Bowman," I say. "Drums."

* * *

RHYTHM

The reception, held in Grandma Millicent's terraced garden – overlooking the Ohio River – is one swingin' party. At first, the Sewickley Heights neighbors huddle in a cautious group on one side of the lawn. They sneak peeks at the Gatehouse boys. But before long, everyone is mixing it up, dancing, eating and drinking, laughing and telling stories. The musicians take turns on the bandstand. Even with the *touch of Lycra* sewn into my dress, there's no way to play the drums in it, so I've changed into the jeans and t-shirt I brought with me. When I'm not playing, I check out Franklin Boswell, former drummer and future heart surgeon, as he takes charge and guides the members of the Gatehouse Band, past and present, through stinging versions of their favorite tunes. He may not be playing much these days, but he sure sounds good. I'd kind of like to dance with him, but since one of us is always playing the drums I never get a chance. We pass each other on the way to and from the stage. He nods, I nod. My skin tingles whenever I look at him. Something about Franklin makes me want to talk to him, to touch him, oh man, to just jump on him right here in Grandma Millicent's back yard. Poor André is oblivious to all of this; he's way into the music.

As the sun sets, Mary Two – full of champagne punch, her royal wedding hat slightly akimbo – takes the stage and grabs the microphone.

"Ladies and Gentleman, Miss Mary One and I have been working for Mr. Bowman for almost fifteen years now. I used to think Jesus was a good boss, but he doesn't hold a fucking candle to Sam Bowman. Anyway, Mary One and I love Mr. Bowman very much and we're ever so thrilled to see him this happy. Miss Olivia, you've seemed like part of our family since the minute you walked into our house. I'm glad that now it's official. So, to celebrate the coming off of your nuptials, Miss

Mary One and I have prepared a little musical selection as a gift to you. André is going to play for us."

I can't imagine what the Marys are about to do. I'm almost afraid to look. André slides in behind his keyboard. Franklin leaves the stage and stands next to me. Mary One, a little bashful, walks center stage and takes the mike.

Look at the blushing moon,
Swimming in cherry light,
How can I feel so fine?
I've just had one glass of wine,
The thought of a simple kiss,
Could light up the sky in shades of bliss,
I'm swept away by your love.

Mary One sings like an angel, doing her very best Lady Day impression. A piano-solo begins, and right then, Mary Two lifts her long skirt, grins, and performs a perfectly rehearsed little soft-shoe dance, while Mary One stands to the side with one arm held out.

The guests go wild, Dad and Olivia embrace each other like they'll never let go, Grandma Millicent cries, Grandpa Jack leans against a magnolia tree with a wistful look on his face, Leo and Octavious lock arms and hope that nobody notices, Franklin places his hand on the small of my back, and I look up at the dusky sky and wonder if it's possible to actually see stardust.

The Very Thought of Her

My chance to move to New York City comes sooner than I expected. I've got a job! I've been hired to play with an all-female band called SOS, which stands for Sisterhood of Soul. What a name – half silly and half perfect, if you ask me. One of the guys at the wedding, a former student of Olivia's named Jordan Gray, knew that SOS was looking for a drummer. So I sent some audition tapes, Jordan gave me a rave recommendation, and Olivia made a few phone calls on my behalf. The only weird thing was when the band manager – some guy named Bernie Brown – insisted on having an 8x10 glossy picture of me. What you look like shouldn't have anything to do with the way you sound, but Leo says that this is the real world and marketing is everything, and besides, I look pretty good, so what have I got to lose. Leo took photos of me sitting at the drum set in our living room. He tried to get me to wear this completely bogus gold lamé top that he borrowed from Spanky, but I refused, opting instead for a black t-shirt. Perfect.

The photo worked, I got the job, and now Leo, Dad, Olivia, and I are packed in the old station wagon and driving northeast, right to the Big Apple. We've stuffed my drums, my stereo, my records, and my collection of framed photos of Mom into a small U-Haul van, driven by the Marys as they follow us along the Pennsylvania turnpike.

This isn't one of those struggling-artist-moves-to-Manhattan stories. Hardly. Lucky Leo and I will be living in my family's apartment in Jack and Isabella's brownstone on the East Side of Manhattan. I feel sort of guilty about the swank factor – part of me almost wishes we could go live in a rat-hole for a year, just to be like everyone else – but I figure it'll be enough of a struggle trying to hold onto my job. Our apartment has three big bedrooms and a sofa bed in the living room, so Leo and I will have plenty of space, even when Dad and Olivia come to visit. Decades ago, Jack and Isabella had built a studio space for mom in the basement – so I'll be able to practice there. But according to the schedule that Bernie Brown sent me, I won't be around all that much. SOS will be on tour much of the next year and a half.

Leo is still waiting to hear if he has been accepted into the architecture program at NYU, but he's coming with us anyway, hoping to get some kind of work to keep him busy until he gets into school. Spanky will fly to New York tomorrow and meet us at the apartment. She has purchased some "darling bed linens and matching draperies" for Leo's bedroom, and wants to be sure the wall coverings and carpets correspond with her choices.

"And you wonder why I'm gay?" says Leo. "The last thing Spanky said to me before I left was something about bath accessories in periwinkle blue with matching floral curtains. I've got to start making my own money, or I'll be doomed to a life of Sister Parish chintz."

We've left André and Octavious behind. Leo will miss Octavious, but they've already planned a couple of reunions over the holidays. André, who's coasting through his second year at the University of Pittsburgh, was relieved to see me go, at least that's the impression I got. We haven't exactly broken up, but we both need some kind of change. Until now, André has been my only romance, and I love him, really love him, in a way. We both dig music and we have really great sex. In my book, that's all a girl needs, but Leo – who seems to be head-over-heels crazy about Octavious – keeps telling me there's more to true love than rolling around in bed and listening to Weather Report records. Maybe he's right. I keep thinking about Franklin Boswell. He stood next to me for about five minutes at the wedding, but, God, the way my heart pounded when he touched my back? Maybe that's what Leo means. I'm hardly ready to settle down.

I've been to New York City lots of times. When Mom was doing the *Curly Dobson Show* we stayed in the city almost every weekend. Even after Mom died, Dad and I still flew to New York once a month or so to visit Jack and Isabella. For awhile after the accident, I was afraid to go back – almost like the city itself had killed Mom, not a fire. But when Olivia helped me realize that a fire like that could happen anywhere, I stopped blaming the city. It was harder to stop blaming myself. I'm still working on that.

As we drive across 42nd Street on our way to my grandparents' house, I lean out the window and try to suck up the sights, smells, and sounds like a newcomer. I'm sort of jealous of Leo, 'cause he's having a real *moving to New York* experience.

"Holy shit!!" says Leo. "Did you see that? Did anybody see that? There was a naked lady in a cage back there on the corner. And nobody was even looking at her. Nobody!"

"That's the lady from PETA," I say. "She's always on that corner. It's a protest against people wearing fur. And besides, she's not really naked, she just looks like she is."

"But, still," says Leo.

At this point three teenagers wielding squeegees approach the car and begin smearing the windshield with oily water, even though Dad has turned on the wipers and started honking his horn for them to go away.

"Tell them to stop!" shouts Leo. "What nerve! Their squeegees are filthy! They're making a mess out of the windshield! Hey! Hey, you with the scummy squeegee! Stop that!"

The boys ignore Leo. Olivia laughs and says, "The Squeegee Boys have their own rules. Actually, if you don't want them to clean your windows, you have to give them money in advance."

"Should have thought of that," says Dad.

"Next time, let me drive," says Olivia. "My, that young man in the red shirt is persistent. Too bad he doesn't have a saxophone to practice."

The boy in the red shirt gives Leo the finger.

"Did you see that?" he yells, like he has never in his life witnessed a gesture that he uses himself about a dozen times a day.

"I just hope they don't mess with the Marys," I say, looking out the rear window of the car. "Or someone is gonna get hurt."

The light changes and we drive through the intersection. I hear Mary Two gun the motor and blast the horn at the boys on the street.

We park the car in Grandpa Jack's garage and the Marys pull the truck into the parking bay. Huffing and puffing, we get everything unloaded and carried upstairs into the apartment in less than an hour. Grandma Isabella is with the night nurse, so Grandpa Jack orders pizza for us and we sit around the glass dining room table gabbing until we run out of steam. The Marys say good-bye and take a cab to the Waldorf – where they'll be spending the night – and Dad and Leo return the truck to the rental company. I take advantage of the quiet and go to visit Isabella.

Grandma's night nurse has braided her long hair. I touch the silky fabric covering her boney shoulders and she shudders. She looks at me, puzzled.

"Hi Grandma," I say. "I'm here. It's me. Jane. I'm going to live here with you now. I'll be upstairs, in the apartment."

Her huge eyes fill with tears, and she smiles. For a second, I imagine she has recognized me. She jabbers and rocks back and forth in her wheel chair, clutching my hand, never taking her eyes from my face. I'm shocked by the strength of her grip, the power of her stare.

I have the distinct feeling she's confusing me with Mom. Maybe, just maybe, she thinks her Helen has returned. I stay with her for thirty minutes, playing with the idea that somehow I've made her happy, until her rhythmic babble stops, her head tilts to the side, and she falls asleep. I kiss her on both cheeks and call for the nurse.

When I return to the apartment, Olivia helps me unpack. For ten minutes, we work side by side, folding sweaters and jeans, hanging skirts I'll probably never wear, placing toiletries in baskets and drawers.

"What are you thinking about?" I ask her. "Are you thinking about her? About Kate?" It bothers me that Olivia never talks about her daughter.

"No, Jane. I was actually thinking about my first apartment, the place Sister Mary Katherine found for me when I was your age and starting at Juilliard. It looked a little different from this."

I remember the bleak room Olivia had described, and then, through her eyes, I look at my new home, the high ceilings and the butter-colored moiré curtains framing the huge windows, the hip mix of contemporary furniture and handsome antiques, the needlepoint pillows and whimsical art. Things, beautiful things, Isabella's things, then my mother's things, and now mine. A soft light bleeds through the rose-colored lampshades.

"I feel guilty," I say. "You know, for being rich. For having so much."

"Come on. Don't you dare feel guilty. You were born rich, I was born poor, and neither of us had anything to do with it. You still have choices to make, just like I did. And bad judgment is not the exclusive property of the poor. You'll have plenty of opportunities to screw up and make bad decisions, just like I've had many chances to make good ones. Honestly, I'm not worried about you, Jane. I think you're an intelligent and caring young woman, with enough sense to recognize the things that are bad for you. Plus you have Leo here, and Grandpa Jack, and you can talk to both of them if you need advice. And you can always call your dad or me. You have so many people who love you. If there's anything I'm envious of, it's that. That's something I never had when I was your age. My fault, I guess, I thought I could handle everything myself. I think if I'd found someone to talk to, someone to trust, that I never would have made all those terrible decisions. You're surrounded by people you trust. Listen to them, and – here's the main thing – make sure they to listen to you."

"Do you think about her? About Kate?" I ask again.

"You're not going to let go of that, are you?"

"No."

"Yes."

"Well?"

"Yes. I do think about her. Not as much as you might suspect. Years ago I hired a private detective to find out what her life was like. He even took pictures for me, but I never looked at them. I couldn't. Basically, Kate seemed to be a happy kid, at least according to the report. She went to a private school for girls and had lots of friends. She took ice-skating lessons, and ballet."

"Will you ever try to contact her?" I ask.

"I don't know."

"Why? Why don't you know?"

"I'm not sure if I want to."

"Don't you want to know if she's okay?"

"Yes. But I'm afraid of finding out that she's not."

"What if she needs you?"

"What if she doesn't?"

Silence.

"I have my new life to protect," Olivia says. "Kate has a life of her own. I think it's best to stay away."

"I don't understand."

"I don't either. Someday you'll realize that not understanding is part of growing up. I don't understand why my mother abandoned me, why no one adopted me, why I screwed up my Juilliard scholarship and dove headfirst into a pile of cocaine, why I gave up music, or why I married Bruce. I don't understand why I didn't run away before I got pregnant, why I allowed him to do those awful things to me. I don't understand why I didn't fight harder to keep my child, or why I was so quick to take his money and leave town. But I also don't understand how I pulled myself together and reclaimed my life. I don't understand how I was persistent enough to get through school, to get the job at the Gatehouse or how I was lucky enough to meet you and your dad. I don't understand why I still have nightmares about Bruce, and why, after all these years of proving myself, I'm still very much afraid of him – terrified, in fact."

A look of fear flashes across Olivia's face, a look I've seen before in unguarded moments when she thinks no one is watching her. I wonder what she's not telling me – which things she keeps hidden, even from Dad. I brush away my suspicions.

"It's all so strange," I say. "If Mom hadn't been killed in that fire, I probably never would have met you. And if Bruce had been a decent human being, you never would have met us. How is it that so much good can come from so much bad?"

"I don't know, Jane. Do you?"

"Well. Yes. I think I do. I think the good returned to our lives because we allowed it to. We took the *recovery option*, as opposed to, say, the stick-your-head-in-the-oven option."

"There you go. That sounds like something Leo would say."

"Yeah, well, I might have stolen it from him."

"How did we get into this discussion anyway?"

"You were giving me the *leaving home* speech."

"I was?" says Olivia. "Look at me, acting like a mother."

"Look at you," I say. "Being one."

A Pink Lace Bra

Random puffs of chilly October wind sweep me across town to White's Rehearsal Studio on West 44th Street. Today's my big day. I'm prepared to spend the morning playing hard and getting to know the musical strengths and quirks of the women I'll be expected to work with for the length of my contract – which is eighteen months, assuming management doesn't decide to fire us. I'm trying to act cool but I have to admit I'm really psyched. Someone is paying me to play the drums! And I love the idea of playing with female musicians. I've spent the last three years with the Gatehouse boys, so I'm looking forward to the new vibe. I guess it will be very different, but still the same.

The sky looks like the cream of mushroom soup Mary Two always makes on Tuesdays. I miss her. As the wind creeps under the hem of my jacket, I heave my cymbal bag onto my other shoulder and walk as fast as I can, looping my way around clusters of strange-looking people. Maybe it's always this way, but today the street seems like an especially scary carnival ride – complete with surprise plumes of smoke, sirens, bells, and pop-up spooky people who jump out of nowhere. A hotdog vendor makes kiss-kiss noises at me and says "hey mama, mama" as I walk by. I check my watch and see I have five minutes to cover this last endless block. Man, these cymbals must weigh about two tons.

As I hustle past the Port Authority Bus Terminal, I pretend to ignore the homeless people sleeping on sheets of cardboard over ventilation grates, and the old-looking young women rummaging though garbage cans for scraps of thrown-away food. I try to distract myself, but no luck. I keep seeing Olivia, and thinking about her days on the street. I keep walking, but my eyes refuse to focus on the sidewalk in front of me. My gloom threatens to ruin my day, my week, my life, but then I reach the studio and the doors slide open. Nothing like an automatic door to shift a mood from bad to good. I coast through, a little surprised by my nervousness.

'Hi, " I say to the security guard. "I'm Jane Bowman. I'm here for an SOS rehearsal? Sisterhood of Soul?"

"Yeah, toots. Take the elevator to the third floor. Sign in here."

The elevator smells like stale cologne and French fries. On the third floor I'm met by a cigar-chomping bald guy in a light green blazer.

"You're Jane, right? Drummer? I recognize you from your picture. Thank God you look better in real life. That picture sucks."

"Gee, thanks, and yes, I'm Jane Bowman. How do you do?" I say, extending my hand with Penn Academy politeness, which he ignores.

"Go talk to Mandy Fantalo over in the corner. She'll measure you for your costume. You get to say if you want pink or purple."

"Excuse me?"

"Your dress. Pink or purple. You pick. I don't know crap about this kinda thing. Talk to Mandy."

"Isn't this a rehearsal?" I ask, waving away the cigar smoke.

"Yeah darlin', it's a rehearsal. But we do costumes first. We can't do the photos till we have the costumes, and the costumes will take a week or two to make. First things first. *Capice*?"

"I didn't get your name," I say, swallowing the urge to kick him in the shins and run.

"Yeah, yeah, yeah, I'm Bernie Brown," he says, not even looking at me.

"So you're the band manager?" I say.

"Yeah darlin', I'm the manager."

"Let's try this again. How do you do, Mr. Brown," I say, extending my hand once again and holding it there for what seems like ten minutes. Finally he shakes my hand.

"Yeah, yeah, yeah, whatever," he says.

"Very pleased to meet you," I say.

"Yeah, yeah, yeah, me too," he says, looking down at his clipboard. "Now could you please get your butt over to Mandy? We got business to do here, this ain't no bingo hall."

"Yes, of course," I say, wondering what a bingo hall looks like. "Pink or purple, right?"

"That's right, darlin'. Pink or purple."

* * *

"Hi," says one of the musicians standing in line at Mandy's desk. "I'm Liz." She's short and curvy, with a big tangle of auburn curls trailing down her back. Her voice sounds like she smokes way too much.

"Hi. I'm Jane Bowman. Looks like we've signed up for a fashion show."

"Looks like."

"Pink or purple?" We burst into laughter. "So. You're an alto player?"

"Right."

"Are we actually going to play today, do you think?"

"I hope so," says Liz. "But first it looks like we'll cover a lot of the production details – like costuming."

"Okie-dokie, next gwoup, come with me!" says the middle-aged bottle blond behind the desk. "I'm Mandy Fantalo and I'll be doing your costumes!" Mandy leads us into an area that has been draped for privacy. She has an unfortunate speech impediment that makes her sound like Elmer Fudd. "Okie-dokie girls, take off your sweaters and dwop your jeans. I gotta get accuwate measurements for these dwesses cause they're supposed to be weally weally tight. Form fitting. Weally form fitting. Like you can't bend over."

Liz sighs and pulls off the backpack holding her sax. She yanks her sweater over her head.

"Isn't this sort of weird?" I say to her. "I mean, we've been here for five minutes and now we're supposed to take off our clothes?"

"This your first girl-band gig?" she asks.

"Yeah," I say. "Believe it or not I've been playing in an all-boy band for the last three years. Pink or purple was not an option."

"All guys? Lucky you. Listen, these girl-band managers are obsessed with costuming. Part of the gimmick, you know. But don't worry, everything is cool here. I worked with Mandy on another gig and she's a little hyper but basically okay. Kinda heavy-handed with the sequins and the hot glue gun if you ask me, but I can live with that. I sorta like the glamour-girl look."

Mandy wraps her measuring tape around Liz's chest.

"37 ½ inches," Mandy says to Liz. "You lose weight, hon?"

"Uh, you shouldn't say that until you check the bottom half," says Liz.

"Oh yeah, I see what you mean. You gain weight, hon?"

"Just shifting it around a little. I've been temping. You know, desk job."

"Okie–dokie, hon, you're finished," says Mandy. "Pink or purple?"

"Pink."

"What do you do there?" I ask.

"On a temp job? Answer phones mostly."

Another musician, a trumpet player named Patti, says, "You oughta try working with me on your down time."

"Yeah? What are you doin'?" asks Liz.

"Topless car wash."

"You shittin' me?"

"No. It's completely easy, as long as you don't mind being topless and walkin' around with a big old hose."

Isn't it cold? I want to ask, but it seems like a pretty stupid question.

"Isn't it cold?" asks Liz.

"Nah, it's inside. Plus at fifty bucks an hour you learn to live with it if it gets a little nippy. Good for the Nortons, you know. Makes 'em stand up nice and proud."

"Fuck," says Liz.

"So what happens? Do the guys look at you while you wash the car?"

"Yeah. I mean I guess they look. I don't much wanna know what else they're doing in the car while they're checking me out. But I found out if you rub soapsuds all over yourself and squish your boobs up against the windshield you can make good tip money. Tits for tips."

"Fuck," says Liz.

"Yeah, well I could probably do that, too, but I have to draw the line somewhere."

Another girl, a stocky electric bass player from Montana named Betty Wimpner, stands next to me while she waits to be measured.

"Okay, Betty. You're next," says Mandy. "Off with the sweater. Nice wool. Hand made?"

"Yeah, I like to knit in my free time." Betty jerks the sweater over her head. She's not wearing a bra. But that's not what I notice first. She stinks. B.O.. Big time. I hope I don't have to sit next to her on the band bus. Holy cow, this is really bad.

"Were you on that Nellie Nigh tour?" Liz asks Betty. "I heard that was a nightmare."

"Yep," says Betty. "Nellie got so drunk she barfed onstage one night, all over my amp. I got stories like you wouldn't believe. She's an unbelievable tramp, that woman. Can't keep her hot pants on. You know, she hired this Brazilian guitar player, Luisa what's-her-name? We called her Lulu. Well, Lulu is like five feet tall and weighs about 70 pounds. Looks like a South American Tinkerbelle. Plays the shit out of the guitar, though. Anyway, Nellie taught Lulu how to lap dance, see? One day, on the bus, Nellie started passing Lulu around to all the musicians. I mean we were literally handing her over our heads from one row to the next."

"That's awful," says Liz, laughing.

"Yep. That kept us entertained for a while, lap dancing with little Lulu. Not that I did it. Not me."

This story has temporarily taken my mind off the B.O..

"Better than those guys on the Buddy Wich tour," says Mandy, with straight pins between her lips. "I heard they got so bored they started whipping each other in the back of the bus, just to see how long they could stand it. Widuculous. They had weally big welts and everything."

"No shit?" says Liz.

"So wait," says Betty. "The Nellie Nigh story gets worse. Last winter we were in Montana and Nellie tried to get it on with the lady bus driver. That poor broad was driving through a blizzard, and Nellie ripped her bra off."

"No shit."

"Wait a minute, did she rip off her own bra or the bus driver's bra?"

"Like it matters. Jesus."

"Really. The worst part was, I think the driver liked it – I mean, it's not like she was yellin' for help or anything. We were swerving all over the road. If it weren't for Carla Sampson grabbing the steering wheel we'd probably all be dead."

"Carla is that singer who did back-ups for Lionel Richie, right? The one with the glass eye?"

"Yeah, that's Carla. Imagine that. A half-blind singer who can drive a bus. Anyway, Nellie had a nervous breakdown ninety days into the tour and had to cancel three months worth of gigs."

"Any cancellation money?"

"I'm not countin' on it, knowin' Nellie. Maybe I should look into the car wash."

Compared to these girls, the Gatehouse boys seem like a church choir.

"Arms up, hon," says Mandy to Betty.

I don't understand how a person can smell this terrible.
I hold my breath. My eyes are starting to cross.

"Oh dear hon. We have a pwoblem," says Mandy.

I'll say.

"These dwesses are stwapless," she continues. "You're gonna have to shave those pits."

"No way, Mandy," says Betty. "I've never shaved and I'm
not gonna start now. My body is my temple."

"That's the hairiest temple I've ever seen," says Patti.

Liz doubles over laughing.

"Okie-dokie, hon, let's see what we've got here," she says
to me. By this point I'm not feeling at all self-conscious, so I
unzip my leather jacket and take off my t-shirt. I'm wearing a
sports bra, which is what I always wear when I play. It prevents
excess jiggle.

"You've got yourself all smashed down there, hon," she
says. "You got a nice figure, what do you want to hide it for?"

"I'm not trying to hide anything, it's just that I play better
in this bra," I say.

"Okie-dokie, hon, we'll build a nice pink lace bwa into your
dwess for the show."

"That's going to be a problem Mandy. I can't play in a dwess. I mean *dress*."

"Yes you can."

"No I can't."

"YES YOU CAN."

"No I won't."

"BERNIE!!!! Get your ass back here."

Bernie, with fear in his eyes, sticks his head around
the corner. I can hardly blame him for being nervous. Look at

us – a gaggle of girl musicians with dropped drawers and an assortment of motley looking bras. Plus it smells like French toe cheese in here.

"The little dwummer girl won't wear a stwapless dwess, and it's going to fucking destwoy my costume plot," says Mandy.

"Excuse me," I say. "The little drummer girl will not wear any kind of dress, strapless or not. OKIE-DOKIE? I'm a drummer. I play in pants, like every other drummer. Otherwise I don't play. Fire me if you want to."

"Fuck," says Liz.

"She has a contwact," says Mandy. "She's gotta pway."

"You have a contract," growls Bernie. "You've gotta play."

"Yeah, and it says nothing about costumes or believe me I wouldn't have signed it."

"You know what?" says Betty. "She's right. I'm sick of having to dress up like Barbie just cause I'm a female musician. We might as well work at the car wash with Patti. Tits for tips."

"Jesus," says Bernie.

"This is widiculous," yells Mandy. "Outwageous!"

"Fuck," says Liz.

The discussion goes around in circles for several minutes. Eventually the other band members join us and we all threaten to quit if we have to wear costumes that make us look like Cher impersonators. Mandy stomps out of the dressing room in a huff.

"Purple," yells Patti. "I'll take purple!"

"You've got balls, girl," says Liz to me. "Way to go. This may be the first gig I've had where I'll get to look like a normal person."

"Get dressed, all of you," yells Bernie, grinding his cigar between his teeth. "We'll meet on the fifth floor to pass out the charts and start playing through the music."

About time, I think.

"And someone open a window," says Bernie. "It smells like a freakin' locker room in here."

* * *

When we finally get around to playing, we sound pretty damn good. The charts are a hodge-podge of mediocre arrangements of soul classics like "Brick House" and "Think," but the musicians are all experienced players who manage to make complete sense out of the music on the stands.

Our leader is a fiery woman named Raj, who plays the alto saxophone and sings like Aretha. I mean, no one sings exactly like Aretha, but Raj gets awfully close, while putting her own spin on the material. Raj is in her forties. Her skin shines like polished amber, and her body is tight and sculpted by intense dance training. I don't understand why someone this talented and gorgeous isn't really famous. I mean, as a singer she's about as great as anyone I've ever listened to. Plus she kicks ass on the sax. You'd think she'd be a big star. Leo is going to have an absolute fit over her.

"Raj is the best," says Liz. "She's demanding but really easy to work with in a way. No diva shit or temper tantrums. She's a pro."

Raj talks us through the charts and we play them, all of us hearing the problem spots we'll need to work out over the next few days. She consults with me about tempos and we make metronome markings when we find a groove that works. In a way, her conducting style reminds me of Olivia's – firm, flexible, in control, relaxed.

The SOS band has a rhythm section, Liz and Raj on alto sax, two tenor players, two trumpets, and a lone trombone. It's sort of a more balanced version of the Gatehouse band, which had way too many altos. Liz sounds great. And so does Patti on trumpet. Betty's bass playing is way beyond anything I ever experienced at Gateway. Forget the smell, I'm hooked up with her, right from the start. Funny thing about drummers and bass players, once the music starts, they're in bed together, like it or not. That's what Mom always said.

Bernie wanders in and out of the rehearsal, looking at his Rolex watch and slurping coffee from a blue and white to-go coffee cup from the Greek diner I spotted on the corner. When we break for lunch, I head over there and order a Spanish omelet with rye toast. I'm starving and I love New York diner food. I don't know why they can't cook like this in Sewickley Heights.

Raj slides into the booth next to me and orders a piece of lettuce with two shrimp on top.

"You sound good," she says to me. "Where have you been hidin'?"

"I just moved here," I say, chomping on my toast. "I'm from Pittsburgh. I graduated from high school last June."

"No shit."

"No, really," I study her perfect bird-face and green eyes and try not to get Spanish omelet sauce on my shirt.

"Where are you livin', little girl?"

"Uh, my family has a house on the East Side. I have an apartment there."

"Good, you'll need it. The way you sound, you're gonna work a lot in this town."

"Thanks. And I love the way you sing. Are you a native New Yorker?"

"No, I was born in Bahia. My mother's Brazilian, my father comes from Bombay."

"Almost as exotic as Pittsburgh."

"Almost." She takes another bite of her lettuce leaf and calls for the check. "See-ya back upstairs," she says.

Cold Sweat

The Emerald of the Sea looks like a floating Las Vegas mega-hotel. SOS will be playing in the Lido Room of the cruise ship for the next three months, as the warm-up act for a dance review, called *Va-Va-Va-Vegas!* The audience doesn't come to listen to our band, they come for the topless dance show, which features half a dozen stick-thin girls – wearing false eyelashes, high heels, ostrich feather hats, and metallic thongs – parading up and down a strobe-lit ramp to a playback of *Saturday Night Fever* music. During their opening number, some of dancing girls strike sexy poses and some of them hang – upside-down – right over the audience – on ropes suspended from the ceiling. This is my favorite part of the show, and I could watch it a million times – mainly because of the danger factor. I gawk at the rope girls every night and realize I could never in a million years do this kind of work, my breasts are too big and they'd end up in someone's linguini. The musicians in our band joke about slashing the cables at a strategic moment – plunging the rope girls headfirst into the laps of the lycra-clad suburban retirees and their drooling husbands.

We actually like the dancers – most of them are pretty nice people – but we hate that they get all the applause and that they're so skinny. Half serious, we suggest to Raj – the only member of our band lean and nimble enough to dangle from the upper deck in her underpants – that she play her sax solo on "Respect" hanging from a rope. Raj doesn't pay much attention to us, though – she's busy hitting on the *Va-Va-Va Vegas* dance captain, a red head nicknamed Kiki who lives on our deck. It seems like Kiki only gets dressed when she has to appear in front of the passengers, and even then – during the show anyway, she eventually strips. When she's not around the passengers, which is most of the time, she walks around topless, swooping into rehearsals, meals, and our dressing room like something out of an uncensored Tarzan movie. Her breasts point straight up and seem to defy gravity. Maybe this is a side effect of hanging upside down all the time. I envy her. I hate her. I want to be her.

* * *

This isn't a bad job, but since it's my first, I'm hardly an expert. It bugs me that I don't get much practice time. I sneak into the lounge early in the morning when the clean-up crew is there, but that's about it. In the afternoons the room is used for a class called *Chase Away Your Chubby Thighs with Jill!*, an aerobic cha-cha class for passengers, taught by one of the bulimic dancers.

My band mates seem to be at once satisfied and disgusted by the gig. We each make 300 dollars a week, and we get free food – lots of it – and Munchkin sized cabins down in the bowels of the ship where the saltier employees refer to the ocean liner as The Mold of the Sea. I'm sharing a cabin with Liz, and we get along just fine. I've never been good friends with a female, and I'm enjoying the experience. She's a real girl-y girl, very concerned about her make-up, her nails, and her tan lines.

"Pay attention," she says. "This tube of mascara is your best friend. Or maybe your second best friend after concealer."

"What am I concealing?" I say.

"Well to start, that zit on your forehead."

"Oh, that."

"And you do have some dark shadows under your eyes," she says.

"Liz, I'm a quarter Cuban. I've got dark shadows everywhere."

"Well you don't need to live with that. Use the concealer. You'll look better on stage. If you use one with a slightly yellow tinge, it'll take the blue out of those under-eye circles."

"You know, you really have to meet my friend Leo, I think the two of you would love each other."

"Straight?"

"Are you kidding? A straight guy who knows about concealer?"

"Forget it."

"Okay."

"I mean maybe we could have coffee or something."

"Right."

"It's just that I'm going nuts trying to find a straight guy in New York who is not completely weird. The last one I dated had an obsession with washing his hands."

"Oh, no."

"Oh, yeah. Every time we had sex he wore latex gloves. You know, like those gloves they wear at the dentist's office. At first I was into it, sort of – I thought it was kind of kinky in a good way. But once I realized he was doing it for personal hygiene reasons I freaked."

"Wow."

"Plus he was married."

"Oh no. Maybe he didn't want to leave fingerprints?"

"Don't worry honey, he's history."

"Don't you meet guys while you're on tour?"

"Not on one of these cruise ships, that's for sure. I mean, have you checked out the guys in the audience? First, they're all with their wives. Second, most of them weigh about 300 pounds. You've seen them up on the pool deck drizzling oil on their big blubber bellies, right? They look like a bunch of barbecued pigs. Not for me. I do one of these cruises; I take a vow of celibacy. Unless there's a drunken sailor type with big biceps. That I can deal with. But even that's a risk. Sometimes they get all lovey-dovey, which is no fun at all. Can you imagine what it's like being stalked for three months by a deck-swabber with a Dutch accent?"

"What about when you're on the road?"

"Now that's different. But dangerous. I met a guy in Oregon five years ago. His name was Luke and he looked like a Greek statue stuffed into a plaid flannel shirt. Muscles like you wouldn't believe. Plus he could cook. I mean really cook. He actually won first place in the Medford Pancake Cook-off, which – trust me – is a very serious event."

"Was he a musician?"

"No. He was a logger."

"You mean a lumberjack?"

"Yep. A friggin' lumberjack, although he insisted that I call him a *logger*. Please. Anyway, I married him and moved to Oregon, where I played about two and half gigs over the course of one year. Luke was the jealous type and didn't like me working in clubs, which sort of limited my employment opportunities, since there aren't exactly tons of concert hall jobs for female R&B sax players in Medford, Oregon. I also gained twenty pounds from eating stacks of blueberry specials. But the sex was great. That's the thing, you get desperate for a little male attention, a nice smooth ride on the golden pole, and the next thing you know you're throwing your career down the crapper and running off with a pancake cookin' lumberjack."

"Logger"

"Right. These days I try to limit myself to one-night stands. But I confess, I'm still looking for the illusive Mr. Right."

With my hands on the wooden desk, I play a rhythm that compliments the *scritch scratch scritch scratch* of the file on her tapered scarlet nails.

"How old are you?" I ask.

Scritch scratch, scritch scratch.

"Thirty-nine." She looks out the porthole.

"Really? I thought you were much younger."

"No, I've been thirty-nine for a few years now."

"Oh."

"So," she says. "You've got a boyfriend?"

"No, not really. Not right now."

"You're not gay are you?"

I hesitate, maybe just a moment too long. "I don't know." Wow. I can't believe I said that.

"Jesus Christ, don't let Raj hear that, she'll jump you in heartbeat. I've seen her looking at you."

"Me? Really?" This scares me a little, but I also find it thrilling.

"Yeah. Don't let it go to your head, though, she checks out everyone new. She's a real skirt chaser. Or in your case, a pants chaser. And what do you mean, you *don't know* if you're gay?"

"Well, I've only had one real boyfriend. We, you know, slept together for a few years, and I really, really, really liked it. But that's all it was. Sex. And music. He's a piano player."

"What, are you crazy? You gave that up?"

"No. I mean, I don't think I'm giving anything up. Not yet. I'm pretty young still. I feel like I need to have other experiences, you know."

"Yeah. I know. That's what I said in my early twenties, too. Got to be careful with that. You start having too many *other experiences* and before you know it you're a forty year-old cruise-ship musician, fantasizing about men in white uniforms with gold braid on their shoulders. So what happened to the piano playing sex machine?"

"He's back in Pittsburgh."

"Got his number?" Liz says. "Just kidding. So why don't you know if you're gay or not?" There are copper streaks in her hair, and strands of it tumble over her green eyes.

"Cause I've never tried it? And it kind of, uh, turns me on to think about it?"

Liz stops filing her nails and looks at me.

"Works for me," she says.

"What?"

"You wanna try it out, I'm game. I might be straight, but I'm also feeling a little needy these days."

"I didn't mean . . ."

"Very needy."

"But I . . ."

"You wanna help me out?"

What to do. I sputter parts of words as she slowly pulls down the straps of her white swimsuit and begins touching herself. I gawk at her heavy breasts and consider my options. Just as I'm ready to say *no thanks let's just be friends*, my gut tells me something different. How do you know what you want until you know what you don't want? How do you know what you don't want if you've never tried it? A million things run through my brain. Yes. No. Maybe won't do. Or will it? Should I be faithful to André? No. Does my desire right at this moment mean I'm gay forever? Maybe. Does my hesitance mean I'm straight? Don't know. Will it matter to anyone in the world if I go through with this? No. Will it matter to me if I don't? Probably. My face heats up as she peels off her suit and places my hand between her legs. She begins moving back and forth, her head thrown back and her eyes closed. Now what? I grab her and push her onto the bed, ripping off my own bikini bottoms and pressing myself against her, kissing her, tasting her, inhaling the mingled scents of salt and perfume.

When I finish, I look down at her, slippery and drunk on that thing that happens after good sex, and I wonder if I've just made one of those bad decisions Olivia had warned me about. Or if maybe I've made one of the good ones.

"Don't go fallin' in love with me," says Liz. "Basically, I like guys, But this will do, for now."

"Sure will," I say. "For now."

"For now. Why not?"

"Why not?"

And just when I think we're finished, I start touching her again.

* * *

"Listen, did Bernie or Mandy set you up to talk to me about make-up?" I ask. Liz and I have gotten dressed and resumed our conversation as if our two-hour erotic adventure never happened. Aside from a wet oval stain on her bedspread, there's no evidence of our tryst. My breasts, harnessed once again in my bikini top, ache from the tug of her lips, her teeth, her tongue. It reminds me of the way I used to feel with André. Different, but somehow the same. Not worse, not better. Just good. It seems like the earth has cracked apart and offered me a silver platter of extra options.

"No, honey, I'm doing this cause I want you to look your best," she says as she applies inky goo to my bottom eyelashes.

We've convinced Bernie and Mandy to let us all wear whatever we want to, as long as it's black. Because of Betty's hairy pits, we do have a rule about sleeves. Our arms must be covered to the elbows, which seems a little overboard to me – I guess Mandy is afraid the pit hair could grow to world-record lengths. All of this gets on my nerves. I know that Bernie really cares about the music. I just wish he'd care less about our all-girl band image. But that's how he gets us work so I sort of understand.

"I hate this," I say. "I just want to make music."

"I just want to make music, too," Liz says. "But there's nothing wrong with having double-thick-extra-long-charcoal-black eyelashes while you play. Use the mascara! On stage, it'll make your eyes look like big white dinner plates."

"I'm going to go check out the employee buffet," I say.

"But I still need to teach you about lip liner," she says.

"No thanks. Maybe next time. Wanna go to dinner with me? Someone told me they're having lasagna tonight."

"Nope," she says. "Diet."

"Oh. Okay, catch you at the Lido Room at seven?"

"Honey," she says. "Not a word to anyone about our, uh, experiment, okay? Let's just keep it between us. And I mean what I say. I'm not looking for romance with a girl. So don't stalk me, okay?"

"Fine with me," I say. "But if you start feeling needy again, you let me know."

I laugh and close the cabin door behind me. I've been seduced. Or maybe I've been tricked. In any case, I've been laid. In a curious way, I feel victorious, but I'm starving, too, so I head up the galley steps to the dining room. I sit by myself and dig into my dinner. Through the huge windows stretching across the far end of the canteen, I watch the endless swells of Caribbean blue – peaking, breaking, again and again – rolling to places I can only imagine.

A Little Respect

We disembark in Ft. Lauderdale and fly to Atlantic City, where we're booked at the Diamond Kingdom Atlantic City Hotel and Casino for the next six months. I had been to Las Vegas and Reno – and even Monte-Carlo – with my Mom when I was a kid, but I had never seen Atlantic City. It's a pretty weird scene, especially during the day. Busloads of old women spill into the casinos every hour. The ladies, with plastic cups of quarters clutched in their fists, prowl around their favorite slot machines like vultures circling week-old carcasses. They stand for hours on end, coaxing the gleaming machines to spit money back at them, swearing like sailors when they don't, crying like abandoned toddlers when they lose the last of their change. I watch them out on the beach, loping along beside the surf in pastel colored double-knit pantsuits and orthopedic shoes. Most of them carry an empty plastic cup in one hand, a vinyl purse in the other. The winners stay inside the hotel – juiced on the constant *buzz buzz buzz* of the casino, the ringing bells, the free 7-UP and salted nuts – gloating over their winnings and praying to Jesus that their luck holds out. Sooner or later, they all end up on the beach, counting seagulls, scooping up the jagged-edged shells they'll give to their grandchildren as souvenirs. They march back and forth like a polyester army of church-lady hobos, scanning the filthy sand, hoping to find somebody else's vanished treasure. At sunset, the enormous charter buses whisk the ladies away. The beach empties, and I go running in and around the odd footprints left on the sand.

This time around our band is the opening act for a fire-eater and a group of belly dancers who call themselves HOT HOT HOT!!!!. The dancers have all been assigned Moroccan-sounding names like Temptira and Slaviana, but really they're a bunch of nice gals from Secaucus, New Jersey.

The fire-eater, whose real name is Ed, is billed as The Prince of Pyrotechnics. He wears puffy red silk trousers, big gold cuffs on his wrists, and no shirt. I can tell Liz is checking him out. Good for her. I'd take a fire-eater over a lumberjack any day. Liz and I have the occasional rendezvous, but most of the time, I'm on my own. At least here I have my own hotel room, so I'm free to have visitors whenever the urge hits me. Male or female, I'm always glad when they leave. I spend a lot of time by myself, practicing, running, working out in the hotel gym.

SOS sounds better and better. After months of playing, we're hitting hard and locking in tight. In AC I've got more opportunities to practice, so I feel like I'm keeping up with my playing. Lots of times I convince my band mates to jam with me, and we'll spend hours in the morning blowing on new tunes, catching a groove and surfing on it like it's one of those nice easy waves cart-wheeling toward the Atlantic City coast.

So far, Bernie's bookings have been pretty depressing. The cruise ship and casino crowds pay good money to see our show. But it doesn't seem like they're into the music at all – they listen to us with dull eyes and jaded smiles, waiting for the real entertainment – the dancers – to liven things up. I know, I know, I'm in the trenches, earning a living, carving a career for myself. I've got a great job – that's what the other musicians tell me – so I try not to let the musical ignorance of the audience bother me. Still. I know the big name male bands working here aren't opening for a fire-eater and group of belly dancers. They're headlining, and that's what we should be doing, too. We're nothing more than a novelty act. I make up my mind to do something about this, someday. What, I'm not sure.

My musical tastes are evolving; at least that's what Leo says. I still listen to my old favorites, but I've added all of the latest Prince CDs to my collection of classic funk records. Prince does it for me. I daydream about playing for him someday. I practice all of his music just in case I ever get the call, but I don't think that's likely to happen with me stuck here in Rocky Balboa's Rock and Show Palace.

* * *

After months of being separated, Leo visits me in Atlantic City.

"I love the way they bill this show," he says. *"SOS, The Prince of Pyro, and HOT HOT HOT!!!!.* Hardly sounds like casino entertainment. Sounds more like an EMT drill."

Leo bunks in my room at the Diamond Kingdom and we stay up all night and half of the next day catching up. It's so good to see him in person. We've been gabbing on the phone since I started the SOS tour, but it's not the same. He loves New York, as I knew he would. Grandpa Jack and Leo have become good friends. Leo helps out with Isabella all the time – she can't stand or walk anymore, so Leo takes her out in the mornings. He pushes her wheelchair and tells her stories, while a nurse tags along in case of a medical emergency.

Meanwhile, Octavious has quit school and moved to New York to be with Leo. The two of them can't stand to be apart.

Evidently Spanky is throwing fits, not because of Octavious, but because Leo has given up on the NYU School of Architecture and wants to go to work immediately for a talent agency.

"Why should I design buildings," he says, "when I can design careers."

Oh, brother. But I think he has a point. I'm just not sure if a twenty-year old rich kid from Sewickley Heights, Pennsylvania is qualified to be the world's next super agent. But once Leo makes up his mind, there's no stopping him.

"For instance, this SOS band of yours."

"It's not my band Leo, I'm just part of it."

"Well it should be your band, you're cookin' like crazy up there. Raj might be out front, but you're the one with the star power."

"I don't want to be a star, Leo. And anyway, SOS is Raj's band. It's her concept. And she plays her ass off. She deserves to be the star. I just want to play the drums."

"Yeah, I know, I know. But SOS should be headlining, not playing the overture music for that Sheik of Araby act."

"At least it's a funky overture," I say.

"It's all in the marketing," says Leo. "If Bernie Brown marketed you gals the right way, there would be no stopping you. If I were your agent, you'd be working in far better places." Leo is wearing yellow flannel pajamas and munching on a club sandwich. It's hard to imagine him as anyone's agent.

"Like where? I've listened to Liz and Raj talk about gigs, Leo. There aren't many jobs out there. The girls in the band think we're pretty lucky to be hooked up with Bernie. Sure beats temping at the Topless Carwash."

"Come on, Jane. There are tons of opportunities! Regional performing arts centers, schools, small towns! Hey, the SOS women would be great role models for little girls who want to play music."

"Role models?" I squirm. My mom was a role model. Olivia is a role model. I'm a drummer.

"This is why I want to be an agent," says Leo. "So I can look out for artists like you. It's my calling."

"Yeah, well, Spanky is gonna freak," I say. "*My son the agent* hardly sounds as distinguished as *my son the architect.*"

After a long pause, Leo says, "Guess what? I told her. I told her I'm gay."

"About time," I say, not mentioning any of my recent escapades. "How'd she react?"

"She knew."

"Oh, Leo, of course she did. Spanky is a smart cookie."

"Sometimes. Mainly she's a good mother."

"We both got lucky that way."

"Yep."

* * *

And now Ladies and Gentlemen, direct from New York City and a recent concert tour of fourteen exotic Caribbean Islands, Rocky Balboa's Rock and Show Palace is proud to present a group of gals who know how to cook, and not just in the kitchen! Some call 'em sexy, some call 'em pretty as peaches, but here in Atlantic City, where we know all about beautiful women, we call 'em Hot, Hot, Hot!!! If you need more SAX in your life, this is just the group to give it you, cause, ooh baby baby, can these girls BLOW! Let's have a steamy round of applause for the loveliest little ladies working the casinos today. HERE THEY ARE—Sisterhood of Soul!"

We stand in the wings, hidden from the audience, holding up our middle fingers in a mock salute to the emcee. Then we rush onstage, smile, and start the show.

We sound great tonight. Really great! Our thirty-minute set flies by, and I'm convinced, more than ever, that our hard work is paying off. Not that the audience notices.

Debbie von Schlippenhaus – who goes by the stage name "Baghira" – prepares to make her entrance. Debbie, or Baghira – what I call her depends on what she's wearing – is sporting a magenta sequined bra with matching veil and bloomers. From faraway the costume looks pretty authentic, but up close you can see the snags in the polyester chiffon, the missing sequins, the telltale signs of a leaky glue-gun.

There's a round of lukewarm applause for our last number – a kick-ass version of "Brick House" – and then a drunk in the back row yells, "Bring on the babes!"

HOT HOT HOT!!!!

Right.

The SOS band hustles offstage, but I stay seated – in the glow of an ugly blue spotlight – to play the transitional drum solo before Ed and the dancers take over. Like last night and the thirty nights before, I start with a nice fat funk groove, and then segue into an odd Arabic meter that's really fun to play. Another spotlight – this one pink – hits Baghira. She shakes her booty and her stomach muscles roll back and forth, distorting her tummy. A couple of guys in the balcony hoot and whistle. Baghira looks like she has eaten an angry tomcat and chased it down with a shot of rum. The crowd goes wild.

I play hard and wonder how much practice it takes to be a belly dancer.

An alarming shriek comes from one of the front booths.

There's a commotion on the floor right next to the stage, but I keep playing and Baghira keeps writhing, because, hey, the show must go on. I spot something spewing – is it vomit? – from the front row. There's a loud crash.

Now what? I hate this. Shit. I'm starting to panic.

Suddenly, the room manager catapults onstage. He stands in front of me and screams: "STOP THE MUSIC!!!"

So I do. But not before a hundred horrible thoughts race through my head. What's going on? I breathe, slowly and deeply, the way Olivia taught me. The house lights snap on and Baghira and I stare at the mess in the audience. A large man, seemingly unconscious, sprawls on the floor, and a waitress, on the steps above him, crawls on her hands and knees, picking up toppled glasses and smashed dessert plates. Looks to me like the poor man had some kind of attack, fell to the floor, and a waitress carrying a large tray of cocktails tripped over him. Guests wipe spilled drinks and chunks of fruit from their shoulders, the bus-boys pick tidbits of restaurant china off the tables.

"Call an ambulance!" screams a blond woman hovering over the Poor Man.

"Is he breathing?" shouts someone from the second row.

"How the hell should I know?" she shouts.

I sigh and slump over my drums.

Here's the thing about working in clubs. Weird shit happens, all the time. Most musicians let these incidents slide by – they even laugh about them – but I tend to overreact. Considering what happened to me when I was a kid, I guess this is to be expected. When I first started playing in nightclubs with SOS, little distractions really wigged me out. My heart would pound, I'd feel nauseated, and my ears would start to ring – just because the lights flickered, I heard a strange noise, or some idiot blew a cloud of cigar smoke in my direction. These days the anxiety attacks don't occur as often as they used to, but they still happen. When they do – *zap* – I flash back to the fire. A mental Ken Burns-type slide show clicks on in my head and images of the fire charge into my consciousness, attacking like soldiers on a revenge mission.

But I'm not going to let that happen tonight. I know better. *Breathe and focus.*

I check out the scene. Olivia taught me that if I can stay in the moment and focus on what's happening, I'll regain my composure.

Focus.

I look out on a sea of painted women and grayish men. The Poor Man lies in a heap on the paisley carpet. Baghira hurdles off the stage and begins thumping on his chest.

I hope he's okay. I take another deep breath and try to stay in the moment, even though the moment sucks. I mean, I don't know the guy, right? He's a complete stranger being given CPR by a belly dancer, for God's sake. He's overweight, wearing thick gold chains around his neck, and he's with a date who is way too young to be his wife.

Breathe.

Focus.

Ed the fire-eater joins me next to the drums, his oiled biceps crossed over his massive torso, a jeweled saber secured in the sash at his waist. Together, Ed and I wait for the ambulance to arrive and the clean-up crew to sponge away the mess. Baghira keeps thumping. Leo, who is seeing the show for the third time in four days, wanders over to the edge of the stage.

"Poor Man," says Leo. "What a mess." Then he turns to me. "You okay?" He knows how these incidents can set me off.

"Yep. Fine, fine, fine."

"Remember to breathe," he says. Leo thinks he's in Monte-Carlo instead of Atlantic City, and he's wearing a tuxedo he bought at Bergdorf Goodman. He holds a martini glass. Three olives. He looks like Cary Grant. Or maybe James Bond. The three of us watch Baghira work on the Poor Man. Her G-string peeks through her magenta chiffon trousers and her big boobs spill out of her top as she administers mouth-to-mouth resuscitation.

"This guy comes to," Leo says, "and he's gonna think he has died and gone to heaven."

"Baghira used to be a nurse," says Ed in a greasy New Jersey accent. "That's how she knows this CPR shit. It comes in handy more often than you think."

"Baghira? Isn't that the name of one of the *Jungle Book* characters?" asks Leo. "Great flick, I could watch it a million times. Love the music in that movie!"

"Wait a minute," I say, not quite calm yet, but at least able to speak. "Baghira gave up nursing to be a belly dancer?"

By this time the paramedics have arrived, which is a good thing, because I sense Leo is about to start singing his rendition of "Bare Necessities." Two guys who look like studio wrestlers carry the Poor Man out of the club. The lady escort scuttles behind them. There's complete silence as we watch them leave.

By this time most of the mess has been cleaned up and the customers – after receiving dry cleaning vouchers – have been wiped dry with towels and settled back into their seats. New trays of piña coladas arrive from the bar.

The manager jumps back on the stage, grabs the microphone and shouts into the quiet room, "EVERYBODY STAY CALM!!!"

We stare at him.

"I HAVE BEEN ASSURED BY THE MEDICAL TEAM THAT THE POOR MAN WILL BE FINE!!!" he says.

We stare at him some more.

"AND NOW LET THE FUN CONTINUE!!! START THE MUSIC!!!!" he yells at me.

The house lights dim and Baghira's spotlight clicks on. She hops back onstage, tugs at the wedgie in her harem pants, and scoots over to her circle of light. "Take it from the top?" she whispers to me on her way past the drums.

"Is he okay?" I ask.

"Probably," she says.

I wipe the beads of sweat from my forehead. I grab my sticks and dig into the music. Baghira gyrates to a groove that's too hip for the room, and the manager mops the floor.

* * *

Three days after the incident in Rocky Balboa's Rock and Show Palace, a private detective from a Long Island law firm shows up backstage – minutes before our eight o'clock show – to investigate a claim that the volume of the drums had caused the Poor Man's heart attack. Mute with disbelief, I look to Leo for moral support. He doesn't disappoint me.

"With all due respect, sir," Leo says to the detective. "An obese man, on a date with a hook – uh, someone other than his wife – who has just consumed four pina coladas, prime rib, French fries, and double order of Baked Alaska has a heart attack while looking at a harem girl with the world's largest knockers, and you're saying the *drums* caused his heart attack?"

RHYTHM

"Let's not get excited," says the Suit with the clipboard. "No one is accusing the drum-lady of anything.

"*Drum-lady?*"

The Suit continues: "We have several eye-witnesses who claim that the drums were, uh, let's see, I quote, *extraordinarily loud, louder than fireworks.*"

"*Louder than fireworks?* I'm sorry, but I played the way I always play,"

"And has this happened before?" says the Suit.

"Are you serious?"

"Let me handle this. I'm Ms. Bowman's representative," says Leo, puffing himself up. Is he standing on his toes, or what? He looks huge.

"Leo – ," I say.

"Put a lid on it, sister," says Leo, elbowing me in the ribs. "I'll take it from here."

"Who are you, exactly?" says the Suit.

"Leo Wainwright of Wainwright, Wainwright and Chubbs," he says, without missing a beat.

"Oh," says the Suit, nodding.

"Now. Has *what* happened before?" says Leo. "That a guy vomits and collapses on the floor right in the middle of Ms. Bowman's "Funky Drummer" groove? No, I don't believe this has ever happened. Although I've heard rumors that an middle-aged woman once hyperventilated and fainted during Jane's solo on "Freeway of Love.""

A concerned-looking Liz steps into the hallway. "You need help out here, Leo and Jane?"

"I think this man is accusing me of a crime," I say. "He's a detective from a law firm in Parsippany and he says my drums caused the Poor Man's heart attack."

195

"You know what?" says Leo, putting his hand over my mouth. "Ms. Bowman is not saying another word about this matter. Please don't talk to her anymore. She needs to prepare for tonight's performance. Jane, go do some push-ups or something."

"But, I – "

Leo pulls me away. We leave Liz standing there with the Suit. I guzzle a Diet-Coke and pretty soon I'm calm again. I look over my shoulder and see Liz flirting with the guy. Sometimes she's pathetic.

"What is the world coming to?" says Leo.

"*Wainwright, Wainwright, and Chubbs*?" I ask. "I know you're proud of your creative streak Leo, but you can't just *make up* a law firm."

"I didn't," he says. "One of those Wainwrights – the second one, I think – is my Uncle Wally."

"Wally Wainwright?"

"Yep. He's a tax attorney, or something like that. Very respected in the Squirrel Hill area of Pittsburgh."

"Who the hell is Chubbs?"

"Oh. Well. That part I made up," Leo says.

* * *

During the opening number of our set I spot the Suit sitting in the front row, next to a guy wearing padded headphones attached to some kind of gadget on the table. *What*? I can't believe it. Are they measuring the decibel levels? Okay, they wanna hear loud – I'll give 'em loud. I hit the drums as hard as

I can, hoping the punch of my kick drum will drive away my evil thoughts.

Here you go, boys, louder than fireworks.

Crash. Bam. Ooooh. Ahhhh.

Check it out. The drum-lady means business.

Love Letters

Dear Jane,

    It's spring again. This time of year always reminds me of your birthday. The day you were born, the wisteria was in bloom, and your grandmother and I sat for hours on end waiting for the phone to ring with news of your arrival. Isabella planted that wisteria right after your mother was born, over fifty years ago. It grew even faster than she did. Each spring, the new clusters of delicate blue blossoms remind me that life goes on. Life goes on and on and on. You and I know this better than most people.

    I miss you. I miss your mom, and I really miss your grandma, even though she's right next to me as I write this. She's here, but she's not. Funny, but the people most absent in my life seem to be the ones who are most present in my thoughts. In the snow globe of my mind, I see the sparkle of your mom's eyes, I hear your grandma's angelic voice, I find myself wondering where you are or what exciting adventures you're having. The three of you have been the dearest people in my life, and you're always with me, even though you're not, really.

    Your grandma's health is much worse than when you left on your SOS tour. It doesn't make any sense to me, this disease. When you're old, you should sift through your memories, rehash them, and file them back in an orderly fashion so they can be pulled up randomly, held to the light, and cherished. What's the point of living an entire life, cutting out and pasting together a mental scrapbook of recollections, if – in the end – all the pages turn out to be blank? What's the point?

Your grandma sits and stares at the wisteria, but she doesn't remember planting it, or why. Hell, she doesn't even know what it is. Until recently, the only thing she recognized was music, but now, even that memory has faded. Her response to her all-time favorite Dizzy Gillespie recording is the same as her reaction to a siren on the street, the chirping of a bird, the hum of the vacuum cleaner. She blinks; sometimes she turns her head a particular way. That's about it.

To be honest, I don't know what's sadder, knowing that she doesn't remember me, or that she doesn't remember us, the two of us, as a couple. If two people share a whole life together and one of them forgets that it ever happened, what happens to those shared memories? Do they disappear? I think that they do, in a way.

I wish many things for you, dearest Jane: a full life with someone who loves you as much as I've loved your grandmother, and as much as she has loved me. I want you to have the career that your grandmother gave up, the career that was stolen from your mother when she was killed. I pray that you'll have a loving and open relationship, always, with your father and Olivia. And I hope that someday you'll experience the beautiful day-to-day reality of watching a child grow stronger in your care.

RHYTHM

You might try planting some wisteria, too, like your grandmother did all those years ago. Years from now, when you're as old as I am, you'll see it clinging to your garden wall, verdant and tenacious, and it will comfort you.

You're my little heaven, forever, no matter what.

Love,
Grandpa Jack

* * *

Two hours after I read the letter, I'm on the phone with Leo, who had been summoned to Jack and Isabella's apartment after the early shift nurse found them dead. Evidently Jack had given the evening nurse the night off, fed Isabella ground up Nembutal in yogurt, waited for her to fall asleep, and put a pillow over her head. He then took his own lethal dose of sleeping pills, lay down next to her, and died with his arms wrapped around her shoulders. That's how the nurse found them, and that's the position they were in when Leo entered their bedroom. The police are calling it a murder-suicide, the press is calling it a double-suicide, and we are calling it choice. Trying to make me feel better, Leo tells me how peaceful they looked, the wrinkles smoothed from their faces, their eyes closed, as if they were bumping into each other in their separate dreams.

I wonder if Leo helped my grandfather, but I don't dare ask.

After a very public memorial service at St. Thomas Episcopal Church in Manhattan, Dad hires a plane to take us to Miami. At dusk, we scatter Jack and Isabella's ashes in an illegal ceremony on the beach where the old Flamingo nightclub once stood. We stand barefoot in the sand, watching the silver sea sweep away the dusty fragments of their romance.

I turn away from the glittering ocean, look at the silhouetted faces of my family and friends, and wonder who's next. I'm the last link to Jack and Isabella. I'm what they've left behind. Me. And the wisteria. Leo takes my hand and we walk in silence for a very long time on the empty beach – the flashy Miami hotels choking the shoreline on one side of us, the vast and humbling Atlantic on the other. We keep going, until our feet and ankles are numb and coated with layers of cool brown sand. The seagulls follow us, chanting a hit parade of cheap songs – their hollow shrieks mocking the thundering rhythm of the crashing waves.

Wide Open Roads

I've inherited my grandparents' Manhattan brownstone, along with several other office and residential buildings in Midtown. I've got no interest in being a real estate tycoon, so Dad helps me sell all of the buildings except for the brownstone, which will continue to be my home. It will also be the future site of the Leo Wainwright Agency, just as soon as Leo figures out exactly what kind of agency he wants to run. When he starts making money, he'll begin paying rent. In the meantime, he lives in the brownstone while I'm on the road. He takes care of odds and ends, feeds Jack's ancient cat Pablo, and supervises the cleaning and gardening staffs. Octavious lives with Leo now, and the two of them often spend their evenings in the library. They lounge in matching brocade winged-back chairs that once belonged to my grandparents, sketching ideas for their office design, comparing fabric swatches, and sipping martinis served in Isabella's crystal glasses. Leo was born to live in a house like this.

I'm left with millions of dollars. It's too overwhelming to think about, so I turn the details over to Dad and his investment bankers. I receive a huge monthly allowance, but I save most of it, preferring to live off of my SOS salary. Leo keeps bugging me to buy a Ralph Lauren wardrobe, a Mercedes jeep, and a condominium in the Dominican Republic – but I'm not interested in collecting stuff. Not yet, anyway. There's a purpose for my money, I just don't know what it is.

When I arrange to have 500,000 dollars put in trust for each of the Marys, I fear they'll take the money and run like hell to get out of Sewickley Heights, but I've underestimated their loyalty to Dad and Olivia. I donate another big chunk of cash, anonymously, to the Gatehouse music program. Olivia knows, but she's good at keeping secrets.

I worry that my band mates will hate me if they find out about my inheritance. Grateful for the work, and happy to have a distraction, I've stayed on the road with SOS, trying to maintain my musical focus. Our gigs have continued to be borderline – casinos and cruise ships, and the occasional week-long engagement in Tokyo where they treat us like big stars. We recorded a CD called *Girls' Night Out* and it got a few rave reviews along with a couple of unenthusiastic ones.

"It's easy to ignore the bad reviews," Mom used to say. "It's a little harder to ignore the good ones. Just play your ass off and forget the rest of it."

A year passes. We tour the country playing one-nighters in school gymnasiums and community centers. I almost quit when an ecstatic Bernie books SOS into a Vegas mega-hotel that features us playing on a tiny mock tropical island – in the middle of a giant fake lake – while twelve topless synchronized swimmers perform aquatic routines to our music. The show – called *Funky Mermaids* – is just awful. I mean, we sound good, but we're so far away from the audience that the human connection fizzles and dies every single night. Plus – even with the ultra-hip choreography and the bare breasts – there's no way to make synchronized swimming funky. Bathing caps and backbeats are not compatible.

"Why Bernie, why?" I say. "Why do we always have to play in tandem with some sort of jiggle show? Isn't there anyone in this country who will book us because they want to hear good music?"

"If they want good music they book the established male bands," he says. "I can't sell you without some sort of tits and ass act. I know it sucks, but hey, that's reality. Count yourself lucky to be workin', darlin'. Most of these places are usin' play-backs."

Unlike my co-workers, I've always had the financial *screw you I'm out of here* option. But I realize that I've gotten way more out of this SOS tour than my meager 300 bucks-per-week salary. I've learned how to hang in there and get the gig done, night after night – dodging flying sequins, horny casino managers, and splashing pool water. I've learned how to survive on stale donuts, cold burgers, and leftover fried rice stashed in a mini-bar fridge. I've adjusted to bad mattresses, bad manners, hideous acoustics, lousy sound systems, and fog machines that make me feel like an asthmatic. I've learned to practice whenever I can, spray my dirty clothes with Fabufresh to make them last one more day, grab a little short-term romance wherever I can find it. But the most important thing is this: I've earned the respect of my band mates. They don't think of me as Helen Bowman's rich daughter – they think of me as a player. I can't quit now, because they need me. I make them sound good, and that's a great feeling. It's something you can't buy, even if you do have millions of dollars. I'll wait until the SOS contract dries up, and then figure out my next move.

Olivia, who has come to hear the band six or seven times in the last year, says my playing is stronger than ever. Having her in the audience always reminds me of how far I've come; how, in so many ways, I owe my recovery to her. I wish I could return the favor by helping her feel more at peace with herself.

Every so often I sense edginess in her that she can't – or won't – explain. Really, she has nothing to worry about. My father loves her, and so do I. She's safe with us.

In Las Vegas, we meet between shows for dinner. Olivia's praise of my playing feels like a much-needed warm blanket in the fake chill of the hotel air conditioning.

"You'll be ready soon," she says, her eyes scanning the crowd in the packed steak house.

"For what?" I say.

"Anything," she says, "Anything at all."

PART III: 1992

Mr. Bigstuff

"Play mother-fucker, play!"

R&B star Bobby Angel yells at all of his musicians like this, not just the females. Leo calls him an equal opportunity asshole. Right in the middle of a concert, he'll screw up his face like a pug dog, strut upstage to the drums and unleash a string of obscenities at whoever happens to be playing them. He's so loud that the mikes pick up his insults and spew them into the audience.

"Louder cocksucker, louder!"

When his drummer quits and moves to Idaho, I get a chance to audition for the drum chair. It's a big deal.

Like most of the important things in my life, this particular opportunity has been arranged by Leo. LWA – Leo Wainwright Artists – has taken off. I invested a lot of money in the enterprise, even though my accountant told me I was crazy. But after all these years with Leo, I know for a fact that he never fails. Never. Last year, with me as his silent partner, he set up shop in the brownstone, lured a couple of hot-shot agents from the best offices in town, and – with their assistance – poached a couple of celebrity clients from other agencies. Bobby Angel, winner of three Grammys and two People's Choice awards, now holds the top client spot in Leo's music division. LWA's signing of Bobby Angel created a real media buzz – *World Entertainment Magazine* called it the "show-biz coup of the year."

First chance he had, Leo told Bobby about me.

"Sure," said Bobby Angel to Leo. "A chick drummer? Sounds good, assuming she can hit. How's she look? Got big tits?" Leo called me immediately and tattled, sure that I'd be angry, surprised when I wasn't.

"Look," Leo said to me last November, "this guy is a major talent but he's also a major jerk. Are you sure you wanna subject yourself to this? I mean, you could have your own band; I could work on that for you. You don't have to spend your career being a sideman, or side woman, or is it side person? Help me out here."

"Sideman will do. And when did you start being so politically correct?"

"Since I started working with a big bunch of divas. You gotta be careful these days. I said *Indian* the other day instead of *Native American* and Dale Hammer practically scalped me."

"Who's Dale Hammer?" I ask.

"Indian – I mean Native American. Cherokee. Or at least he claims to be, although I have my doubts. Actor. Chief Giant Eagle. Everyone says he's the next big thing, so I don't ask too many questions."

"Well look, I don't wanna be a diva, or an Indian, or the next big thing. I still have a lot to learn. I'm happy being a sideman. And don't think that just because I've spent the last couple of years on tour with a group of women that I've been sitting around trading cupcake recipes. These gals are tough, Leo, you know that. There's nothing Bobby Angel will throw at me that I haven't handled before."

"Good. Here's the deal. The Bobby Angel gig currently pays five grand a week, even when you're not working. I can probably get you more. It's a retainer thing – you'd be on call fifty-two weeks a year."

"Like a doctor."

"Like a doctor. And you might need a doctor after working with this maniac."

"What? Because he screams at his musicians? I'll just scream back. If I have to, I'll grab the little anorexic weasel and toss him into the mosh pit; he weighs, what, about 100 pounds? I can put up with his ranting Leo, the guy plays and sings like no one else out there these days. Okay, okay, he's no Prince, but he's got a really tight band. Those guys can build a groove solid enough to get a whole arena shaking. I mean, imagine what I could do with that! Please keep working on getting me an audition with Prince or Lenny Kravitz, but Bobby Angel is a good start for now, even if he acts like an idiot."

"He does, indeed. I got a complaint that he called his last keyboard player a turd in front of 15,000 people. Then, get this; he insulted the female pyrotechnics specialist. Used, you know, the dreaded C-word. I told him, 'Bobby, never, ever mess with the pyrotechnics expert, you're just askin' for it.'"

"What happened?"

"The pyro-lady rigged a flash pot much closer to Bobby than planned. Damn near caught his cape on fire."

"He wears a *cape*?"

"Just for the opening number. Then he does, you know, the sequined cat suit thing."

"Okay fine, back to the point. I'd really like to experience playing for a big star for a while. It'll be cool to play in arenas and stadiums and check out that scene. I saw a tiny bit of that with Mom when she did that *Blood Sweat and Tears* tour, but mostly she played in smaller places – plus the T.V. show."

"The money okay for you?"

"Leo, I'm making three hundred a week with SOS. The Bobby Angel money sounds fine."

"Not too shabby."

"Not too shabby. But I want you to do one thing for me."

"Shoot."

"I want you to get Liz on the gig."

"Whoa. I thought you were going to ask to have a turkey dinner rider put in your contract or something. I don't know, Jane. Bobby Angel already has an alto player."

"He can use another one."

"Liz is a looker, maybe he'll go for it. You know, I had a feeling there was something going on between you two."

"There's not."

"Oh please. Everyone has a thing for Liz. Even I have a thing for her."

"Okay, we had a little fling, but it wasn't ever serious. We're friends. Look, she's a great player, and it's kind of now or never for her. She deserves a gig like this."

"I'll try my best. But first you've got to do the audition and get the job."

"I'll get the job, Leo. Don't worry."

* * *

Even if I don't get the job, I know it's time to leave SOS. Bernie ran out of casino and cruise ship bookings, so we've spent the last six months criss-crossing the country in a bus driven by a two-hundred pound red-head named Dagmar. Each day unfolds pretty much the same way; we drag ourselves onto the bus and drive, stopping every four hours for toilet, ciga-rette, and food breaks. With Dagmar pointing at her watch, we hustle into truck stops with names like Mo's Family Best – restaurants with cracked orange plastic seats and tattooed men sitting at the counter – and scarf down gravy-smothered mystery mounds served with delicate packets of saltines. Then we climb back onto the bus and drive some more. Eventually we get wherever we're going. Exhausted, we shuffle into the hall, argue with a soundman determined to ruin the natural mix of our band, play the concert, sign a few autographs for sad little girls in puffy dresses, and pack up. Pathetic, really. After the gig is even worse; we're forced to beg for food because – even though it's supposed to be in our contract – the backstage caterer either forgets to come, or worse, shows up with nine ham sandwiches for thirteen people. By the time we get off the stage, Bernie and Dagmar have eaten most of the grub, leaving us with scraps, crumbs, and spit-backs.

Often, after fighting over crusts of bread, we talk Dagmar into driving us to the nearest seedy bar, so we can pig out on cheese puffs and beer. Liz hits on the bartender, Raj hits on the waitress, I sit in the corner with a diet coke and a bowl of stale peanuts and watch the action. Sometimes Betty and I bet on who will score first. On a really good night, Liz and Raj both get lucky, and Betty and I con the manager into cracking open a dusty old bottle of Wild Turkey. Then we drink shots and arm wrestle.

Yeah, it's time to move on.

Usually the alarm wails at five in the morning, which is pretty brutal if we haven't gotten to bed until three. We crawl back on the bus – which Liz has nicknamed The Grey Ghost – and doze the morning away as Dagmar exceeds the speed limit and hauls ass over rough patches of highway. Pale and sleep-deprived, we stumble into the next place – a nightclub, a community center, a high school gym, a church basement, all the time moaning about how the venue looks just like the one we played the night before. Sometimes it seems as if we've spent the day driving in circles around a municipal parking lot. But the tour isn't all bad. I've grown up during this last year-and-a-half – musically and emotionally – and I've formed some friendships that will last forever. I'm not sure if anything else in my life will ever compare to the SOS tour. I've even managed to get used to the way Vapor Betty smells. She grooves so hard on the bass, I stopped noticing the stink. And besides, she's a damn good arm wrestler. I'll miss her.

But it's time to move on.

Raj and Bernie try to convince me to renew my SOS contract, but they're not surprised when I tell them I'm quitting. There have been rumors circulating about Bobby Angel's search for a new drummer, and Liz, who knows I'm auditioning, has blabbed it to all the musicians in SOS. To Liz, a chance to play for Bobby Angel means a one-way ticket to the R&B Hall of Fame. When she's called for an audition as well, we celebrate with a spaghetti dinner, a bottle-and-a-half of cheap red wine, and one very drunken and meaningful kiss.

We fly to New York, nail the audition, land the gig, and start the next chapter of our lives.

* * *

When Liz and I show up at our first Bobby Angel press event, we're swept into a makeshift salon by a team of frenzied stylists clad in black. Two middle-aged guys named Buzz and Josh spackle our faces with a lard-like paste, then they tease and spray our hair until it's stiff and smelling like fake raspberries.

"That's the biggest hair I've ever seen," I say to Liz. "It's got a real Don King vibe."

"I like it," she says. "I don't know about this black lipstick though. What if it wears off on my teeth?"

"Quiet ladies! We need to finish," says Buzz. "The photographers want to be out of here in an hour. If Tess from *Rolling Stone* shows up we shouldn't keep her waiting."

"Here we go again," I say. "Another damn beauty pageant disguised as a music gig. Some things never change."

"Don't fret, darling," says Josh. "I saw your audition tape. You can really do those drums, girl. Plus – you're going to look just foxy fabulous.

"Aggggh," I say.

"Listen, it's not just a girly thing. Bobby Angel was in here and – *entrée nous* – I put more make-up on him than I do on most women. Deal with it, darling, this is the big time. You're being paid to cope with the media frenzy and just be all-around wicked. The music comes second."

"Great," I say.

"You know with your dark skin that gold powder looks really special on you," says Liz.

"Shut up," I say.

"Excuse me, Mizzzzz Bowman," says Liz.

"Bowman?" says Josh. "Oh-my-god, oh-my-god, oh-my-god. Are you any relation to Helen Bowman?"

"She was my mother," I mutter, as he blots my lips with a tissue.

"Get out of town, girlfriend!" says Josh. "I did her make-up for the Curly Dobson Show. Every week for years. I loved her. I think I must have met you way back when."

Josh's hands run over my cheekbones, smoothing creams and powders into my hairline. I think about those same hands touching Mom's face.

"She was a beauty," he says. "I mean, I know she was a brilliant musician, but faces are my business, and hers was something else. Cheekbones to absolutely die for. She once showed me a photo of your grandmother. Same bones. I'll never forget that picture. Your grandmother and mother were standing, nose to nose, looking down at a baby, which I guess must have been you – little baby Jane."

"I know that photo," I say. "I have it in my apartment."

"You have the same bone structure," he says. "Just a little softer around the eyes."

"On the table in my bedroom."

"Maybe your lips are a little fuller."

"In a silver frame," I say.

"Looks like you're carrying on for her," says Josh. "With the music. It's too fabulous! Okay darling, you're ready. Just slip into that bronze dress."

"I can't play in a dress."

"I know that. Your agent worked it into your contract. Smart guy. But there's no playing today, just photos. You can wear your own boots – they'll look just wild with the dress."

"I always forget that you're Helen Bowman's daughter," says Liz. "I mean, you don't act like the daughter of a music legend. You act like you."

"Thanks." I think this is a compliment, but I'm not sure.

Buzz puffs my hair. Josh checks my nails, squeezes my hand, and escorts me to the entrance of the studio. A man growls into a walkie-talkie and I hear an amplified voice announcing Liz and me as the newest members of the Bobby Angel Band.

Liz grips my elbow and whispers: "Here it is, honey, the big time. Are you ready?"

The heavy metal door swings open, and dozens of flashes go off.

Taking baby steps, with hair as big as a full-blown moon, I slip with surprising ease into the spotlight that once belonged to my mother.

Step Into the Light

"By the way, Jane," says Leo, when I call from the Bobby Angel tour to check in with him. "Remember that guy from your Dad's wedding? The one who used to be the drummer in Olivia's Gatehouse band? The one who was giving you the glad-eye at the reception?"

"*Franklin Boswell*?"

"Yeah, Franklin. He called."

"What do you mean, *he called*?"

"Jane, we're speaking English, right? That guy named Franklin called. On the telephone – which is still an accepted way for people to communicate these days."

"Yeah, and?"

"He called the apartment. Olivia gave him our number. He said he was in town on business and he wanted to ask you to lunch."

My heart starts tap-dancing. Or maybe it's clog-dancing.

"Really?" I ask. "*Really?*"

"Really," says Leo. "Miss Jane, do I detect a little *hot and bothered* quality to your voice?"

"What did you tell him? Did you tell him I was on the road? Did you get his number? Did you tell him I would call him back?"

"Yeah," says Leo, "but that was three days ago. You really should check in more often."

"Leo. I'm gonna get bitchy in a second."

"Okay, sorry. Yes, he knows about your Bobby Angel gig. He saw your photo in *People* Magazine. And the entire world saw that *Primetime Live* piece on female rock drummers. Since there are apparently only about four of you in the entire universe, you were a huge part of the segment. It aired last week."

"I didn't see it. Did I look okay?"

"Since when are you worried about how you look?"

"Since Franklin Boswell saw me on TV, that's when! Quit it, Leo. Stop torturing me. You know I have a major crush on this guy. He put his hand on my back for about two seconds at the wedding, and I've had the shivers ever since."

"Hey, aren't you playing Boston next week?"

"Yeah. Should I call and offer him tickets?"

"That's that I would do. In your shoes, I mean. You've got the shivers, you've gotta go for it."

"Thanks, Leo. Now give me the friggin' number."

* * *

I call Dr. Franklin Boswell and leave a message on his voice-mail.

"Franklin, it's Jane Bowman," I hope my voice doesn't sound as squeaky as it feels. "Leo said you called me and I'm sorry I wasn't there but I'm doing this Bobby Angel tour and we're sort of all over the place right now. So. I looked at the schedule and I see we're in Boston next week at the, uh, whatever the big arena there is, I don't have the name on this list. These shows are usually sold out, but I can always get a couple of house seats. So look, I'm guessing you're a Bobby Angel fan, cause who isn't, right? Yeah. I'll leave two tickets and a backstage pass under your name at the artist entrance to the arena. If you can make it, fine, if not, well, I'll catch up with you some other time. Hope the, ummm, doctor business is going well and that you're digging doing all that surgery and that you have lots of patients. Not that I want people to need heart surgery, I mean, I just hope you're happy. I guess that's what I'm trying to say. Man, I sound like a moron. Okay, look, I'd really like to see you, so I hope you can come to the concert. Bye."

I spend the entire week thinking about Franklin. I even babble to Liz about him. Liz, true to form, has taken up with Bobby Angel, even though she's ten years older and thirty pounds heavier than he is. She's having the time of her life, but insists her relationship with Bobby isn't serious.

"How can I be serious about a guy who runs up to me onstage and screams PLAY HARDER YOU COCKSUCKING BITCH," she says. "Is this any way to talk to your girlfriend? Nope, I don't think a long-term relationship is in the works."

"What a pig," I say.

"Yep. But he makes up for it when we're alone."

"Spare me the details."

"Jealous?"

"NO."

"So what's with this Franklin guy? Didn't you say you've only seen him one time? At your Dad's wedding? Like a hundred years ago?"

"Five years ago. Yeah. But I've never stopped thinking about him."

"What does he look like?"

"He's dark, like Olivia. And tall. And he has the most beautiful hands. And his eyelashes are about a mile long.

"Oh honey, you've got it bad. You start noticing eyelashes, you're in trouble."

"He's smart; I mean you've got to be smart to get through Harvard Medical School right? And he's such a great drummer. I got to hear him at the wedding."

"Is he still playing? I love the idea of the doctor-drummer combo. He grooves you to death and then resuscitates you slowly, one stroke at a time. Ahhhh . . ."

"Oh, come on, Liz. I don't think he's still playing, but what do I know, I haven't seen him for years. I can't imagine that a person could play with so much heat and then just quit cold turkey and start doing triple bypasses. You know, what I really liked about him was the way he treated Olivia. There's so much love between those two. Almost like a mother and son. I'll never forget the looks on their faces when he walked her down the aisle at the wedding."

"Okay, so what are you gonna do with the good doctor when you see him? You can't just hang backstage – it's like a circus back here."

"First of all, I don't even know if he'll show up."

"He'll show up."

"If he does, I'm going to play it cool. I was eighteen – still a kid – when I met him. What if he's not really as great as I remember?"

"Maybe he is."

"Maybe he isn't. We'll see."

* * *

A lot of musicians I know have a couple of drinks to chase away their nerves. I don't much like to drink – except when I'm bored silly – and I usually don't get nervous, so I actually enjoy the feeling when it sneaks up on me. Tonight counts as one of those times, and it has everything to do with Franklin and nothing to do with the Bobby Angel music. After two years of touring with him, I could slam out this show blindfolded if I had to. So it feels nice to have butterflies in my stomach for a change.

Tonight, like every night, Bobby wrangles the band and stage hands into a prayer circle and asks the good Lord to cast a favorable blessing on our performance.

"Bobby," I say. "If the show sucks, I don't think the good Lord has anything to do with it."

"No, when we suck, the Lord is out of it."

"Well doesn't that same principle apply when we sound good, too? I mean, if the good Lord . . ."

"Look, babe," he says, tugging on the crotch of his spandex pants, "I only bring the Lord into this shit because it makes us look respectable and the press people eat it up. Those cocksuckers are always standing around backstage before the show, looking for an angle. They fuckin' love this religious crap. Look, there's an NBC News crew right over there in the corner," he says, glancing away quickly, pretending not to see them. He smiles and talks through clenched teeth. "Or are you so *into the music* that you haven't noticed?"

Steaming mad, I stomp away from him and wonder how much longer I can put up with this nonsense. I'm getting sick of trying to balance my dignity with what's good for me musically. Bobby's music is so great, but I really wish he would chill. And I wish the media circus would lighten up. At almost every concert there's at least one camera crew, filming a segment for yet another *Bobby Angel Live* documentary. I don't know who watches this stuff. For the last backstage docu-drama, an obnoxious producer with dyed black hair and an over-sized clip-board followed me around with a camera crew to find out what a power-drummer *eats*. A lot, it turns out. I looked like Miss Piggy in that film, sitting down to plate after plate of mashed potatoes and gravy.

"Never, ever eat anything while you're being filmed or taped," says Liz. "Unless you're fond of seeing yourself with a chicken leg hanging out of your mouth or with pieces of sal-ad stuck to your chin. That's the footage they always use, the sloppy stuff. There's this one TV segment of me wolfing down a banana?"

"Oh no, don't say it."

"Yep. It looks like – "

"Don't say it!"

"Well, let me just say that people are still talkin' about that particular film clip."

After the prayer circle, Bobby leads us in a sort of rhythmic East Indian chant that grows gradually louder, until we're all standing there with red faces, screaming like banshees. Then we jump up and down – supposedly to get ourselves *pumped up* for the show – before charging down a narrow ramp and onto the stage. I can't imagine that any of this helps our performance, but evidently it looks good on film. And at least no one is eating.

This evening, I think about Franklin and the time that has passed since I've seen him. He performs heart surgery, I per-form music. When we met, five years ago, we were both in training – apprentices; refining our skills, figuring out what we want. Maybe now we've got an idea.

The fog machine kicks in, blasting a frosty chemical draft onto my shoulders, and I get the cue to start playing the drum

RHYTHM

solo that opens the show. Soon, when the lights heat up and I've played half the set, I'll be sweating buckets, but right now, I'm freezing. The Megatron screen jumps to life, and I sense my giant video image looming behind me. I check the tempo light blinking on my metronome, listen to the click coming through my headset, and slam into the first few bars. Man, that feels good. The off-stage announcement blares through the stadium while I continue to play.

"*Hello Boston!*"

"Hello!"

"*I can't hear you!*"

"Hello!"

"*Louder!*"

"*Hello BOSTON!*"

"Hello!"

"Say Y-E-A-H BOSTON!"

"Y-E-A-H"

The groove feels really solid now, and the crowd, estimated to be somewhere around 20,000 people, is clapping along with my backbeat. Cool.

"*Give it to me!*"

"Hello!"

"*Give it to me!*"

"Y-E-A-H!"

"*Are you ready for the show of a lifetime?*"

"Yeah!"

"*I can't hear you!*"

"Yeah!"

"*Say it louder!*"

"Yeah!"

225

It's so hip when the announcer goes on and on like this, it gives me more time to dig in. Man, I love this.

"*Are you ready?*"

"Yeah!"

"*Who do you want?*"

"Bobby!"

"*Who do you love?*"

"Bobby!"

"*Bob-by! Bob-by! Bob-by! Bob-by! Say it with me now!*"

But in my head, I hear *Frank-lin! Frank-lin! Frank-lin!*

I imagine the evening ahead; not just the concert, but the after-party. The show might be predictable, but beyond that, who knows?

"*Bob-by! Bob-by! Bob-by!*"

This much I do know: A weird musical force churns deep inside of me. It bashes and thrashes around inside me and drives me to hit the drums harder, to find the beauty in a groove, to breakdown complex patterns into precise rhythms that breathe and move. But at the core of this force lies a liquid center of muted sounds. This part of me, this undefined middle soft-spot, begs for time that can be counted in moments, not measures.

Bobby Angel, wearing a lime-green cat suit, leaps onto the stage. The crowd roars, and the whole arena throbs with excitement. In my headset I hear my cue to ease up for Bobby's first chorus of "Soul of a Singer."

Surrounded by the darkness, you hear music in the night,
You fight off all your shadows, you step into the light,
Your future's far behind you, your past comes rushing in,
You've got the soul of a singer.

I catch a close-up of myself on the video monitor, and I see her – Mom – sculpted arms and wild hair, focused on the task ahead, loving herself, loving her life. But it's not Mom, it's me. Just me.

You orchestrate your moments,
And repeat the second verse,
The bridge you love to take
Is both a blessing and a curse,
The coda seems much bolder,
But you're older than your years,
You've got the soul of a singer.

I steal one last look into the trippy haze of tonight's audience, and then, after taking a deep breath, I dedicate my performance – not to my mother, like I usually do – but to Frankin Boswell, a man I barely know.

"GET YOUR TIGHT LITTLE ASS TO THE BRIDGE!" Bobby screams at me.

I smile in Liz's direction. But she's preparing for her solo, and besides, there's too much smoke and fog for her to see me.

I lean into the groove, allowing it to swallow me whole.

* * *

After the show and a much needed slug of cold orange juice, I wipe the sweat from my face and neck with a fluffy white towel. Then I race to the visitor's area and scan the blur of eager faces. At least a hundred backstage guests lurk behind the velvet rope, sipping the caterer's cheap champagne, waiting and hoping to meet Bobby. I search and search, but Franklin isn't there. I ignore the cluster of fans waving plastic-covered autograph books and programs for me to sign, and march back to my dressing room, cursing Franklin, cursing crushes, cursing love. But when I open the door, there he stands, holding a giant bouquet of red roses.

"Franklin!" I say. "Oh wow! I just went to find you and I thought you hadn't come after all. How did you get back here?"

"Your friend Leo made arrangements with security. He called me and said it would be nicer than waiting outside with the other fans. I believe he called them *the great unwashed*."

"That's Leo."

"I told him I thought waiting in your dressing room would be presumptuous on my part. But he insisted. I hope it's okay."

"Of course it's okay."

"Leo can be quite persuasive. He said to tell you that sending me back here had something to do with 'the shivers,' and that you'd understand."

"Uh, yeah, Leo knows me really well. He knows what I want." As Franklin glides closer to me, I notice how handsome he is. Graceful. Elegant. Confident.

"You're playing so well, Jane. You're all groove and raw power up there. Your solo on "Cool Cat" was unbelievable – I've never heard anyone play a kick drum like that. You've got the fastest feet in town, girl. And you're beautiful. Just like I remember, but more."

"You didn't see that mashed potato documentary did you?"

"That's not what I meant, but yes I did see it, along with all the other media coverage. I've been, uh, following your career. I even showed up at one of your SOS gigs in Atlantic City."

"Really? Why didn't you say hello?"

"I was with a date, and she was having jealousy issues after I raved too much about your playing. Listen, I'll bet you could use some dinner right now. I remember how hungry I used to get after a concert. I've made reservations at Antonio's, home of Boston's best mashers. Oh, and these are for you." He thrusts the flowers into my arms, then brushes a damp strand of hair away from my throat. Someone knocks on the door.

It's Liz. I make introductions, but my voice shakes. I can feel my right knee trembling.

"Bobby and I are headed to the Wine Bar," she says, "You wanna come?"

I look in Franklin's direction, fearful for one second that this whole thing has been a ploy to meet Bobby, the star.

Like he's reading my mind, Franklin laughs and says, "No thanks, Liz. Some other time. Jane and I have a lot to talk about." He puts his hand on the curve of my back, right where he touched me all those years ago. The exact same spot. Whoa. My legs seem to dissolve, and I crumple onto the sofa behind me.

"Oh boy," says Liz. "Looks like you two are gonna have some fun tonight."

"Yeah," I say.

"Hey," she says, flashing one of her famous flirty grins at Franklin. "Nice eyelashes." Then she winks at me and whirls out of the room.

"Are you okay?" Franklin asks me, pulling me to my feet.

"Yeah," I say. "It's just that I've been thinking about this evening for a very long time."

"Me, too," he says, curling his velvety fingers around my calloused right hand. "Let's take it slow, okay?"

"Yes," I whisper. "Slow is good."

Sail On

Because Franklin lives in Boston and I live out of a suitcase, taking our time turns out to be our only option. I've fallen in love with him and he tells me he feels the same way. I only manage to push him out of my thoughts when I'm playing – if I allowed my fantasies to follow me into the studio or onstage, I'd unravel. So I force my romantic notions to stay in a separate place, just outside the edges of my playing, where I can visit the dream of him whenever the music stops. When it does, another kind of rhythm takes over; intense and sweet enough to carry me through a million nights. I want to be with him forever – no one else, just him.

I know Franklin's story, but just the hazy version, the one he has chosen to tell me. His dad was a drummer working in the Hill District of Pittsburgh. His mom was a drug addict. Both of them died when Franklin was a boy – the result of an accident with a gun. Franklin has never revealed the details to me, and I've never pushed him. Years ago, Olivia yanked him from one side of his grief to the other, and, like me, he has learned to seek revenge by clinging to his career like it's a lifeboat.

Work hard, live well, keep going.

As a member of the thoracic-cardiac staff at Boston Memorial Hospital, Frankin doesn't have much free time. We're the king and queen of long distance phone calls, last minute flights, and passionate trysts in five-star hotels. It's fun, that's for sure, but we want more time.

When the Bobby Angel tour screeches to an end, after three years and two CDs, I quit. I move back to New York City, exhausted, exhilarated, and looking forward to a freelance career. In the meantime, Franklin starts searching for a position in the city. I move into the main part of the brownstone, preparing for the day when we'll live together. Leo's agency has grown, and he and Octavious have rented a larger office space in Chelsea. They'll continue to live in the extra apartment in the house.

Liz has signed on for another Bobby Angel tour, not for the romance, but for the money, or so she claims.

"Look honey," she says. "I'm up to six grand a week with him. Another year and I'll have enough saved to do whatever I want. Maybe I'll retire from the road and just go live and play somewhere peaceful. Like Ohio or something."

I can't imagine Liz living in a suburb of Columbus but maybe she has a point. She confesses to me that she'll be fifty years old this year, and swears me to secrecy since Bobby thinks she is thirty-five.

"Honestly, I don't know how I'd survive if I wasn't on tour. I'm such a road rat. Except for that one awful phase with the lumberjack, I've been touring for almost thirty years. I might as well tattoo my passport to my forehead."

I can't imagine thirty years on the road. Between SOS and Bobby, I've been out for five and even that seems like forever.

It's hard to say goodbye to Liz and we both cry, even though we swear that someday we'll play together again. But it won't be the same as touring. On the road, your band turns into your family. You snap and snipe at each other, you tussle around in the mud, you eat together, sometimes you sleep together, you gossip, you laugh, you triumph, you fall flat on your asses, you tease and taunt, you creep over borders and forget your manners, you linger longer than you should, you expect too much, you give back too little, you drink too many Black Russians, you build grudges, burn bridges, scorch fingers when you can't find a decent roach clip, and batter each other with cynicism disguised as humor. But then the lights dim, the music starts, and *wham!* you're locked in tight, to a place that feels like an outer-space version of home.

"Take care of yourself Jane," she says, her arms tight around my waist. "And hold on to Franklin."

"I'm not quitting Bobby's gig for a man."

"Yes you are."

"No I'm not. Really. I've gotten what I need out of Bobby Angel. It's time for the next thing."

"And the next thing is Franklin."

"No. Yes. I don't know. I mean, he's a part of it, for sure."

"Don't be embarrassed, Jane. Live your life. Sometimes people like us get too hung up on playing. We bury real life in the cellar and hope it doesn't pop up and scare us when we're not looking. Pay attention to life the way you pay attention to music. Every single detail. And pay attention to love; it doesn't come around all that often."

I feel like I'm listening to Mom. Or Olivia.

"Music is a kind of love," I say. "Right?"

"Yeah, of course it is. And it'll be there for you, whenever you need it. It gives back everything you put into it. You can't always count on people. You can love them, but you can't always count on them to be there."

We stay locked together and think about this.

"I know. Thank you, Liz. For everything."

"Honey, I don't deserve any thanks.

"Yes you do. You taught me to go after the things I want."

"Nobody had to teach you that, Jane. But do me a favor, okay?

"Sure," I say. "What?"

"Keep going."

"My mother used to say that. *Sigue adelante hija*. Keep going."

"Well, she was right." she says. "Don't stop. Just keep going."

Come Love

"So let me get this straight," I say to Franklin, "the resting human heart rate averages between 60 and 100 beats per minute? That's a pretty wide range, isn't it?" We're having dinner together in the brownstone; take-out Chinese that we're eating in candlelight on Isabella's good china. A single white rose bends over the side of the tall onyx vase Olivia gave me for my birthday.

Franklin has taken the shuttle down from Boston. He'll leave again before the sun rises. It won't be much longer before we're able to live together. Franklin, who has become a hotshot specialist, has accepted a senior surgical position at Mt. Sinai, where, starting in six months, he'll join the cardiac surgery unit. I'm so proud of him I could burst.

"Right," he says, stabbing a water chestnut. "Athletes are on the low end of the scale, kids on the higher end. Generally if the heart's resting rate is outside of that 60–100 scale, there's a problem. A resting rate above 100 beats per minute is called tachycardia. Under 60 is called bradycardia."

"I got accused of bradycardia today." I pile more rice on my plate. "We were right in the middle of the bridge section this tune called "Save Me" when Jake stopped playing, pulled a big hissy fit and said that I was slowing down. Me. Slowing down. Like I've ever slowed down in my life. I mean Betty used to call me Steady Eddie."

I've spent almost eight hours at the studio today, recording for Jake Waters, a quirky singer songwriter with a laid back R&B style. Leo signed him last year and then nailed a three-record deal for him with Virgin. People seem to dig the way Jake sings – there's a lot of buzz about him. But to me, he sounds like Donald Duck. I'm discovering that a freelance career means taking some cool sounding jobs that turn out to be big fat duds. Like this one. I'm scheduled to be holed up in the studio with sniveling Jake-y boy for the next month.

"Were you working with a click track?" asks Franklin.

"No. Jake refuses to play with a click. Says the music won't breathe with a click. I tried to explain that there's plenty of breathing room between the clicks, but he didn't buy my argument."

"So what did you do?"

"I got out my metronome and proved to him that the take hadn't slowed down at all. I'm telling you Franklin, at the point we stopped we were almost exactly at the same tempo as when we started."

"Almost exactly?"

"Yeah, sort of. We were actually a bit faster. Our start tempo was eighty."

"On the quarter-note or on the half-note?"

"Half-note. We sped up to eighty-four."

"Not quite Steady Eddie."

"Give me a break, it was the first take. Plus, you know how it goes, sometimes the whole thing feels better if it speeds up just a little." I should know better than to start a conversation about tempo with a drummer turned heart surgeon.

"Baffling, isn't it, the range of interpretation? We all hear things differently. Jake thought it was slowing down, you thought it was perfect, and a reality check told you it was rushing."

"Are you ever happy to be away from these stupid tempo discussions?"

"I listen to heart beats all day. I'm surrounded by tempo discussions."

"But it's more clear-cut isn't it? Not much room for interpretation?"

"Interpretation is everything in the heart biz. The detection of potential valve abnormalities relies on a creative analysis of two very basic sounds. *Lubb-dupp*. Actually, it's three sounds if you count the silence that follows."

"*Lubb-dupp*?"

"Yeah, those are the sounds the heart makes with every single beat. It's sort of swinging, once you get into it." He smiles. "Listen." He pulls my head to his chest. "The first sound, *lubb*, is usually lower and thumpier. The second sound, *dupp*, is higher pitched."

"Cool."

"There's a pause after each *lubb-dupp*, then the beat starts over again. Sometimes these sounds are called the first and second heart sounds. You ever think about what makes those sounds?"

"Love?" I ask, only half joking.

"The first sound results from the pressure in the chambers – caused by the contraction of the heart muscle. The second sound is due to the closing of the aortic valve. That's the sound of the valves slamming shut."

"Love must happen when they open up again."

"Which they do. That's the silent part, and it happens about 100,000 times a day."

"Wait a minute," I say. "You remember I took a workshop a few years back with Ed Thigpen? He talked about exactly this thing. He told me a groove should be like my heartbeat. He didn't say *lubb-dupp*, he *said bu-duh-rest, bu-duh-rest*, in a triplet feel."

"There you go. Like I said, it's swingin'."

"So we're all carrying a human-groove in our hearts?"

"That's why people respond so strongly to rhythmic music, yeah. And when a bunch of musicians play together you've got all those human grooves working as a team to make a musical groove, which can be miraculous if it works, or a complete train wreck if it doesn't. A human groove machine comprised of multiple musicians only functions when the trust factor kicks in."

"Trust?"

"Trust."

"So," I say. "What do you listen for when you hear a person's *lubb-dupp*?"

"Hopefully I hear a nice clean steady triplet, without any snaps, clicks, or murmurs."

"Hopefully. What controls the actual beat?"

"The heart's four chambers beat in a systematic way. An electrical impulse controls that system. That's one reason, as an ex-drummer, why I'm not so opposed to metronomes or click tracks. I figure if the human heart needs an electrical guide, then maybe a musician does also, at least sometimes."

"What do you mean the heart is run by an electrical impulse? I didn't exactly pay attention in biology class, but I don't know how that slipped by me. You make it sound like we're being zapped all the time."

"True, in a way. See, there's this little package of highly specialized cells in the right atrium. It's called the SA Node. It's sort of a natural pacemaker – and it causes the heart to beat."

"Steady Eddie."

"Yep."

"What about when your heart speeds up, like during exercise, or . . ."

"During sex?"

"Yeah. Like that."

"Emotional reactions and hormonal factors can affect the rate of the electrical discharge."

"That's a good argument for not using a metronome, and just letting the your impulses guide you."

"Right. Except sometimes in music, like in the studio today, you don't want to be controlled by your emotions, or God forbid, your hormones. Sometimes it's like that with your heart rate, too. Like sex, for instance, you can speed up and get it over with, or you can hold the tempo steady and make it feel better."

"And you, Dr. Boswell? Applying what you know about the mechanics of your own heart to music, if you had to produce a recording session right this instant, would you use a click? Or would you listen to the natural *bu-duh-rest* of the music and keep it as clean and tight as possible?"

"Depends," he says.

"Depends on what?" I ask.

"On who the drummer is. If it's you, I'll go with clean, tight, and natural every time. It doesn't get any hipper than that." He pulls me onto his lap, wraps his arms around me and places his head firmly against my heart. "Keep it steady now," he says. "You're in control."

No wonder I love this man.

* * *

In 1996, Franklin and I plan our wedding – a small ceremony on the beach in Bermuda. Dad and Olivia will attend, along with the Marys, Grandma Millicent and Grandpa Vernon. Franklin doesn't have any family, aside from two distant aunts. Leo and Liz will serve as our official witnesses.

The morning of the wedding I sit with my father on a veranda overlooking the ocean. He reaches for my hand. "Seems like a couple of days ago you were running off to Penn Academy with Leo. Now look at you, twenty-six years old and getting married."

"I never thought this would happen, did you?"

"Yes. No. I mean I always hoped you would fall in love and marry someone perfect. But I – "

"What?" Dad's eyes are glassy, like the sea. I'm not in the mood for a sloppy sentimental discussion. But I sense it's about to happen.

"I worried that losing your mother would – "

"What, Dad? Screw me up forever? Make me afraid to love someone because I'd be afraid that person would disappear?"

"Whoa. I wouldn't put it that way exactly, but yeah, I was worried."

"I'm fine, Dad."

"You fought so damn hard against all those shrinks I sent you to."

"I didn't need them."

"Yes, you did."

"They were pretty awful. I'm sure they were trying their best, but I hated them."

"Jane, I'm sorry. I wanted you to be able to talk to someone about what happened. I couldn't do it myself. You kept pushing me away. Plus I wasn't in the greatest shape, you know. I wanted someone, anyone, to help you. Leo was the obvious choice – since he was the only one you'd listen to – but I couldn't very well ask a thirteen-year-old to play therapist. "

"Yeah," I say. "He could have borrowed a notepad, a pipe and one of those tweed jackets with the suede elbow patches. You know Leo, even back then he was never one to miss a costume opportunity."

All of the sudden I realize that Olivia – the only person alive who knows what really happened to me in the fire – has never told my story to Dad. It doesn't seem fair that she knows and he doesn't. But at the same time I realize Dad doesn't need to hear the details of that night, he only needs to hear that I'm okay. Almost fourteen years have passed since the fire, I have a promising career and a wide-open future with a man I love, and poor Dad still isn't sure if I'll ever recover.

"Dad," I say. "Look at me. I'm okay. Really. I did talk to someone all those years ago. Olivia. When I was fifteen I told Olivia the entire story. She helped me. She guided me through that whole swamp of memories, and helped me understand what happened. She let me know that it was okay to start feeling things again, not just in music, but in life, too. Things like anger, or ambition. Like desire and passion. She showed me that it's okay to love another person, no matter how much you've lost. I mean, look at her. Look at what she's been through. Look at the way she loves you. And look how she cares about me. I'm surprised you didn't know that I talked to her."

"Olivia is very loyal," he says.

I'm on the verge of telling Dad what happened in the fire, but the look on his face tells me I shouldn't.

"Are you happy?"

"I'm as happy as I've ever been." His voice is a careful mix of confidence and embarrassment. "Seems like our Olivia Blue is very good at rescuing Bowmans."

"Not just us, Dad. Look at all those Gatehouse boys. Franklin says he owes his life to her."

"She's like a sorceress. I just wish she could work some of that magic on herself."

"What do you mean?" I ask, but I know. I've seen the fear in Olivia's eyes. She thinks no one picks up on it, but I do.

My Dad takes a moment to answer. "Nothing, Jane. Olivia's fine."

Dad can be loyal, too. "I'm proud of you, Jane."

"I know. Thank you, Daddy."

"I've gotten married twice now. Both times, a beautiful beginning waited for me at the end of the aisle. Beginnings are enchanting, Jane. But without endings, we'd never appreciate their magic."

"Oh, Dad," I say. His words touch me, but I roll my eyes so he doesn't know.

"Good luck, sweetie," he says, with tears running down his handsome face. "How I wish your mother were here."

"She'd tell me to kick ass."

"She'd tell you she loves you."

"That, too."

"That, too," he says. "I'd better go and get ready. We've got a big day ahead of us." And with that, my aging father touches the tip of my nose with his index finger, stands up, and – smiling – ambles back into the shade of the hotel.

* * *

Later, at the ceremony, it seems the entire world has been painted the color of a perfect twilight. The sand is pink, the clouds are copper, and the potted flowers lining the walkway to the sea are shades of apricot, crimson, and cherry red. The glowing faces of my family reflect the gilded sky, and I wonder if – during our afternoon naps – we've all been carried away by wedding fairies and dipped into buckets of liquid sunset.

In the moment right after the magistrate pronounces us husband and wife, I stare into Franklin's loving eyes. Deep brown, flecked with green, they remind me of an overflowing stream. He brushes his fingers against my cheek, and I feel all of the world's goodness protecting me. I feel my mother's love for my father, Grandpa Jack's devotion to Isabella, Dad's passion for Olivia, and Leo's commitment to Octavious. Now, I understand.

An open sea of forever-ness.

Franklin kisses me and I shiver. Like everyone else who has ever been in love, my heart beats in a triplet rhythm 100,000 times a day. With each beat it makes two loud noises, then, on the third part of the triplet – the silent part – the valves open. That's when life, golden and mystifying, comes rushing in.

Day Dreaming

As Grandpa Jack used to say, "I'm in a pickle." I've established myself as a big-bucks first-call drummer, and now everyone is afraid to hire me for the low-profile jobs I'd love to do. I want to work in smallish rooms again – clubs, bars, little theaters – but no one calls. Even though I do a fair number of recording sessions, the live jobs close to home aren't happening. I'm offered another major tour, this time with a hot young soul singer named Lovie Smythe, but I turn it down. Been there, done that. So I stay home and practice and wait for my husband to return from the hospital. It's a great life, but I miss playing in a group full time.

Enough. I've got the money. I'll start a band of my own.

Leo – whose agency now competes with all of the major offices – goes nuts. He wants to negotiate a record deal with one of the big labels. But I don't have a clear concept yet. I don't even have a band.

So I do what I always do when the subject is music. I call Olivia and ask her for advice.

"Look, you've got talent, you've got a big pile of money, and you're semi-famous, to boot," she says. "Do the thing you want to do. But do you know what that thing is?"

"I think so," I say. "I want to write, rehearse, and record. And then I'd like to play live in some local venues. No more touring."

"Good. You know what you want. Find the players and do it."

"I don't want to get into any of that marketing nonsense, and have to worry about image and all that."

"It's your band Jane, do what you want to do. Don't look for excuses before you even start. You'll find a hundred of them."

"I mean, maybe this sounds obnoxious, but I want to get the best players around. I want them to play at least as well as I do, or better. I don't care if they're old or young or male or female, whether or not they're famous, or what color they are. I just want the best."

"How is that obnoxious?"

"How do I know if they'll work with me?"

"You don't. You have to ask. And then you have to offer them a lot of bread."

"I don't want people signing on just I cause I've got money."

"What better reason is there? Look Jane, don't fool yourself. I don't care how good you are; no pro is going to play with you for low wages. You have to offer them something substantial. Don't test a musician's values or intentions by offering too little. If you do that, you'll never find anyone decent. You don't need to worry about money, but practically no one else in the biz has that luxury. You can afford to invest in yourself and your band, so do it. Offer your musicians what they're worth and you'll be a happy bandleader."

* * *

I start with Liz and she turns me down flat. She won't leave Bobby, which doesn't surprise me. Still, it pisses me off. She says she's on the five-year plan with him. I tell her that five more years with Bobby will buy her a one-way ticket to the loony bin, but she pretends not to hear me. Liz likes to play the role of the wise village elder when I'm in a dilemma, but she's a disaster when it comes to listening to her own advice.

So I call Raj. I need a singer, and I can't think of anyone better. Plus she plays the hell out of the alto. If I hire Raj, I get two musicians wrapped into one steamy bundle.

"Hey, Janey," she says. "I always knew I'd hear from you again. I saw you on MTV a couple of nights ago; I think it was the last video you made with Bobby. You sounded great. And you looked awesome. You ready to give me a try?"

"You're still a slut, I see."

"And proud of it," she says.

"What's happening with SOS?" I ask.

"We're dying a long slow death," she says. "Hasn't been the same since you left. Still doing a couple of cruise ships here and there, but Vegas and AC have dried up, almost all the shows are using playbacks these days. It sucks. Mostly we're on the bus, driving a billion miles a day, playing in towns with one restaurant and a church. What can I tell you? That we're lucky to be up to three-fifty a week now? I make four, but only cause I know how to guilt-trip Bernie."

"That's terrible."

"Oh yeah – we're back to wearing Mandy's strapless dresses because Bernie is desperate for bookings and he thinks the only way we can get work is to look like a bunch of Barbies. It's the lowest. And by the way, there are like no female funk drummers out there. At least not very many good ones. At one point Bernie was threatening to hire that fat guy from the Crisis Soul Band and put him in an evening gown."

"Now there's a gimmick," I say.

"Yeah, right. So what's the bread on your gig? You want a rehearsal band, or what?"

"At first, yeah," I say. "But then I'd want to record and start playing some around town. I'd don't want to go far from New York."

"New York gigs all pay about 50 bucks a night."

"I know."

"You're not gonna get rich doing that, but I guess you saved some money from the Bobby Angel tour."

"Uh, yeah."

"I heard you found yourself a guy – a nice rich doctor. Liz told me last time we talked."

"I did. We got married a couple of years ago."

"And here I thought you were saving yourself for me."

"Maybe in another life, Raj."

"Hey, my mom comes from India, don't forget. Half of me believes in reincarnation"

"You never know," I say.

"So. What's the deal on the gig?"

"Three grand a week. How's that?"

"Are you serious?" she asks.

"Damn straight. I'm completely serious about this, and I've got the money – just don't go asking a lot of questions. But there are some strings attached. You'd have to quit SOS and your first obligation would be to my band. I won't go nuts with scheduling or anything. But we'll play a lot. And you won't have to wear one of those awful dresses."

"Holy shit," she says."

"What?" I say.

"When do I start?"

"I want to get this thing going six months from now. It'll take me that long to organize everything else. But I'll put you on a retainer as soon as you give notice to SOS. Then we can brainstorm – I've got some big ideas, and you can help me."

A week later I track down Vapor Betty, the ace bassist from SOS. She had left Sisterhood of Soul about the same time I did, and began freelancing around Chicago, occasionally touring with Natalie Cole. Betty agrees to sign on with me, and I'm thrilled. She's the best bassist I've ever heard, especially for my kind of music.

Raj and I talk a lot about musicians. After a month of e-mail arguments hashing out the good and bad sides of all the candidates, we come up with a pretty impressive list. I force myself to call Ted Roblas, the pianist who was playing with Mom the night of the fire. He's a Latin-jazz musician, but lately I've been hearing him on some Latin-funk fusion records. His playing knocks me out, plus he plays keyboards – he's not just a piano purist. I try to talk myself out of hiring a musician who used to work with Mom, but no matter how many times I shuffle the list of the best keyboardists, Ted's name stays right on top. So Ted gets the call.

For the guitar chair, Olivia recommends Freaky Nash, and Raj agrees. I've never worked with him, but I've been listening to his old records for years. He had a major heroin problem a few years back, but he found God, cleaned up, and now he's playing better than ever.

The tenor position proves to be more complicated. At first I think I want to hire Dave Plank, but I end up with Steve Swain when Dave gets weird on me and starts ranting about girl musicians getting all the breaks. Nothing I haven't heard before, but I'm not going to tolerate that kind of talk in my own band. I've got a choice this time around. Steve gets the gig.

Steve tells me about his pal Wilson Rogers, a hotshot jazz trumpet player who wants to cross over and mess around with R&B. I've been reading a lot about him, so I check out some of his recordings and dig what I hear. He sings too, and Raj has worked with him and says he has a great attitude.

What a group: Betty, Freaky, Ted, and I in the rhythm section, with Raj, Wilson and Steve on horns. Seven musicians, and two of them sing. I start writing lyrics, working on grooves, pounding out melodies and chord changes in my studio at home, imagining how my band will sound. Man, I love saying that – my band. My band. My band.

PART IV: 2001

Planet Funk

Three busy years have passed, and Franklin – the amazing and still very sexy Dr. Boswell – has become a specialist in heart-lung transplants. I've become a specialist in my own right – an expert in my own kind of music. I turned thirty-one in June, and the two of us are thinking about a baby. Actually, Franklin is thinking about a baby. Seems like it's time, but I'm not sure. I'm too selfish. I have my band, I have Franklin, and I don't want to lose my groove. But I look out the window at the wisteria, recall Grandpa Jack's last letter to me, and think again.

My band – *Planet Funk* – is flying high. I've started my own record company, hiring, on Olivia's recommendation, Emmanuel Pritchard – the lead trumpet player from our old Gatehouse band – to run it for me. Emmanuel, aside from being a good musician, has a business degree and a strong computer background. Since most of our sales are on-line, that's important. The record company doesn't really turn a profit, but we manage to break even. Fine with me; we're up and running, and I've got control.

It sounds simple – my goal is to play and record the music I love. That's enough for me. In spite of what Leo says, I don't need to be a star. For what? So I can be rich? So I can be loved? I already have those things.

Mom thrived on her fame, but Grandma Isabella bolted when the celebrity monster knocked on the front door. She pulled the shades, hit the floor, and hid until the beast went away. I used to think she was forced to quit singing because it wasn't her place as a Cuban-Catholic woman to be a star. Now I know better. She quit because it wasn't her place as a human being. Some of us aren't cut out for stardom; it distracts us from our real intentions. It's weird; most people think that if you're in the music business, being famous is the ultimate goal. But really, for most of us, the only goal is to keep playing, to keep cranking it out, to keep getting better until the day we play that last hit and die.

Money sure helps. I hid my resources from my band for a long time, but eventually I got sick of the questions and confessed. Funny thing about being rich, even the people who like you resent you just a little bit. It doesn't matter if you're doing some good with your money. I mean, I'm not exactly using my cash to fund any kind of charitable save-the-world cause, but I do support seven musicians and an office staff. And we're making music that moves us and moves our listeners, so how can that be wrong? I pay my band very well in return for a full time commitment. Our debut album, *Planet Funk: Locked In*, made a big splash in 1997 by being the first R&B CD by an indie company to make the top ten on the Billboard charts.

Raj, who really does want to be a star, sang her ass off on *Locked In*. She gets frustrated with me because I'm not busting my butt booking world tours and splashy television shows, but I think after five years of good money and the squishy kind of fame that comes with a nonexistent marketing plan and consistently good work, she understands my reluctance to enter the celebrity game. I keep saying no to the big tours. We rehearse, we record, we sell CDs on the Internet, and we play small clubs in and around New York City. It's a good life. It's not a rock-star life, but it's good.

RHYTHM

Franklin's hellish schedule often keeps him away at night, and I like to be around when he comes home, no matter what time it is. Because we've built a recording studio in the basement of the brownstone, I'm almost always somewhere in the building, either messing with new tracks in the studio, or in the office with Emmanuel.

One day, as I'm finishing up the mix on a new song, Leo calls with an interview request from New York Magazine. Since I've never hired a publicist, the press contacts Leo. He knows I hate these things, but he also knows we have a gig coming up next month right here in Manhattan, at the Colony Club on West 76th Street. The club is new on the scene, and the owner – a friend of Leo's – has asked me to do this interview to help fill the place.

"Sure, Leo," I say. "Tell the reporter to meet me here at the brownstone."

"Is tomorrow okay?" he asks.

"Yeah," I say. "Tell him to come for lunch."

"It's a her."

"Good. One o'clock works for me."

"Her name is Alex McCoy."

"Got it. Are you coming to the Colony gig? You and Octavious haven't heard us play for a long time."

"We'll be there," he says. "I've got a table booked in the front."

"Good," I say. "Olivia and Dad will be there, too. You can sit with them."

"Can't wait," says Leo.

"Yeah," I say. "It'll be a great show."

* * *

Alex McCoy sits in the dining room and rubs her manicured fingers over Isabella's creamy Irish linen, while Jeanette, our housekeeper, slams down plates on the mahogany table. Jeanette, a sour-looking cookie-face woman who insists on wearing an Aunt Jemima rag on her head, comes from Poland. It's unusual, a cookie-faced person who is pissed off. Usually cookie-faces are jolly types. Leo says Jeanette is a freak of nature. I miss the Marys. I'd like to get one of the two of them to live here in New York with us, but they refuse to be separated. This strikes me as odd, since they never seemed to like each other – but who knows. So I stay out of snarling Jeanette's way and try not to let her bad mood bug me too much.

"Hope you're not a vegetarian," I say to the reporter, slicing into a piece of roast beef.

"Well, to be honest, I am. But that's okay; I'll sacrifice my diet for today. This roast looks lovely. It's, uh, so pink."

"That's the way I like it. *Chase the cow through the kitchen and cut off a slab.* That's what my Grandpa Jack used to say," I say.

"Do you mind if I record our conversation during lunch?" Alex asks.

"Not at all. In fact, it's better that way, don't you think?"

Alex is tall and rangy, with a horse-face that is actually attractive. Lately, Leo's face theories are being dashed to smithereens. Right here in this dining room we have a glum cookie, and a cute horse. I make a mental note to tell him, he'll have a field day with this.

"You mind if we start?" she asks.

"Shoot." I say.

"Let's get right to the point, then," she says. "You're Helen Bowman's daughter, right?"

Here we go, I think.

"Right," I say.

What's it like to live in her shadow? How did her death affect you? You were there the night of the fire, what were your feelings at the time? How do you feel about being the daughter of a glamour girl? What's it like to be a woman in a man's world? Why the drums – it's such a macho instrument – do you have something to prove? Do male musicians hit you on? How do you feel being compared to male drummers? What about your mother? What about your mother? What about your mother? How do you feel? How do you feel? How do you feel?

I feel like the top of my head might blow off, that's how I feel.

Just as I'm sure she couldn't possibly ask another stupid-ass question, she surprises me with a good one.

"Who do you credit with your success?"

Or maybe it's not her question that surprises me, but my answer.

"Olivia Blue," I say.

"Who's that? Never heard of her."

"She's a teacher."

"Oh."

Her boredom angers me. "Nobody ever talks about good music teachers, but they're the real heroes of the business," I say. "You listen to a good player and just assume that her talent has surfaced on its own. Like it's some kind of magic trick. But I can tell you from my own experience that's not true, at least not all the time."

"Oh, come on," says Alex. "You were born with talent. A natural. Your mother's daughter."

"Talent is imagination. We're all born with imagination, some of us with more, some with less, but it's there."

"Please," says Alex. "I took piano lessons for years and I was terrible."

"Did you practice?"

"Uh, no, not really."

"Well . . . maybe that was the problem, then, you never learned the technique of playing the piano, and as a result, your talent could never blossom," I say.

"I guess I just didn't have an aptitude for it," she says.

"Look," I say, "people always confuse technique and talent. Technique, or skill, differs from talent, because it's learned. If a kid works hard – like you did not – she'll learn the technique of an instrument. That's when her talent will start to shine, when she has built a strong technical basis for her talent. Think of it this way: Technique is the frame. Imagination, or talent, is the picture. For determined kids with normal lives – assuming the kid works her tail off to learn the technique – filling up the frame with imagination is easy. But for kids who have been through some sort of major trauma? It doesn't matter how hard we practice or how skilled we become. When it comes to that last step – the imagination part – we get lost."

"Why?"

Noticing that I have Alex's attention for the first time in the interview, I continue my little dissertation while trying to smooth the contemptuous tone of my voice. "Because imagining anything hurts too much. Little things might set us off – smells, tastes, colors. For me it was the clinking of glasses, the smell of smoke, the taste of strawberry ice cream. Traumatized kids protect themselves by turning off their imaginations, shielding themselves from evil memories. But they shut out the good along with the bad. It's tragic, really."

"So you were on your way down the tubes when you met Olivia, uh, what was her last name?"

"Blue. Olivia Blue. And don't put words in my mouth, I wasn't *going down the tubes*, I was just sort of numb. Anyway, Olivia found me when I was all frame and no picture – a big gilded chunk of chops with absolutely nothing inside. Empty. How do I say this? She was half psychologist, half music teacher, and she showed me how to pour my feelings into that empty frame. That's how she turned me into a real musician – by helping me retrieve my imagination. Teachers like Olivia are called music therapists, and believe me, we need more of them."

"Wow," says Alex.

"Wow is right. She's pretty amazing. I had a great drum teacher named Bruce Hammill, and my mom influenced me like crazy, but all of that would have meant nothing if Olivia hadn't stepped in."

"Where's she now?"

"She's still at Allegheny Gatehouse in Pittsburgh, Pennsylvania, teaching music classes to teenage boys and running an R&B band for kids who excel. It's her life's work. And by the way, she's married to my dad."

"Really? Your dad is Sam Bowman, the novelist, right?"

"Yeah."

"What a hunk. I love his books."

"Yeah, he's good, isn't he? Anyway, Olivia Blue is my stepmother, actually she's my mother now, and has been for a long time. She saved my life. If she hadn't helped me, I'd probably still be sitting in my childhood bedroom, listening to old records and thumbing through scrapbooks of photos."

"Do you do any writing?" she asks.

"Sure – I write music, if that's what you mean. But I also keep journals. Someday maybe I'll write a book. You know how that goes. Someday. Right now I'm having too much fun playing. There's nothing else I really want to do."

"Well, that's about it," she says, snapping off the recorder and pushing away her untouched plate of food. "I hope I get to meet this Olivia Blue someday. And that handsome Dad of yours, too."

"They'll be here next month when I play at the Colony Club with *Planet Funk*. You really should write about Olivia Blue. Everyone should know about the work she does."

"Once this article is published, they will," says Alex. "*Everyone* reads my features, you know. I promise you, Olivia Blue will be a big part of this story."

Later that evening, as I'm standing on my balcony overlooking the garden, it occurs to me that maybe this is not a good thing. I'm not sure how Olivia will react to such notoriety. But I let go of the bad feeling – at least I think I let it go – and listen to the uneven rhythm of the soft city night.

Rock Steady

Leo and Octavious lounge backstage in my dressing room at the Colony Club, sipping Taittinger Rosé and acting like power agents. The jacket of Leo's perfect black suit – Prada, I'm guessing – is draped over the back of his chair. Octavious massages Leo's neck. I look at these two gorgeous men, a solid fifteen years after they first met, and wonder how some people get so lucky with love the first time around. As far as I know Leo has never had another partner.

"When is Franklin coming?" Leo asks.

"Probably halfway through the first set," I say. "I was hoping he'd be here on time, but the hospital is nuts this week." As I'm talking, I scan the Alex McCoy article in this week's New York Magazine. "Did you read this?" I toss the magazine across the table.

"Only about twenty times," he says. "I think it's fabulous. And I love that old photo they used – the one of you with Olivia and your dad at the wedding. That dress you were wearing that night was something. Yeow! Brick house!"

"Don't remind me. If it was up to you I'd never be seen in anything but red spandex."

"Mighty, mighty – "

Octavious laughs, Leo drinks, I do some side stretches to warm up. My back isn't quite as strong as it was in my brick house days, and I have to be careful.

"Come on, Leo," says Octavious, "We ought to go claim our seats before that greedy-ass manager sells them."

"That Alex McCoy article did the trick," I say. "We're sold out for the next week, and they want to add on a couple of shows."

Leo throws his hands up in the air. "Marketing, my dear! You ought to try it more often."

"Leo," I say.

"Okay, I know. Thanks for doing this interview though, it really helped out the club."

"Sure," I say. He kisses me on the cheek.

"Play good, Janey," he says. He stands up, grabs his jacket, and turns to go. I'm so lucky to have him in my life. I count on him to surprise me, to make me laugh, to show me the beauty of clear thinking. Little Leo, the inventor of the Elixir of Youth and the Lego Eliminator, has grown into a stunning man of the world by staying true to himself and loyal to his friends. Awesome. He stops and swivels around, like he knows what I'm thinking.

"Have I told you lately how much I love you?" he asks.

"No. You're due."

"I love you."

"I know. I love you, too, Leo."

"But you really could use some kind of flashy accessory with that outfit. You're bordering on bland. Perhaps a brightly colored wrap or one of Isabella's sapphire brooches, or . . ."

"Leo. You're the only dude our age who uses the word *brooch*. And I can't wear a wrap, I'm a drummer for God's sake – I'd strangle myself."

"Sorry," he says, grinning. As Octavious drags him out of the dressing room, I hear him shout: "A simple pair of diamond pavé clip earrings?"

I look in the make-up mirror and apply enough goop to make me look respectable onstage. I grab a tube of mascara. Ah, Liz. To this day, I can't pick up a cosmetic product without thinking of her. Liz and I haven't talked for years. I saw her in a music video a couple of months back, and she looked sort of cartoonish. Her face was tight and sculpted, her lips puffy, her cheeks inflated. She had lost a ton of weight, and her breasts seemed pumped to the point of popping. Last I heard she was still working with Bobby Angel, but there are rumors circulating that Bobby dumped her and has taken up with his twenty-two year-old back-up singer. I wonder if Liz is pissed or sad or relieved. Or if maybe the rumors are wrong and Liz is the one hanging with the twenty-two year-old. Who knows. Funny, isn't it, how friends slip away from each other. I've been meaning to call her for a long time, but I haven't. I thought I'd bring her into *Planet Funk* someday, but now we're such a tight band I don't dare hire anyone new.

Since I'll be spending so much time at the club in the next week, I've decorated the dressing room with photos of my family and friends. I've always had a thing for photos, and when I started touring with Bobby I got in the habit of taping a few of them to my dressing room mirror. Tonight, Dad and Olivia smile from the snapshot directly in front of me. Another picture features the Marys – all dressed up and standing in front of the Waldorf – peering out at me with a whacky mixture of pride and suspicion. A wedding photo of Franklin is propped on the table against the wall, and an autographed photo of Leo sits opposite it. Leo is the only agent I know who autographs 8×10 glossies of himself. Maybe the stars were crossed when nature was distributing diva genes – he was certainly meant to be an opera singer, a movie star, or at least a news anchor. "Celebrity is a state of mind," he always says. "It doesn't matter if you actually do anything."

Two framed photos of Mom rest on my right side, close enough that I keep brushing against them with my elbow. After years of studying all of her pictures, I've decided these two are my favorites. In the first, she's playing at the Fillmore West in San Francisco, sweating and hitting her congas so hard that the sides of the photo threaten to curl. In the second picture, she's the age I am now, and she's pregnant with me. She's sprawled on her back in the rose garden of the Sewickley Heights house, knees bent, her eyes closed, her arms stretched towards the sky, fingers spread wide apart, like she's trying to touch a cloud.

My cell phone rings. It's Franklin.

"There's a problem with one of my patients," he says. "I'll be there towards the end of the first set, assuming the traffic isn't too crazy."

"Okay," I say. I'm disappointed, just a little. But at least he'll get to hear the second set, which will probably be better.

"I love you," he says. "Have fun, and play one for me."

"I love you, too Dr. Boswell. Now go save some lives."

"I'll do my best. Keep it steady, Janey."

"You, too."

From the main room of the club I hear chairs scraping, glasses and silverware clanking, people chattering and laughing. When I was a little girl this pre-show racket thrilled me. For many years after the fire, the same sounds made me want to hide. Now, I understand they're just sounds, nothing more than noise – the random clatter of too many human beings stuffed into a space that's too small; eating, drinking, telling old stories, having first dates, or endless arguments, holding hands, touching knees, worrying about their children, complaining about their parents, wondering when the rain will finally stop. They shift in their seats and jabber, checking their watches, and waiting for the entertainment to start, as if their own lives weren't enough of a show.

I take one last look at myself in the mirror and slip out of the room to talk through the set list with my band.

Take Me There

"And now Ladies and Gentlemen, the Colony is proud to present one of the hottest bands on the scene today. You all know drum star Jane Bowman from her years with Bobby Angel. Jane has been voted best R&B drummer three years in a row by Musician Magazine. Now, she's tearin' it up with her own band – Planet Funk! Planet Funk topped the charts last November with their debut recording Locked In, *coasting in the number-one spot in the R&B category for a record-breaking seven weeks with their powerful single 'Give it To Me Now.' In the last six months, they've – "*

My phone vibrates. I glance at it and see that it's Franklin. "Hi!"

"I'm on my way, just wanted to let you know. You hit in a minute, right? Whose voice is that?"

" – and internationally, Planet Funk has received record of the year awards in Japan, Germany, and Sweden. Ladies and Gentlemen, they've won – "

"I'm backstage," I say. "Leo wrote some sort of epic introduction for the club owner and he just keeps going on and on. I hate to admit it, but I like it. It's so cool having my own band announced like this. There's some kind of buzz in the air, I can feel it!"

" – they've also won the iTunes Best New Band of the Year award, and recently appeared on the MTV Hot-Mix Live

Showcase. This year they're nominated in not one, but two Grammy categories for their latest recording Take Me There. *So let's not waste another moment – "*

"Gotta go! Love you."

"– and let's have a big New York City Colony Club welcome for Jane Bowman and Planet Funk!"

We race onstage. We start with "Playin' For Keeps" and the band sounds hot. Raj is positioned down front, and she's the focal point for the audience – teasing, wailing, and throwing down hot licks. I might be the bandleader, but she's the eye-and-ear-candy for the audience. Vapor Betty is my reliable workhorse on the bass – without her, the whole thing wouldn't groove and click like it does.

I don't much like to break the mood of the music, but I force myself to make some announcements – it's my band after all, and Leo tells me that people want to hear that I can put a sentence together, not just whack the drums. I tell a couple of silly stories, like Leo has coached me: *And then when Raj and I sat in with Sting – blah blah blah – and you know my favorite part about playing for a real New York audience like you guys is – yeah, yeah, yeah.*

I look down at Leo and he gives me the thumbs-up sign. I think I sound ridiculous, but the audience seems to like what I say. I'm pretty sure I hear my dad laughing at one of my stupid jokes. But really, I just want to shut up and play the drums.

Steve plays a smokin' solo on a sexy ballad called "Back to You." By the time we get to "Queenie," a song I wrote a long time ago for Liz, the band is cooking so hard I swear I can see steam coming off the floor. Raj grinds out the "Queenie" lyric, fierce and wild, flexing her vocal muscles, twisting and bending phrases that serpentine through the tune like a jewel-covered serpent. Every once in awhile – when things are really tight – Betty looks over at me and winks. The band pounds through the set, pumping out groove after groove. The really cool thing about this kind of music is that when it's played right, it feels easy and sensuous, even when it's forceful. The smoothness of the groove disguises the complexity of the rhythmic line; it's a feel-good vibe that sounds simple, but isn't.

We bust into my tune "Night Owl," and the rhythm section hammers it out while the horn players trade ballsy solos. Sweat rolls down the back of my shirt, and flashes of copper and bright silver leap over my cymbals as the solo section reaches its peak. I think the lighting guy likes this tune – he's getting awfully creative during the solos – but this strobe effect is way too much. I have to tell him to chill; it's not his show.

Olivia and Dad sit at a front table, holding hands, next to Leo and Octavious. As we finish the set, they leap to their feet with the rest of the crowd, cheering and stomping. Leo blows a kiss to me before he scoots away to meet and greet. Looks like Franklin still hasn't arrived. Too bad, he would have loved that last number. With the crowd still hooting, I slide out from behind the drums, and head to the edge of the stage.

"Yeah!" says Raj, as she hugs me. "Doesn't get any better than this!"

"Yeah," I say. "Yeah!"

Joining hands with Betty and Raj, who in turn grab the hands of the other musicians, we laugh and take a deep bow together. I bend over, my head and heart bursting with joy. Cutting through the applause, I hear a razor-sharp clatter – loud and crisp. Maybe someone has dropped a tray of glasses. Or maybe something has blown on the mixing board. Shit, I'll have to deal with a pissed-off soundman during intermission. But then I hear it again, that same jagged noise, this time followed by screams. As I lift my head, the brittle snap of automatic gunfire pulls my attention to its source. I think for a moment that it can't be gunfire . . . it's another drummer . . . it's someone playing a weird single stroke pattern. No, I don't understand – it must be a gun.

A large man stands in the aisle, several tables away from the stage. Because of the spotlights shining from the back of the house, I see him in silhouette as he staggers towards me. My legs are numb, and my heart begins to thud.

Breathe.

Focus.

Stay in the moment.

The weapon looks tiny in his swollen arms, like he's carrying a toy machine gun won at a neighborhood carnival. Why is everyone panicking? *I am the one who panics; everyone else stays calm.* That's the way it works, isn't it? The shots and screams sound fake, like sound effects on a scary amusement park ride.

Breathe.

I'm confused. I stay frozen in place, thinking my imagination has gotten the best of me, that my perspective is being warped by an anxiety attack, that if I stand here long enough, people will begin to applaud again, I'll take another bow, and get back to my dressing room where I'll be able to calm down and maybe even laugh about this. But everyone around me is diving for cover, scrambling under tables and chairs, behind racks of keyboards and amplifiers. Chaos breaks out in the back of the club by the exits – as people struggle and push through heavy wooden doors.

What the fuck is going on?

A bloated silence, broken by whimpers and moans, followed by another round of gunfire – the man shoots at people huddled on the floor near the stage. From the back of the club I hear screams and panicked shouts for help. But in the area on the stage and close to it, the silence, the stillness, is terrifying. The man has made it clear that he will shoot anyone who moves or speaks.

Breathe.

This is real. I turn my head, looking for a way out.

He swaggers towards me. The quickening thump of my own pulse slams against the inside of my head. As the man approaches, I hear bodies shuffling behind him, the sounds of people crawling on their hands and knees, trying to leave the stage area. I shudder.

Breathe, damn it Jane, breathe.

The man approaches. Something crunches under his feet.

I search the house for Dad or Leo, but it's too dark to see anything more than odd shapes and shadows. I remain center stage. Alone. Where is everybody? Why am I standing here by myself? The others must be hiding under tables and chairs. I clutch at an imaginary table leg, and hold on, tight, just like I did all those years ago, the night of the fire. But I'm grabbing at air.

Someone groans.

"Where is she?" he says, the gun pointing up at me. My knees tremble. He moves closer and I can see him clearly. My shaking body wants to collapse, but a strange force holds me upright.

"Who?" I say.

"That fucking whore," he says.

"I don't know who you're talking about." My voice is high and wobbly.

I see the hatred in his eyes. And I know. I know who he is. My stomach lurches.

Strange phone calls, Olivia's worried face, and my father's unease, all leading to this one, horrible moment.

"My wife," he roars. "My fucking whore nigger wife."

I choke back the bile rising in my throat. It tastes metallic, like dirty coins.

"I don't know," The muted colors of the room spin around me – over me, under me, through me.

"Tell me. I know she's here. Tell me where she is or I'll splatter your fucking brains all over those fucking drums of yours."

"I'm here, Bruce," says Olivia. Her calm voice chills me. "Don't hurt her."

Breathe.

Focus.

Stay in the moment.

Olivia limps out of the shadows and to the edge of the stage. I can see blood splattered on her jacket. My legs shake harder, my vision blackens around the edges and my heart pounds, louder and louder, so loud that I'm sure he can hear it. I look at the floor, but the dizziness gets worse, so I look back at him again.

Breathe. Try to breathe.

"I'll do what God tells me to do," he says. "I've got a shit load of explosives strapped to myself." He turns, pulls open his jacket, and reveals a vest with wires and sticks of dynamite held into place with silver duct tape. "Anyone makes a wrong move, I'm blasting the whole fucking lot of you straight to hell."

"Bruce, your problem is with me," says Olivia. "Let these other people go. They don't deserve this."

"They're sinners," he says.

"Yes, we're all sinners," she says, "but I'm the worst one. Let the others go."

"Not until they watch you die. Get up on the stage," he says to Olivia, prodding her with his gun. "Next to the other whore." He aims the gun back at me.

"Olivia?" I say. I'm crying now, afraid to move, afraid not to, afraid that he's going to shoot me, afraid that he'll shoot Olivia, afraid that I'll have to watch. I've lost one mother – I can't lose another. I try to extend my hand to Olivia, but I'm too weak."Focus, Jane," she whispers, her eyes steady and straight-ahead. "It's okay. Stay cool. Just stay cool. "

"On your knees," he says to me. I look at Olivia. She nods. I kneel.

"Take your clothes off," he says to Olivia.

"Bruce . . ." she says.

"Now!" he screams. "Or I shoot your little whore step-daughter."

I try to focus but my mind is racing. Why doesn't Dad do something? Where is Leo? And why isn't Franklin here by now? Please, please, someone help us. *Please.* The other musicians are all cowering onstage – pretending to be dead, trying to stay invisible. I'm freezing cold, as cold as I've ever been in my life. My knees, pressed into the floorboards, have stopped quivering, but the solid muscles in my upper thighs seem scrawny and limp. I glance again at Bruce and spot the desperation and rage surging though him. It doesn't matter what Olivia does, he'll kill all of us. I'm certain of this.

Breathe.

Focus.

Stay in the moment.

I hear a distant voice.

Forgive me, Jane. I look to Olivia, but she's fumbling with the buttons on her jacket. She has not spoken.

Forgive me, Jane.

When Olivia catches me looking at her, she blinks twice.

I hear it again.

Forgive me, Jane. Again. *Forgive me, Jane.*

It comes from someplace inside me, a place that is quiet and safe.

Forgive me, Jane.

The voice swoops through my body, calming, soothing, chipping away at my panic, slowing my heartbeat, clearing a path for whatever lies ahead.

Forgive me, Jane.

It's the voice of my mother, just the way I remember it. Or is it? No. No. It's Olivia's voice. I look back to her. She's not speaking, but still I hear her calling to me.

Forgive me, Jane.

Abruptly, every light in the club switches on – full force – flash flooding the room with agonizing brightness.

Shielding my eyes, I look down at the tables in front of me, and see my father's body, collapsed over the table, blood seeping from the back of his head and out of his mouth onto the white tablecloth.

My father.

"DAD!!!"

I feel the force of my leg muscles pushing my body away from the ground, and I fly off the stage through a dazzle of lights, free-falling – in slow motion – like a child tumbling from a jungle-gym, hoping to land in the outstretched arms of her parents.

Instead, I land on top of Bruce. He's slippery with oily sweat and freshly smeared blood. He howls in my ear as my fists pound against his face. I kick at his shins with all my strength – hard, harder. I bite down and I feel something in my mouth. I think it's his cheek, or is it his neck? Harder – bite harder. *Now*. I taste blood. I spit the flesh back into his face as I gag.

I put my thumb in his left eye and he screams – so I push harder. My legs lock around his upper torso and I pin his arms. He pushes back – don't let him – fight harder, fight. His gun fires into the floor. My hands are around his throat and I press, harder – harder. More – press – push. His hair smells like kerosene. If I can knock him to the ground, I can take him. I have to kill him. But he won't fall. As I continue to gouge at his eyes and tear at his flesh, my thighs squash up against the thick belt of explosives tied around his waist. There's a shout. It's Leo. I can't see him but I can hear him, yelling *Jane, Jane, Jane*. From the corner of my eye, in a blur of confusion and desperate chaos, I spot Olivia at my father's side. Someone jumps on Bruce from behind – is it Leo? – and the three of us topple to the floor.

My bloody hands push harder against Bruce's throat. I hear myself screaming my father's name, and then, suddenly, a blast rockets me through the room. Huge blue and yellow chunks of debris, wind, and light rush past me, and I hear distorted segments of unfamiliar music fading in and out of my awareness, as if I'm playing with a car radio, searching for the perfect song.

Now it stops. It's too quiet, too dark.

As I fight against the shadows, a dense silence begins to smother me. I smell something wet – earthy, and I feel myself slipping deeper and deeper into a noxious crevice of no return.

Breathe.

Again.

Breathe.

Stay in the moment.

Look – oh, yes, I see something – a single tiny beam, like a pin-spot. I focus on the spot and it grows larger, drawing me away from the dimness, into a lush haze of amber light above me. I float past the wreckage and smoke, and hover over the bedlam on the nightclub floor. Looking down, I can see the madness below me, but I can't hear it, and the scene unfolds like a silent movie version of everything that's wrong with the world. Dead bodies, broken spirits, musical instruments blown to shreds, glazed eyes, human beings who – if they survive at all – will build barbed fences around their tortured memories.

All of this destruction, in the name of one hateful man's God.

Franklin leans over my body, giving hushed commands to frazzled rescue workers. Leo – his mouth wide open in a soundless scream – cradles Octavious in his arms. Two men, their faces gray and resolute, cover Dad's body and prepare to carry him away. Olivia crawls through the chaos and rubble. She reaches my body and stretches out her hand to me, but I don't take it. Franklin leans across my chest, takes her hand and places it on my heart. He strokes her hair and settles her on the floor next to me.

The light in the club intensifies as I watch all of us – even Bruce – become whole again. We morph into the children we once were: innocent, beautiful, quirky – singing songs and dancing in rows, jumping in evaporating puddles, playing in damp sand, chasing rays of sun with magic wands – full of music, laughing, unaware, alive.

Locked In

"How close did I come?" I ask Franklin, who sits next to my hospital bed. Startled, he leans closer to me. These are the first words I've spoken in weeks.

"What, Janey?" he says. "How close did you come? To what?"

"To dying."

"Very close. I love you, Jane. You'll be okay; you know that, don't you? I know this is terrible for you, but you'll be okay. Keep talking. Please keep talking to me."

I turn away from him and stare at the wall. I can't cry anymore. The physical pain is fading, but I still have phantom pain where my right arm used to be. Sometimes it's an unrelenting itch; sometimes it burns so much it makes me scream. But usually it's an ache, a low-grade throb that keeps me awake at night and tricks me into thinking that my arm will come back.

The first few days after the surgery, groggy and unable to move because of the traction devise on my leg, I thought I was dreaming, that perhaps I was dead, that I had entered an alternative afterlife where everything was hushed, sterile and covered in layers of gauze. It was only later, when the nurses cut back on the morphine and removed the IV from my left arm, that I was able to reach over and touch the bandaged stump. That's when I knew I was still alive.

"I wish I died."

He listens.

"If I had known, when I was outside of myself – that moment when I had a choice to live or die – if I had known my arm was gone, I would have chosen to die."

"What did you see?" His hand touches my face. "You weren't conscious, Jane, you couldn't have really seen anything."

"I saw them carrying Dad away. I saw Leo holding Octavious's body, I saw Olivia crawling over to me. I saw you take her hand and put it on my heart."

"But you didn't see the damage to your arm. Interesting."

"I'm not a fucking medical experiment Franklin."

"I'm sorry," he says.

"I couldn't see that my arm was mangled," I yell. "You were blocking my view of that part of my body. I was above you, looking down."

"I was applying a tourniquet."

The phone rings. Franklin answers. It's Leo.

"She's talking," says Franklin. "Please. Come.

* * *

The hospital air smells like spoiled cafeteria food, chlorine, and urine. Leo arrives with a huge bouquet of yellow roses and a take-out container of mashed potatoes. "For you," he says, kissing me on the cheek. "I hear you're talking." He glances at Franklin, and pulls a chair over to my bedside.

"Fuck this," I say, flinging the potatoes across the bed with my left arm. I burst into tears. "Fuck this."

"Good," Leo says. "That's a start."

* * *

Dad and Octavious were both killed in the club that night. They died instantly, the backs of their heads blown away by

Bruce's first round of shots. They were murdered while they stood and cheered for me – this is more than I can fucking stand.

Leo had gone to the back of the club to meet Franklin, who had arrived during the last number of the set. Waiting for the police, they watched the onstage drama from behind the service bar, helpless, trying to figure out the right strategy to save us. It was Leo's idea to throw the master light switch, hoping the glare would distract Bruce long enough for Olivia and me to get out of the way, and for Franklin and Leo to tackle him from behind. I destroyed their plan when I dove on top of Bruce.

There were two explosions. The first one – the device around Bruce's waist – killed Bruce, mangled most of my right arm, and blew me across the room. The second – planted under one of the tables and detonated by an apparatus attached to the first bomb – exploded a second later. The police say that the second bomb did most of the damage – it killed six more people and injured twenty-three others, most of whom had been closest to the stage. The other musicians, who had taken cover as soon as the gunfire started, suffered wounds and broken bones, caused by a large ceiling beam that crashed to the stage when the second bomb exploded. Olivia sustained horrible internal injuries, and remains in intensive care, in a coma. Franklin tells me she may never recover.

After the second explosion, Leo and Franklin raced to the front of the club. Franklin put the tourniquet on what was left of my arm, did what he could for Olivia, and then, taking charge like the doctor he is, attended to the other victims. The rescue teams were there within ten minutes. In that time, Franklin watched six people die.

I wish I had been one of them.

As for Bruce, he was honored by a quiet burial service at his church in Mount Laurel, New Jersey. One of the New York newspapers called him a barbaric monster, reporting that he had been arrested on abuse charges a total of six times in the last five years – each time escaping a prison sentence because the victim refused to testify. The last arrest had resulted in a conviction, but Bruce avoided jail by committing to an eight-month stay at an upscale New Jersey rehabilitation facility. After his release, he resumed his activities at the Mount Laurel Fundamentalist Church of Christ. The Post printed a photo of him at a church function, and ran it next to a picture taken by a tourist's video camera from the back of the club minutes before the blast.

At Bruce's home in Mount Laurel, police department investigators found a large box of newspaper clippings, reports filed by private detectives, and photos of Olivia. He had been stalking her for over twenty years, waiting for a chance to strike.

* * *

A therapist has been teaching me how to write with my left hand. When no one is watching, I practice my signature. It looks like the careful scrawl of a second-grader. I wonder if I'll ever be able to dress myself, go to the toilet alone, eat a meal without someone having to cut it for me.

The orthopedic surgeon tells me I'll limp for the rest of my life. Most of the bottom part of my right leg was crushed in the explosion. I'm walking a little now, with help, but I can't support my weight on crutches because of my missing arm. The Marys have moved to New York to help, and the two of them take turns going back and forth between Olivia's room and mine. They beg to assist with my physical therapy, but I'm too ashamed to let them see me try to walk. Instead, I depend on assorted therapists and nurses – kind strangers in white coats with coaxing smiles.

I used to look in the mirror and see Mom staring back, but she's not there anymore. With my jutting bones and healing wounds, I see a person I can't recognize, pulled from almost certain death, dropped back into life like an unwanted penny tossed into a wishing well.

I want my Dad to be alive. I want Octavious and everyone else murdered that night to live again. I want Olivia to get better. I want my mother. I want all these things, but most of all, I want my arm back. I hate this. I hate myself. I hate this world.

If I can't be a musician, then I don't know who I am.

* * *

Visitors rush to my bedside but I can't tell which ones are hallucinations and which ones are real. The medication makes me feel like I'm swimming through deep, murky water. Most days, I can't seem to surface.

The Marys, always the Marys, flitting in and out of the room, bringing me food I can't eat, films I won't watch, CDs I can't bear to hear. Mary One sings until I want to scream, Mary Two makes big pots of English tea that nauseate me. I push them away with silence, but still they come, night and day, pestering me with loving gestures.

Grandma Millicent and Grandpa Vernon spend a week in the city, visiting me and supervising the cremation of Dad's body. I can't even look at them, let alone hold a conversation. There's a makeshift memorial service for Dad in my hospital room. I pull the pillow over my head and refuse to listen to the

Episcopal priest hired for the occasion. From under the covers I catch muffled segments of phrases. *Tragedy*, I hear, and *heartbreaking, loving husband, brave, unique, good father, good father, good father.* Stop. Just stop.

I won't talk to my grandparents. They leave with my father's ashes.

* * *

Raj arrives one day, her arms full of CDs. Why does everyone think I want to listen to music? Raj's wrist is still in a cast and she has a nasty scar over her right eyebrow. Leo has paid the band's salaries for the remainder of the year, and terminated the contracts. Raj talks about doing a benefit concert.

A benefit concert? For whose benefit?

"I don't need the damn money," I tell her.

"I *know*," she says, "I was thinking about the families of the other victims in the club that night. There were other victims, remember? Other people died. Other people were injured."

I almost forgot.

I think about killing myself. I don't know what I'm feeling. Everything. Nothing.

Liz doesn't visit, but she sends flowers with a card that says *keep going.* Fuck you, Liz.

* * *

"Jane," says Leo. "Look. I know the last thing you want is another pep talk, but I promised Franklin I'd do my best. He doesn't know how to help you. I don't either, but I told him I'd try."

Leo looks worn out. Rugged creases run across the contours of his once smooth face, turning him from an old boy into an old man in the space of a summer. I saw the same thing happen to Dad when Mom died.

After the bombing, Leo flew with Octavious's body back to Pittsburgh, where old friends from the Gatehouse mourned his death. Spanky Wainwright stood at Leo's side when he spoke at the memorial service. I should have been there, but it will be a long time before I'm allowed to leave the hospital.

I don't understand how Leo can wade through his misery and still find the energy to try and help me, but that's exactly what he's doing. Except it's not helping, it's just making everything worse. I wish I could help him, but I can't get it together to say anything nice.

"Go away Leo."

"No."

"I'm sorry."

Silence.

"Octavious had a perfect bird-face, you know," he says.

"Yeah."

"Sort of like Olivia. All the best people have bird-faces."

"Stop," I whisper. "How can you be so damn normal?"

"I don't feel normal, but at least I'm making an effort, okay?" Leo begins to yell. "I feel like shit. I still cry about every five minutes. I can't set foot in the office, I can't walk through the front door of our apartment without feeling like I'm having a nervous breakdown, but what am I supposed to do? He's gone. Just like your dad is gone. We can't change that, no matter how many gallons of tears squirt out of our eyes. No matter how pissed off we get. You should know better, you've been through this before, with your mom. We've got to move on."

"Back then I still had music."

"You still have music, Jane."

"How the hell am I supposed to play Leo? I'm like a god-damned cripple, here. I can't walk and I only have one arm, and you're telling me to *move on*?"

"You've got a loving husband. You've got me."

"Great. Just great."

"Listen, you want to know what I think?"

"No."

"The way I see it, you've got three choices. One, you could commit suicide. That would probably take the least amount of effort. Two, you could go loony and let them dope you up and put you in an institution. Three, you could work your butt off and try to get on with your life. Your career might be over but your life is not."

"Yeah, right."

"Life won't be the same, but that doesn't mean it won't be worthwhile, in some way that you can't possibly imagine at this moment. You'll have to take a different path, that's all."

"That's all? Which path? All I ever wanted to do was play."

"I don't know which path. There are a million roads to take; you just have to find one that makes sense."

"Yeah, it'll say: One-armed gimpy drummer, limp this way."

"Maybe the prosthesis will help you play again."

"Leo, if I'm lucky, the prosthesis will help me pick up a glass of juice. It will not help me play the drums. Shut up about the goddamned prosthesis."

Leo laughs.

"What's so damn funny?" Big teardrops splash onto my sweatshirt.

"You," he says. "It's the first glimpse of the old Jane I've seen since this happened."

"Alert the media."

"Well, you know – "

"Leo!"

"Just kidding."

"I know."

"Want to hear my one prosthesis joke? I've been practicing it for just this moment."

"No."

"So I said to the girl with the wooden leg, Peg . . ."

"Leo. Stop." But I'm laughing, sort of.

He hugs me, wipes the goop from my nose, and begins to cry. As I hold his hand and squint through the hospital window at the September morning, the clear and cheerful blue sky fractures my heart.

I wonder how long we'll stay here, waiting to be rescued.

Listen and You'll Hear

On September 16th, five days after I watched the World Trade Center towers tumble to the ground like too-tall columns of children's building blocks, I lie in bed and stare at the television. The stunned nurses on my floor – several of whom are missing relatives and friends – keep their eyes on the TV, completing their chores, checking my blood pressure, administering meds, wheeling me to therapy sessions, coaching me to try harder, to push myself a little more. But their voices are hollow, their faces gray.

Towers fall. Even the biggest and strongest of them.

One nurse, whose sister is missing, comes to work each day with swollen eyes and shaking hands. I know how it is, I want to tell her, you can't sleep, you can't think, you can barely breathe. I sense her agony, but I'm too worn out to offer anything more than a whispered *I'm sorry.* I'm sure she doesn't hear me.

The newspapers stop talking about Bruce and the nightclub bombing. Everything in the city revolves around the 9/11 terrorists, the missing people, the city at a standstill, the nation in crisis. From my hospital bed, I flip through the channels, cringing as I watch families taping pictures to walls and makeshift bulletin boards.

I gaze at the photos on my nightstand, the ones that had been retrieved from my dressing room the night of the bombing. I lay them face down, then turn them over again.

"Hold on to your photos," I say to the television screen. "They might be all you have left."

Angry, I grab the remote control to turn off the TV, but right before I hit the OFF button, the location switches to a provisional canteen that's providing food and shelter to exhausted Ground Zero rescue workers. What I see and hear takes my breath away.

A young woman in a blue denim jacket, seated on a folding chair on the side of the hall, plays the cello. As her bow sweeps across the strings, the clarity of her music punctures the quiet of the tension-filled room. The camera pans across the ashy faces of the workers, and I watch them, one by one, take in the small miracle of her performance. Just like the men and women in the makeshift cafeteria, I find my spine straightening. My heartbeat slows and my breathing becomes more even. I close my eyes. For the first time since the bombing, the anger fades. Just a little. I listen to the music. And I hear.

There is still beauty and courage in this world.

Listen.

* * *

Because of the chaos in lower Manhattan, it's almost impossible to get around the city. But Franklin and Leo always find a way to visit me. When they arrive this evening, the story about the cellist appears on the national news. We watch together in silence as the camera goes to a close-up of the musician. Her coiled hair wraps around the top of her head, accenting the sharp contours of her golden-brown face. Long-boned, regal – bird, pure bird, catching hold of the melody and soaring through the room.

It can't be, but it is.

"Leo?" I ask. "Do you see it?"

"Yeah. I was afraid to say anything."

"Franklin?"

"Yes. She looks like Olivia."

My face grows hot.

"Are you okay, Janey?" asks Franklin. "You need some water?"

"Shhh, listen," I say.

The reporter's voice-over says: "The musician claims she felt compelled to help. Because of the lack of public transportation, she carried her cello from her Murray Hill apartment down to Ground Zero. She refused to be interviewed and would only tell us her first name – Kate."

"It's her. It must be. It's Kate, Olivia's daughter."

"Shhh," says Leo.

The reporter continues: "According to some of the people here at the hall, she performs occasionally on the Lexington Avenue platform of the Grand Central subway station. Other than that, she remains a mystery woman."

I think of Olivia, three floors away from me, and wonder what she would make of this – her own daughter, a musician.

"Leo," I say.

"Shit," says Leo.

"What?"

"I know what you're thinking," he says. "And I can't do it."

"You have to find her. You have to find Kate and bring her to Olivia. Please, Leo."

"Franklin?" asks Leo.

Franklin nods, too choked up to speak.

"Please, Leo. Find her."

"Okay, and assuming I do find her, what do I tell her? Kate has a good reason to remain anonymous."

"Tell her the truth. Kate's not like her father, I can tell just from what I've heard and seen. She needs to know about Olivia. She needs to know who her mother is. Please, Leo."

"Jane, I – "

"Please. Leo. For me. For Olivia."

"For all of us," says Franklin.

"Okay. I'll try." Leo looks out the window and tries not to cry.

"Could you help me into the wheelchair? I'd like to go visit Olivia. There are a few things I need to tell her."

"She can't hear you, sweetie," says Franklin.

"She'll hear me," I say. "She will."

Still

The respirator controlling Olivia's breathing hisses at me as I enter her room. As often as I've been to visit, I still can't get used to the sound of it – clanking and insistent, the sounds you'd expect to hear coming from an automobile assembly line or a furnace room, not from a machine attached to a human being. Franklin helps me settle next to Olivia's bed and asks the nurse to leave me alone with her for a few minutes. Franklin leaves, too.

The Marys have been massaging her limbs with thick moisturizers, but her skin seems parched and chalky. Her long arms curl inward; her fingers are twisted into tight fists. Stretched over the pillow is her thin blue baby blanket, washed and pressed by Mary Two. Against her dark skin, the faded color of the blanket looks washed out, almost white.

The Marys have decorated Olivia's room with photos – those damn photos – of Dad, of me, of Leo and Octavious, and even one of Billie Holiday. Maybe Olivia will never wake up and realize that half of us are gone. But maybe she knows. Franklin says that before she lost consciousness at the club, she saw every horrible thing that had happened.

Like a complicated electronic score for a dance of death, the equipment monitoring her heart rate beeps in syncopation to the respirator. I take her hand, and begin: "Olivia, I know you can hear me. Of course you can hear me, you're the best listener I know. But for once, I'm not gonna talk about me. This is about you, and it's very important, so stay with me, okay? Olivia, we know where your daughter is. She's okay, Olivia. Listen to me. Your daughter is alive and healthy and playing the most beautiful music you've ever heard. We saw her on television. She plays the cello. And she's like you, Olivia. She's helping people. There are so many terrible things happening all around us right now, and Kate is helping people. With music. She looks just like you, too. Leo has gone to find her, to bring her to you. Are you listening Olivia? Kate is okay. She has survived. She's a musician."

I repeat these words over and over again, until my voice begins to crack and strain. Just before the nurse asks me to leave, Olivia's right fist opens, reaches for something – perhaps her mother, maybe her child – then curls up again, like a flower closing its petals at dusk.

* * *

Leo finds Kate and tells her the whole story. I imagine an emotional mother and daughter reunion, with Kate weeping at her mother's bedside and Olivia waking from her coma. That's the way it might play in a movie, accompanied by a gushy orchestral score with French horns and swelling strings. But it's not to be.

Kate refuses to see Olivia, but she agrees to talk to me. I'm daydreaming when she arrives. I see her reflection in the small mirror opposite the door. She sneaks into the room with the hesitance of a third grader called to the principal's office, and stays far away from me, at the foot of my hospital bed.

"Thank you for coming." I struggle to sit up straight in my bed.

"I've had nothing to do with my family for a very long time," she says. "I'm only here because I wanted to tell you how sorry I am. For what my father did. I'm so sorry."

"Thank you," I say. "But you're not your father."

"Maybe." Her eyes shift. "He's still inside me, though, like some sort of chronic infection, you know? I can't make him go away."

I stare at her, but don't say anything. I can't connect the woman standing in front of me with the twisted man who killed my dad. But I can't quite connect her with Olivia, either. Physically she resembles her mother, but that's where it stops. Without her cello, she seems timid and apprehensive. Broken, almost. She glances over her shoulder as if she's afraid of what might happen next.

"I'm still freaked out by the news that my mother is alive," she says. "My father always told me she was dead, that she was a pathetic junkie who died of a heroin overdose right after I was born. I never even knew her real name, it turns out. My grandparents told the most awful stories about her."

"They weren't true," I say.

"Maybe it would be better if they were," she says. "Your friend Leo tried to sugar-coat the whole thing, but it sounds like my mother deserted me; left me there with that hideous family, in exchange for a pile of cash and her own secure future. How do you think that makes me feel?"

"She did it to save you."

"She did it to save herself."

"She wouldn't have been able to protect you if she had stayed in town."

"She sure as hell couldn't protect me by leaving."

"It would have been worse for you if she had stayed."

"It couldn't have been worse than what it was."

"The court ordered full custody to your father."

"She could have fought for me."

"She did. She lost. You father's family paid people to lie on his behalf."

"The church people?"

"Yeah. Did you attend that church?"

"Yes. Until I was thirteen. I hated it. I hated them."

"Why?"

"The hypocrisy – I hated the hypocrisy. My father behaved one way at home and another way at church. He would show up at church and be charming – you know, everyone adored him – then he'd come home and beat me. It was sick. Finally, when I was thirteen, I ran away."

"You never went back home?"

"Not voluntarily. He found me. He drove me home, dragged me out of the car by my hair, beat me up, and threw me down the basement steps. Broke my leg. My stepmother took me to the emergency room three days later. Like always, she drilled me about what to say to make it look like an accident. But that time, when the doctor at the hospital asked me what happened, something in me snapped, and I told the truth."

"Did they arrest your father?"

"No, he squirmed out of it. Like always. But they put me in protective custody. Eventually I ended up with foster parents. They changed everything for me. They're church people, too, but in a good way. My foster Dad is a minister of music. He got me into playing the cello."

"You know that Olivia – your mother – is also a music teacher?"

"Yes, Leo showed me the article in that magazine and told me all about her. It's great that she has helped so many kids. Great. Very admirable. She's out there rescuing the world, but me – her own daughter – she threw me away."

"Please don't say that, Kate. She didn't throw you away. She loved you."

"Right."

"Please. She's in a coma. She's dying. Won't you please go and tell her – "

"What, that I love her? That I forgive her?"

"Yes."

"No. I won't do that. I can't love her, ever. Maybe someday I can start to forgive her. I know about forgiveness. My foster parents have instilled that in me, and it's probably the most important part of any faith, especially mine. But forgiving my mother will take some time and a lot of hard work on my part. She abandoned me, I don't care what you say."

I get what she's saying. "Will you at least tell her that you're okay? Will you let her know that you've grown up and survived? That you're still in one piece?"

As soon as the words escape my mouth, I realize how perfectly wrong they are.

"Are you crazy?" she shouts. She begins to cry. "Telling her I'm okay would be the same thing as forgiving her. I told you, I'm not ready to do that. And let me tell you something, Miss Jane Bowman Boswell, I didn't grow up in one piece."

"I know," I whisper. "I know."

"Not even close. I'm a million little shards of a person, held together by a lot of cheap glue. My mother could have saved me from that fate, but she chose not to. I'm functioning now, but only because I've been cared for by a loving foster family with genuine beliefs and good intentions. The people who saved me are my heroes, not Olivia Blue. She sold out. No. I will not talk to her. Right now I don't care if she dies in the next five minutes or the next fifty years. I don't care."

I stare at her. She stares at the floor.

"I'm sorry. I'm sorry about the attack. I'm sorry about your arm, and your dad, and all of the other victims. I'm sorry I'm the daughter of a man capable of so much hatred. But I'm not sorry about Olivia."

I can't argue with her. As much as I love Olivia, I cannot bring myself to challenge Kate's hard-earned rage.

"I'm sorry, too," I say. "For what you've been through. Please forgive me for asking so much of you. I should have known better."

Her head snaps up, and I gaze into her eyes.

Dark. All-knowing. Determined. Scared. Her mother's eyes.

How I miss Olivia.

"Please forgive me," I say again. "I shouldn't have asked you to come. I'm sorry."

"Right – uh, thank you," she says.

"Your music is beautiful."

"It's the only thing I have that's really mine."

"Yeah," I say. "I know the feeling."

Time Passes On

On the night of October 15, 2001, Olivia Blue Bowman – one more victim of the failed domestic violence policies of the American judicial system – dies, with Franklin by her side. Her death, overshadowed by the events of September 11, slips past the attention of most newspaper and television reporters.

At the end of October I return to Pittsburgh to take part in the memorial service for her. Back in the Sewickley Heights house, on my bedroom dresser, I spot the business card Olivia had given me on the day we first met. Perhaps one of the Marys left it here for me to find.

Olivia Blue, Music Teacher, it says.

Music Teacher.

To me, she was a hero.

Olivia didn't believe in cremation, so her body will be interred in the Bowman family mausoleum next to the urns containing Mom and Dad's ashes. In a private moment before the service, we stand before her open coffin. Mary Two covers Olivia's chest and hands with her blue baby blanket. Leo and Franklin place long stemmed roses in her casket, and Mary One lays a Billie Holiday CD on top of the blanket. It's my turn. I reach into my shoulder bag and pull out one of the old silver-framed photos, the last picture taken of Mom, Dad, and me, on my twelfth birthday, right before our lives careened off course, and – miraculously – collided with hers. I place it in the casket and wait for the lid to close.

* * *

Expecting a large crowd, Leo has organized the memorial service at my grandparents' home in Fox Chapel. Over two hundred of Olivia's students are jammed into the crowded room – many of them successful graduates, some of them current students still in shock and shaken by her sudden absence from the school.

Just like they did at her wedding, the young men walk to the front of the room and announce themselves and the instruments they played under her guidance.

"Yoriah Washington, trombone."

"Patrick Russell, electric bass."

"Devaun Henderson, tenor sax."

"Hussein Mohammed, lead trumpet."

And so on. I walk to the back and get in line. With a crutch tucked under my left arm, I struggle down the aisle to the very spot where Dad and Olivia were married. Leo jumps up to help me, but I give him the evil eye and he sits back down. This much I can do alone. I'm conscious of being watched, not by the crowd, but by myself. The empty sleeve of my black sweater swings by my side and the crutch tip squeaks on the wooden floor. Glancing behind me, I remember the way Olivia floated through the doorway of this room on her wedding day. I remember the cling of my red dress, the perfume of the flowers, the way Dad beamed at her, and me, from the front of the mahogany paneled room. I remember how warm sunlight cascaded through the windows and cleared a path for the bride.

I look for friendly ghosts, but they're nowhere to be found.

Olivia's students recite their names, many of them looking to the sky as they touch her casket.

"Vincent DeFade, saxophone."

"André Kenyon, keyboards"

"Jane Bowman," I say, "Drums."

I notice the small wreath of pink roses leaning against the side of her casket. It had been delivered earlier in the day – sent by Olivia's last group of teenage students, the young boys who would miss her the most. The narrow satin ribbon tied to the top says *Teacher*.

I return to my seat, bury my head in Franklin's shoulder, and cry through the rest of the service.

Outside, the autumn sky seems as hard and cold as pale gray marble. Dwarfed by the granite columns of my grandparents' home, a Gatehouse alumnae band plays "Til You Come Back To Me," an old Stevie Wonder tune. I remember Olivia's arrangement; I played it with the Gatehouse boys back in 1986, the year I met her. I breathe in the brittle October air and watch the teenagers in the crowd checking out the older, cooler guys as they perform. They play with passion and – no denying it – a solid groove. Dusty brown leaves dance in a circle around Olivia's casket as Franklin, Leo, and four other young men lift it into the waiting hearse. The Marys stand on one side of me, leaning into each other. The boys in the band keep bopping through the song, while elegant tears fall onto the stiff collars of their best white shirts.

At this moment, I want very much to believe in heaven. I want to believe in a pearly-gated concert hall that rocks with soulful tunes played by the hippest players on the scene. I want to believe that even in paradise, the band isn't perfect, that there's room for improvement. I want to believe that Olivia gets the call.

"Hit the backbeat a little harder," she says. "Give it some juice. Come on, let me hear you *feel* that groove. I want this music to speak to me. Hell, I want it to be so alive it screams, you got it? Power! Give me as much power as you've got. Then give me more. Sit up straight, kids, and remember who you are! You're fighters, you're workers, you're musicians. Take it from the top, and let's kick some ass."

In my imagined heaven, the celestial colors of the music grow bolder and brighter as Mom swings from a nearby star and dazzles us with her conga playing. Isabella – wearing a too-tight red sequined dress – sings like a groovy Latino angel, while Dad and Grandpa Jack float past on a silky magic carpet, listening, always listening. The trumpets soar, the saxes wail, and the drummer – a skinny little girl with braided hair – holds it all together with blind faith.

I look up, the sun peeks around the edge of a patchy cloud, and a thousand pulsing beams of pure golden light polish the sky with the gentle rhythm of trust.

It's not heaven I believe in. It's music.

Epilogue

Twelve years have passed since Olivia's funeral. I think about her often, and about Mom and Dad; but the razor-sharp images of the past have blurred. Every so often, I feel a mysterious tap on my shoulder. When I spin around to look – hoping to finally make some sense out of the past – there's nothing there. The tormented voices of my nightmares have been reduced to murmurs, and they speak to me in gibberish I've stopped trying to understand.

The silver-framed photos of Mom balance on Mary Two's perfectly polished tables and granite countertops. For years after the bombing, I kept them hidden in dresser drawers, stuffed under dense piles of worn socks and soft sweaters. Then one day Mary One, while putting away the laundry, took the pictures out and set them up again, all over the house. Just like that. Now I'm able to see them for what they are – beautiful old snapshots of a little girl and the mother who loved her. That's all.

No secret messages, no hidden meanings, just the truth.

Our daughter, Helena Olivia Boswell, was born fourteen months after the memorial service for Olivia Blue. When Helena celebrates her twelfth birthday next year, she'll be the same age I was when Mom died. It seems impossible that any twelve-year-old child – balancing on the brink of adolescence – could ever survive the loss of a parent. And yet, because of Olivia, because of music, I did.

When I look at Helena it seems everyone I've ever loved is visiting me. They're all there – Dad, Mom, Jack and Isabella, Leo, the Marys, and Olivia Blue. Love, like good music, travels well from one generation to the next. This simple idea keeps me going.

Before Helena was born, Franklin and I left New York and moved back to the old Sewickley Heights house. Defeated by selfishness, it took me awhile to realize that Olivia Blue's death had also devastated my husband. As we waited for the baby, Franklin and I – desperate to move on, but not sure how – agreed that a change of scenery would help both of us. It was time. I lost one arm and three parents in New York; I didn't need to lose my sanity as well.

I know. It's just a place. But still.

Franklin accepted a senior surgical position at the University of Pittsburgh Medical Center, I prepared for the birth of our daughter, and we both began taking tiny steps forward.

As Leo so wisely conveyed to me in the hospital all those years ago: Three choices; you kill yourself, you go crazy, or you take the recovery option. I know Olivia would approve of my choice. So would Mom and Dad. And Grandpa Jack.

With Mary Two's help, I planted a wisteria vine in the back garden.

Through my pregnancy and well into the first few years of motherhood, I worked on reclaiming my body and calming the storms in my mind. The Marys, for better or worse, kept the household running smoothly while I continued the grueling therapy sessions intended to help me walk without a crutch. I never did lose the limp, but Leo convinced me to accept it as part of my new look, calling it a kind of reverse makeover. I still can't put one foot in front of the other without looping my right leg in a small arc off to the side, but I when I move quickly enough I notice a swinging sort of triplet rhythm to my gait. Helena, in a fit of pre-puberty dark humor, once referred to my limp as the Quasimodo Stride.

It took me a lot longer to get used to the loss of my arm. I tried the prosthesis, or *the claw* as Leo called it, but it drove me crazy – having a big creepy hunk of flesh-textured plastic hanging on my side seemed worse than having no arm at all. Because the bomb severed my arm almost to my shoulder, there was never any hope for the nerve regeneration necessary to control prosthesis movement. So I bailed on the fake arm. I learned to write and eat and accomplish most physical activities with my left arm, assisted by my teeth, my feet, my knees, and whichever parts of my body I could use to grab onto things. Planned physical movement, with a lot of practice, became second nature. I've always been good at that kind of thing – practicing something a zillion times, until I get it right. The more difficult task was training myself not to respond to emotions that made me want to reach for things with an arm that was no longer there. For years, I'd hear my daughter crying and try to reach with my right arm to comfort her, I'd see my husband after a hard day of surgery and I'd want to embrace him, I'd look at Mom's drum set and ache to play it.

A drummer can play with one arm. There are a few of them out there, and some of them sound pretty good. I thought a long time about giving it a shot. I even set up the drums in the basement, and tried, really tried – every day for a week – to play. But all I did was cry. It seemed wiser to give up playing, rather than risk the self-abuse involved with lowering my standards.

Olivia Blue, Music Teacher. Night after night, I stared at Olivia's old business card.

I wasn't quite sure what a one-armed drummer could offer the world of music students, but when I remembered what Olivia had taught me, I realized that in all the years we worked together she hardly ever touched an instrument to demonstrate a technique or a pattern. She got me to improve by acknowledging my talent, by listening, by being there to answer questions, by singing any part of any arrangement to drive home her point. She moved me to the next level by knowing when to hold my hand and when to nudge me into the returning tide of my imagination.

I enrolled at Duquesne University and completed my Music Therapy degree in three challenging years. The Board of Directors at Allegheny Gatehouse hired me to run the music department and lead the Gatehouse Band – Olivia's old job. Over the years, Franklin and I had continued to contribute big chunks of money to the music school, so I knew they gave me the job for reasons that were less than pure, but still, I felt proud and excited about starting a new phase in my life. The music department had floundered after Olivia's death, and I thought – I hoped – I could turn it around. I wasn't sure I could help the Gatehouse kids, but I knew if I tried I stood a chance of helping myself.

On my first day in the band room, I leaned on Olivia's old wooden podium and stared at the cynical faces of fifteen teenage boys who had never met Miss Blue, but had heard of her and gossiped about her, the way kids do.

"I'm Jane Bowman Boswell. You can call me Ms. Boswell."

"Wasn't Olivia Blue your step-mom?"

"Yes," I said.

"I got a step mom," said the student, staring past me. "In fact I got three."

"You got shit," said another boy from the back of the music room.

"Mo than you got. You got nuthin."

"You gonna have a face fulla pain if you don't shut yo' fuckin' mouth, muthafucka."

"Stop right there," I said in my sternest voice. "You're wrong. You've got music. All of you are here because you can play."

"Hey lady, what happened to your arm?"

"My name is Ms. Boswell. I lost my arm. Actually, that's bullshit. I didn't *lose* my arm. It was ripped off. In a bombing. While I was playing a gig. I was one of the lucky ones. A lot of people died in the club that night. Truth is, part of me died, too. But I came back."

"That's some heavy shit. I mean, that's low."

"Yo, Mizz Boswell! Who the fuck would do something like that?"

"Someone who was never given a chance to turn his life around."

Silence.

"How you deal?"

"I cope because I have to. But I can't play anymore. Not like before."

"So you teach."

"Yes."

"Excuse me, but you can't teach music if you can't play music."

"That's right Mizz Boswell, how you gonna teach if you can't play?"

"How you gonna play if you can't feel?" I shouted.

More silence.

"That's why I'm here."

And so it started, my enthusiastic stab at giving back, at trying to help these boys the way Olivia had once helped me. At first, unable to let go of my personal drama, I stumbled. But then, one student at a time, I began to notice small changes. The key, it seemed, was listening.

Through the act of listening, I discovered Olivia's secret: A child with a passion for music will develop a passion for life – if given the honest encouragement of a caring adult. I've watched six classes of my boys graduate, some of them going on to college, some of them going to work right away. One of my former students is now teaching at the Gatehouse. I've also had some failures – boys lured back into drugs, crime, or abusive homes – but I do what I can.

Our music program has expanded. Five years ago Franklin and I funded the construction of a separate wing for the Olivia Blue School of Music. We established a trust fund to pay the salaries of two full-time music therapists and a scholarship fund to help kids continue their music studies at college. Spanky Wainwright – Leo's Mom – handles the administrative work. I just fork over the money and show up to teach. Spanky flies all over the country, raising money and talking to local politicians about setting up Olivia Blue music schools in their own neighborhoods. So far, using the Gatehouse as a blueprint, she has managed to raise funds and establish schools in Atlanta and Cleveland. She's also working on a program for girls in Louisville. Even the federal government has kicked into action, matching funds from private donors with government grants.

And what about my best friend Leo? Leo has remained single. He bought the brownstone from us several years after we left Manhattan. The upstairs apartment stays empty, in case we visit. Helena and Franklin have been there a bunch of times, but so far, I haven't returned. Maybe some day. Leo hangs out with us in Sewickley Heights at least one weekend a month. His thriving talent agency has a new division, one that he calls the Octavious Ramone Young Talent Office, dedicated to promoting unknown artists who need a break. Several of them, with Leo's coaching and grooming, have become big stars. It's what he tried to do with me all those years ago, only the performers are a little more cooperative.

Through everything, the Marys have continued to delight and aggravate me. Mary One sings Lady Day from the guest bathroom, Mary Two cusses at every opportunity, and I give thanks every single day that the two of them are still around. When we moved back to Sewickley Heights I was surprised to discover the two of them had been sharing a bedroom for years. Franklin was shocked I hadn't figured this out; he said he knew they were partners from the first day he met them – when they performed their little song and dance routine at Dad and Olivia's wedding. They're both in their seventies now, and – keeping with a Bowman family tradition – we're thinking about hiring yet another housekeeper to clean up after the two of them. Helena would very much like to find someone named Mary.

Aside from Leo, the Marys are the only people left who knew me before the fire. When I'm feeling sorry for myself, I long for those days and for what might have been. I just wish I could figure out how to be grateful for what I have and still hold on to my gold badge of sorrow. I long for both. Most of the time, I watch the sadness slip away, like a child's forgotten sand toy drifting out to sea. If I squint, I can spot it in the distance, bobbing up and down in the glassy water – a sun-faded yellow bucket with a broken handle. I know if I swim as fast as I can, I might still retrieve it. But most of the time, I'm too content to try.

We sit together every night, at Mom's old mosaic table, listening to Mary One hum while Mary Two scolds us for spills and splashes. Talking for hours, we peel back the gift-wrap of each day. By repeating old stories over and over again, buffing the details until they sparkle, we're able to keep Mom, Dad, and Olivia illuminated in our imaginations, hopefully forever. I hold Franklin's hand, he catches my eye, and we know, more than anything, that there's no music as profound as the contrapuntal chatter of a happy family.

Helena plays both piano and drums. When her delicate fingers run over the keys of the Steinway, or when she bashes away on Mom's old drums, her playing carries me backward and forward, all at once. She and Franklin jam together and play house concerts the way I used to with Mom. I'm in the cheering section now with the Marys, hooting and hollering just the way Dad used to.

Sometimes I sit at the drums and try to show my daughter a trick or two. Franklin says I can still play a funkier groove with three limbs than most drummers can with four, but Helena doesn't seem too impressed. She wants to learn things her own way, on her own terms, without her old mom trying to one-up her.

"Tu eres mi cielo," I tell my daughter.

You're my little heaven.

I've learned to play music, I've learned to teach it, I've even learned to touch it, to reach into the core of a song and find the gentle throb of its subtle meaning. Here's what I tell my students: Life can be a songbook of your greatest hits. You play through your repertoire, trying to keep the tempo steady, but unexpected comedies and tragedies cause you to speed up, slow down, jump to the coda, end the tune before you've resolved the cadence, or come to a grinding halt because you've veered out of control. You hesitate, you threaten to rip the score into a thousand scraps of nothingness, and you want – more than anything – to kick over the music stand and quit. But then, surprisingly, you feel the pulse of life coursing through your veins. You take the recovery option and move onto the next tune. Shaken, you pick up the sticks, the horn, the bow, the conductor's baton, and give it another shot. You work through the music, taming the chaos of a difficult phrase by playing one simple note after another, slowly moving forward, practicing until you get it right. Maybe your last groove was the best you'll ever play. Or maybe the next try will turn out to be better.

"Breathe," I tell the kids. "Focus. Stay in the moment."

My students have shown me the tragic beauty of human resilience. With a messy stack of music clutched under an arm, an enormous instrument strapped to a back, a weighty cymbal bag slung over a shoulder, a guitar case swinging dangerously low to the ground – these kids leave for grown-up land, determined and strong, holding onto songs that will guide them through the obstacle courses of their lives. They don't always look back at me, but when they do, my heart aches with pride and respect for all they're about to accomplish. I know where they're heading, because I've been there. And back.

"Keep going," I whisper. "Whatever you do, keep going."

Author's Note

Rhythm is a product of my imagination. As in all fiction, my literary perceptions and ideas are shaded by elements of experience. But Jane's story is just a story and the characters do not represent real people, with the exception of several famous musicians who play fictitious roles in invented situations.

I offer my sincere thanks to jazz musician Karolina Strassmayer for her encouragement and belief in *Rhythm*. Karolina's honesty and willingness to answer endless questions helped shape Jane's character, both musically and emotionally. If you're not yet familiar with Karolina Strassmayer's music, check out *Adventures,* her newest CD as a leader.

Heartfelt thanks to the musicians who contributed their technical expertise and historical knowledge to *Rhythm*: Peter Erskine, Hans Dekker, Arturo Sandovar, Dave Horler, Adam Nussbaum, John Riley, Steve Gadd, Steve Kiener, John Goldsby, Bob Rawsthorne, Pinky Rawsthorne, Ray DeFade, Ludwig Nuss, Mattis Cederberg, Joyce, Greg Thymius, Emilee Floor, Robin Spielberg, Betsy Hirsch, Liesl Whitaker, Fabian Weiland and Michael Abene.

A tip of the hat and a big bouquet of roses go to fiction editor Susan Roth. I'll be forever grateful for Susan's organizational skills, talent, and willingness to jump into Jane's world.

Thanks to Emilio and Carol Delgado for their help with Spanish translations.

Many thanks to Gretchen Abene for teaching me that a field of yellow flowers can bloom forever in the imagination of an orphaned child.

Sincere thanks to Peter Fessler for sharing his first-hand knowledge of a childhood rescued by music.

Special thanks to pianist, author, and talk show host Marian McPartland for her support of my work. The queen of jazz piano just celebrated her 90th birthday, and she's still inspiring listeners with her unique music and well-chosen words.

Many thanks to William Zinsser for his encouragement and no-nonsense advice.

I'm grateful to AWCC's *Writing Women*, an English-language writers' group in Cologne, Germany, for their help with the last draft of *Rhythm*. We continue to meet every two weeks in an old German fire station, an appropriate locale for a quirky group of writers hoping to spark their stories with well-chosen words.

A nod of thanks to Thomas Althoff, Benedikt Jaschke, and the team at Schloss Lerbach in Bergisch Gladbach, Germany.

Rhythm reached the semi-finals of the Amazon Breakthrough Novel Awards. I offer my sincere thanks to the men and women who wrote inspired reviews of the book for the contest: Kristin Kovacic, Kevin Becketti, Daralene Dobbins, Sharon Reamer, Phil Bowler, Dina Blade, Andrea Hall, Greg Thymius, Margaret Whitmer, Mark Koehnke, Frank Lamberto, Nina Lesowitz, Michele Cozzens, Joanne Rogers, Rebecca Kyle, Michael Tracy, Kona, Amanda Richards, Mark Plank, Emilee Floor, Peter Alexander Trivelas (the son), Peter Trivelas (the dad), Noreen Nanz, Gretchen Abene, Jane Franklin, Richard Siegel, Evelyn P., Silverfish, Dave Wieczorek, Susan Roth, Marion Winik, DCD, Hedda Sharapan, John Riley, Marilu Enterline, Leslie Brockett, Priscilla Thomas, Bob

Sinicrope, Robert E. Ashley, Mia Jacobs, Robin Spielberg, Gladys Casper, Karolina Strassmayer, and Andre Wagner.

Big hugs to the unofficial president of my Pittsburgh fan club, the indomitable Marlyn Koehnke.

A big thank you to the *Piano Girl* Dream Team: Kevin Becketti, Nina Lesowitz, and the talented Richard Johnston. Wherever I go, there they are.

Big hugs to my good friends: Joanne Rogers, Andrea Goetze, Jutta Schmitz, Katja Bröcher, Pamela Johnson, Peter and Claudia, Betsy Hirsch at Steinway Hall, Debra Todd, Harlan Ellis, Carol and Emilio, Daralene Dobbins, Emilee Floor, Jean Ewing, and Pinky Rawsthorne.

The decision to write this book meant embarking on a three-year journey, not just for me, but also for my two best friends, Leslie Brockett Wohlfarth and Robin Spielberg Kosson. Both women – living an ocean away – stayed by my side in spirit while I wrote. They read early drafts of *Rhythm*, cheered me with phone calls and emails of support, and hung in there with Jane (and me) through the entire process. I will be forever grateful for their love and friendship.

Special thanks to my brother and sister, Curtis and Randy Rawsthorne, and to my parents, Bob and Ann Rawsthorne. We were a great family. We still are.

Many thanks to my children, Curtis and Julia Goldsby. I hope they hold onto the miracle of music as they enter young adulthood and begin to hear the rhythm of the real world. To my husband, John Goldsby – my live-in take-no-mercy editor, house bassist, chord doctor, friend, critic, cheerleader, and love of my life – I offer Mary One's basket of silken magnolia petals, to be counted every spring, along with the many blessings in our lives.

Also by Robin Meloy Goldsby

Piano Girl: A Memoir
(Backbeat Books)

Solo Piano Recordings:
Songs from the Castle
Twilight
Somewhere in Time

www.goldsby.de

Praise for Piano Girl: A Memoir

"Goldsby has a wicked sense of humor and a keen eye for the absurd. This is a bighearted, funny, truly eye-opening memoir."
Publishers Weekly (Starred Review)

"Goldsby has seen it all from her piano and she dishes it up with a true storyteller's gusto. As refreshing as a frozen daiquiri . . ."
Jeff Yanc, Book Sense Picks and Notables

"Piano Girl is certainly one of the funniest books I've ever read."
Marian McPartland, NPR host, *Piano Jazz*

"Goldsby quicksteps from bumptious to bawdy to trenchant with impeccable timing in this hilarious, truth-telling memoir. Brava!"
Betsy Burton, *The King's English*, Salt Lake City, Utah

"When I was a girl, I devoured behind-the-scenes books about movie stars, airline stewardesses, and other glamorous, jet-setting divas. Reading Robin Goldsby's funny stories of her life as a cocktail lounge entertainer – the blonde at the piano who knows everybody's favorite song – gave me a delicious grown-up version of that long-ago pleasure."
Marion Winik, NPR commentator, author of *Above Us Only Sky*.

"Be it a ballad or an up tune, this plucky lucky lounge pianist arranges her memoir-medley for us and plays it in the key of life."
Cheryl Hardwick, *Saturday Night Live* musical director, 1987–2000

"Punchy, inspirational and juicy – imagine Carrie from "Sex In The City" playing the Marriott"
Daryl Sherman, cabaret artist and pianist, New York City

"Goldsby's wide-ranging stories possess a low-key, party-girl sense of humor. *Piano Girl* is exuberant, keen, and at times very funny."
Adam Bregman, *Seattle Weekly*

"What's most remarkable about this memoir is Robin Goldsby's singular and life-embracing voice. I dare any reader not to recognize himself or a loved one in at least one of Goldsby's many predicaments."
Bill Brent, *Author's Den*

"Individual vignettes perfectly capture timeless moments in this enthralling and honest personal story."
Midwest Book Review

"Nightclub gigs and life lessons dot Goldsby's circuitous path, making this collection of essays especially readable."
Jennifer Meccariello, *Pittsburgh Magazine*

"Goldsby is a great storyteller. You will feel as if you sat beside her on her piano bench for the past 30 years, observing all the people she recalls with such intimacy and personal warmth."
Barbara Cloud, *Pittsburgh Post Gazette*

"One of the funniest reads I've had in a long time, and each of the nearly 50 brief chapters can stand on their own as model short stories, complete with moral."
Ernie Rideout, *Keyboard Magazine*

"Goldsby's tales are often laugh-out-loud funny, sometimes poignant, and always abundantly human."
Kathy Parsons, *MainlyPiano.com*

"Robin Goldsby has written an engaging book with amusing descriptions of her encounters with audiences, employers, mobsters, lounge lizards, stalkers, crazies, and good friends. She has an appealing way with a story and finds the human interest in every situation."
Bill Crow, *Allegro*, Local 802 AFM

"Evokes the funny, sad, and just plain strange life of the cocktail pianist with wit and eloquence. A thoroughly entertaining book."
Maggie Williams, *International Piano*

"Piano Girl is a charming collection of episodes from Goldsby's life as an entertainer. It's not really fair to label her as a lounge

musician. She also sings, acts, and dances in a well-known cabaret (and in one incident must "tastefully" strip), plays one-handed flute, saves a choking victim from a pancake, almost joins the circus, and tours with Sesame Street. There are many laugh-out-loud moments in this book."
Lauren Baker, *Music Educator's Journal*

"Piano Girl is a charming look into the real life of a performer who has done quite well in one oft-ignored corner of the music world, and has enjoyed herself all the way."
Paul D. Lehrman, *Mix Magazine*

"Designing agents, questionable bookings and embarrassing situations are all described here in glorious detail, but above all, the colorful, eccentric and certifiably crazy characters encoun-tered in *Piano Girl* make for an enjoyable reading experience."
Amanda Richards, *Amazon Top 50 Reviewer*

About the Author

Robin Meloy Goldsby is the author of *Piano Girl: A Memoir*. A professional musician for over three decades, she has performed around the world and recorded three solo piano CDs. She is a Steinway Artist. Robin currently lives in Cologne, Germany with her husband—jazz bassist John Goldsby—and their two children. *Rhythm* is her first novel. For more information, visit www.goldsby.de.

Made in the USA